Acclaim for Joanna Scott's

MAKE BELIEVE

"As is made dazzlingly clear in *Make Believe*, Joanna Scott is a Michael Jordan: she has talent to burn. . . . Scott inhabits the souls of the least articulate characters and makes them sing. . . . Perhaps her most impressive achievement is in finding a voice for Bo that is neither twee nor limiting. . . . What we get is one of the most convincingly impressionistic versions of a difficult childhood that I have ever read. . . . There are occasions when the author's ingenuity and command of her craft make you want to laugh with pleasure. . . . One cannot help urging anyone who loves writing to read this book."
— Nick Hornby, *New York Times Book Review*

"Opening with a spookily pitch-perfect description of a car accident as experienced by a three-year-old, Joanna Scott varies the pace but never lessens the momentum in *Make Believe*." — *Elle*

"A powerful novel. . . . As *Make Believe* builds in emotional intensity to its dramatic conclusion, Scott's narrative probes the psychological states of her characters and explores how a single decision can completely change lives."
— Joan Hinkemeyer, *Denver Rocky Mountain News*

"Scott breaks free when the novel goes into the mind of Bo, in one of the finest streams-of-childish-consciousness since Conrad Aiken's classic short story 'Silent Snow, Secret Snow.'"
— Bill Marx, *Boston Globe*

"A strikingly original work. . . . Joanna Scott is a powerhouse. . . . She succeeds in creating a vivid portrait of a child sadly misused by the adults who should have been his refuge and strength. . . . If Joanna Scott's depiction of Eddie Gantz is a *tour de force*, then her depiction of Bo verges on genius. . . . Her ability to capture the complexity of the human condition in prose that dances on the edge of poetry is a gift that deserves wide acclaim."

— Ron Carter, *Richmond Times–Dispatch*

"There's something particularly magical when a full-fledged grown-up author is able to tell a story as if the words were coming directly, innocently, from the mouth or mind of a child."

— Patrick T. Reardon, *Chicago Tribune*

"A fascinating, powerful story. . . . Joanna Scott is a magician. . . . *Make Believe* is magical with themes and symbols and wonderful rich characters like the fairy tales we read as children, just as frightening, just as entrancing. . . . It is a fearsome trip we take with this charming, plucky, and very lonely little boy. . . . The second-by-second account of Bo's father's death, two months before the boy is born, is one of the most harrowing and beautiful descriptive passages I've ever read. . . . Scott's final pages are very satisfying. . . . [Bo is] a little boy I will keep with me for a long, long time."

— Diana Pinckney, *Creative Loafing*

"Scott creates some wonderful effects with Bo's limited viewpoint and embryonic perceptions. . . . The tactic of revisiting the same event from varying perspectives works superbly. . . . A risk-taking book, unafraid to court sentimentality and melodrama in an effort to show how profoundly well-meaning people can unintentionally shatter one another's lives. Scott just keeps getting better."

— *Kirkus Reviews* (starred review)

"Joanna Scott is one of the really important contemporary voices. *Make Believe* marks a departure from her earlier work, one that both preserves and amplifies her reputation. This is vital, passionate fiction about how we live our lives now."　— Rick Moody

"Gripping. . . . Scott keeps the narrative tension high throughout."
　— Starr E. Smith, *Library Journal*

"Scott is a skilled portraitist, subtle and generous. . . . *Make Believe* is filled with life's tragic randomness, the telling split seconds that divide all right from all wrong. Each character clings to the narrow precipice over life's maelstrom into which, Scott suggests, circumstances may pitch anyone at any moment. . . . This book is deeply satisfying as one of fiction's chief pleasures: to see, in literature, events and predicaments that mirror our own deepest uncertainties."
　— Judith Dunford, *Los Angeles Times*

"A tour de force. . . . Scott opens her magician's bag of tricks again and again. . . . *Make Believe* is concerned with the power of the story, the saving grace of the human imagination in the face of unbearable realities, the tales we tell ourselves so we can believe everything will be all right."
　— Stewart O'Nan, *Minneapolis Star Tribune*

"*Make Believe* signals a fresh turn from this inventive writer. . . . Scott's story's hooks are those of daytime talk shows — grandparent's custody, interracial romance, teenage pregnancy, malpractice suits, and child abuse. But at the center of this up-to-the-minute buzz is a very old fairy tale about a preternaturally wise child and a wicked stepparent."　—Albert Mobilio, *Newsday*

"Scott grants integrity to people trying to lead decent lives amid hardships. Her attempts to describe events through Bo's eyes sensitively reflect a child's innocent, flawed understanding of the world. This is a compelling story that will leave readers haunted by Scott's powerful moral vision."   — *Publishers Weekly* (starred review)

"Joanna Scott is the absolute cream of our generation."
— David Foster Wallace

"Scott masterfully balances the perfection of the child's imaginative interior world with the errant turbulence of adult life. . . . Her brilliant prose resonates with awe at the wondrous 'ability of life to sustain itself.'"   — Trey Strecker, *Review of Contemporary Fiction*

"Where the novel succeeds, Scott's writing soars: It's elegant, rich, and completely spellbinding. . . . Scott demonstrates a rare talent for creating a character who is evil but entirely human. There's no question that Joanna Scott is a skillful, self-assured writer."
— Deborah Sussman Susser, *Washington Post Book World*

"Joanna Scott is the real thing, an artist with huge ambitions and the means to realize them. Her novels are astonishingly beautiful, subtle, profound, and unlike those of any other writer I know. She sets a standard for the rest of us; when I begin to wonder why I labor at writing novels I often turn to Scott's work and am reminded of what it's possible to do with ink and paper."
— Michael Cunningham, author of *The Hours*

"Scott's portrait of a vulnerable child escaping from a troubled world into the realms of imagination will stay with you long after the book is read."   — *BookWorks*

Make Believe

Make Believe

A   NOVEL

Joanna Scott

Little, Brown and Company

Boston   New York   London

Originally published in hardcover by Little, Brown and Company, February 2000
First Back Bay paperback edition, February 2001

The characters and events in this book are fictitious. Any similarity to real
persons, living or dead, is coincidental and not intended by the author.

Leonard Lopate's interview with Joanna Scott, excerpts from which appear
in the reading group guide at the back of this book, was originally aired on
"New York & Company" on WNYC.
The partial transcript of the interview is reprinted with permission.

Library of Congress Cataloging-in-Publication Data

Scott, Joanna.
    Make believe : a novel / by Joanna Scott. — 1st ed.
        p.   cm.
    ISBN 0-316-77616-5 (hc) / 0-316-77666-1 (pb)
    I. Title.
PS3569.C636M34   2000
813' .54 — dc21   99-31277

                10 9 8 7 6 5 4 3 2 1

Book design by Barbara Werden Design
Q-FG
Printed in the United States of America

For Kathryn and Alice

PART ONE

Maybe he fell and that's why he was hurting and dangling upside down like a pair of jeans on the wash line. He hurt and his face was wet with warm milk that got sticky as it cooled. But it smelled more like swamp mud than milk. Mud, then. It didn't taste like mud. His lips were covered with it, and his tongue caught what dribbled up from his chin. Sour juice straight from his mama's green bottle? He'd always wondered what was in her green bottle. Sour mudjuice, and now he'd turned the world upside down and made a real mess, such a bad boy, he hadn't meant to, just as he hadn't really meant to climb out of the grocery cart back at the store. It was his fault, everything was his fault, even the cage full of pink and blue bunnies at the end of the aisle. The bunnies were put there to tempt little kids, and he was a little kid, so the bunnies were his fault. *Get your goddamn ass down!* She couldn't have been madder back at the store. But she always got as mad as she could be, never just a little mad. He had cried, and that was his fault, too. He'd cried because if she were really that mad she might have left him sitting on his ass in the grocery cart and walked away. If she ever left him it would be his fault. Please don't go! He hadn't meant to do whatever he'd done and if only she'd give him the chance he would take it back, make it up, tell her whatever she wanted to hear!

Now up was down, down was up. He cried because his belly hurt and because his mama had strung him up like a pair of jeans and left him hanging there. Just left him hanging there while she slipped off —

Where?

To bum a smoke?

To search for hundred-dollar bills stuck to the wet road, hoping that she'd find a fortune if only she kept on looking?

Or maybe she'd gone off to search for Bo.

"Mama!"

Look at him hanging there, a small, helpless child dangling upside down, strapped to the seat by the lap belt. And how quietly it had all happened. You'd think there would have been clanking, clashing, squealing, an explosion of sound. Instead they'd spun around and around, the earth had lurched with a series of dull thuds like the thuds Bo made when he slid under his mama's bed and kicked the mattress, glass burst into stars, and metal bubbled with a noise that reminded him of secret laughter. And then the quiet of night when everyone else was asleep and he lay awake on his own bed wishing he had the courage to get up and go outside and roam the dark streets.

Mama's little Hobo, she liked to call him, because he'd wander out the door in his bare feet, down the front porch steps and up the sidewalk, collecting bottle caps and pinecones along the way. Sometimes when he was searching the curb for treasures a car would pull alongside him, and he'd see a shiny brown boy staring back from the hubcap. He wouldn't answer when the driver called, "Hey, kid, anybody watching you?" Instead, he'd throw a handful of gravel at the car, and the driver would drive away.

Don't you ever go off with a stranger, his mama had said too many times to count, and though he didn't understand what a stranger was, he did sense that when he wandered up the street he'd better keep to himself. He didn't mind if neighborhood kids joined him, unless they tried to steal his treasures — then Bo would scream and his mama would eventually appear. He'd scream as loud as he could, and she'd hang up the phone or turn off the TV and come fetch him, slapping him hard on the side of his head and saying, *Get on home!* or scooping him up in her arms, covering him with kisses while she sang a song about her sweet little Hobo, Ho-bo-bo!

Or else she'd say, *You're just a baby, for God's sakes!*

Straight ahead a line of light cut into the darkness, and he wondered if he'd taken the flashlight from the kitchen drawer to play with it. Maybe that's why his mama was so mad. He'd done something terrible, that was for sure. Maybe he'd pulled the place mat off the table and brought her plate and glass crashing to the floor — that was something he'd always wanted to do! If he'd actually done it, well, that would make her plenty mad. Oh, what a bad boy, bad! But it was about time for her to get over being angry, please. *Time for kisses, please!* He called, "Mama mama mama mama mama," kept calling her until his mouth was too tired to work, then stopped and listened for her answer.

He became aware of a new sound, or an old sound that he hadn't noticed before. *Tickatickatickatickaticka.* It was the sound of waiting. *Tickatickatickatickaticka.* It was the sound of the car when they were waiting to turn right or left, and Bo could almost imitate it with his tongue: *tahdatahdatahdatahdatah.* The sound made him feel better about waiting, made him realize how tired he was, and wouldn't Mama be happy if he went to sleep without a fuss! He narrowed his eyes but didn't close them, since he found some comfort in the beam of light shining across the wet road. The light, the waiting sound, the rain . . . he let himself drift, felt the scare diminishing as he thought of things he knew perfectly well. Six dots on a ladybug mean the ladybug is six years old, salt tastes salty, blue is neither red nor green, a tower is fun to knock over, snow is cold like a sticker is sticky like now is right now, Gran and Pop live on Sycamore Street and Gran sings, "A B C D E F G," sings, "H I J K L M N O P," sings while she makes pancakes, he likes peanut butter on pancakes but he doesn't like green beans or hamburgers or eggs.

What kind of kid won't eat hamburgers?

No no no no no!

Just a bite, sweetpie. One big bite for your ole grandma, and you can have a Fudgsicle for dessert. You can have two Fudgsicles! See, I can't help but spoil my babies, and they know they can do just as they please. Ma, says Kamon, here's my girlfriend Jenny, don't mind that she's white, okay? So he goes out two months before his son is born and gets himself killed on the street. I didn't even have time to understand what I was missing when Jenny says, Mrs. Gilbert, I got a mall job so can you watch Bo? Sure, I say, and Sam and I feed him Fudgsicles for lunch and dinner and let him watch television till he falls asleep on my lap, and when Jenny comes by after work she's so tired she can hardly stand, but still she insists on stopping first at the grocery store for her carton of cigarettes and whatever else, powder donuts for the morning, a quart of milk, she's so tired she can hardly drive, still she drives like somebody's chasing her, twice the limit, drives like there's no tomorrow, and all I can say to her is, one of these days, girl, one of these days.

A B C.

A B C.

A B C.

She was stuck in her song, and Bo wanted to give her a pinch to help her along. But he couldn't move his arms because he was shrinking toward the center of himself so there was hardly space left inside him to draw in air, hardly room in his belly for the soft rain, the night, the *tickatickaticka* and his grandma's song.

A B C.

A B C.

Why, it wasn't Gran singing at all, it was the TV, and Mama had turned the volume up in order to hear the band music better, she'd started to dance along with the TV dancers and like them spun around and around so fast Bo could only see a blur of color, the turquoise streaks of her blouse and jeans, around and around like the fan that blew hot air into her bedroom all summer long.

A B C.

A B —

Someone, Pop maybe, had turned the TV off, so Mama stopped dancing, but by then she'd danced herself to nothing, and when Bo looked for her he saw only the upside-down world glistening in the flashlight beam.

Voices, the murmur of voices behind a closed door, voices of grown-ups deciding whether or not he should be punished for making a mess, then a tap-tap on the window beside him, the delicate crinkle of glass, and a hand reached in to yank up the handle on his door.

"We got a kid here!"

Tugging, grunting, creak of yielding metal, and Bo was eye to eye with the upside-down face of a stranger.

"We got a kid! Take it easy little fella we got you we're gonna get you out we're gonna give me a hand there yeah the collar first we're gonna help if you what's taking so long with that goddamn sneaker I see shit a lady's sneaker shit oh shit give me that now take it easy take it easy here you go little man."

A stranger. *Never go nowhere with a stranger!* As soon as he could he'd start kicking and screaming and his mama would come to find out what was wrong. Wouldn't she be sorry when she saw her sweet Bo in the arms of a stranger, arms like chains of a huge crane lowering him, lowering his aching body, turning him right-side up and settling him back upon a board as though he were going to be made into a house, nailed into the frame of a great big house.

With the sky back in its proper place above him, he decided to scream. He shut his eyes, started flailing and stamping the air with his heels but gave that up because they'd taped him to the board and he couldn't move, though he kept on screaming as loud as he could, drowned out the voices of the strangers with his own voice while he waited to smell his mama's lemon and cigarette smell — only when he smelled her close to him would he open his eyes again. Where was she? He knew that what could happen was always worse than what he could imagine, and for that reason he never wandered farther than calling distance away from home. Never, never had he called for his mama and she hadn't come — except when he was staying with Gran and Pop, and then one of them would come instead of Mama, which pleased Bo to no end, for they'd bribe him to stop crying with chocolate kisses and Fudgsicles and sometimes even a trip to the toy store. No, he wouldn't mind at all if Gran or Pop showed up right now instead of Mama.

Or even Uncle Alcinder or Aunt Merry or Ashley who lived with her five kids in the other side of the house or their next-door neighbors Pat and Sonny or Mrs. Kelper across the street. Anybody who was not a stranger would do just fine.

"Come on, settle down there."

"Get him in, let's go!"

Now he was a key being fit into the lock of a door, slid in, turned, click.

"Can you tell me where you hurt? Does it hurt when I press here? Here? Now you're going to feel a squeeze on your arm. You'll feel this band get tight and then it will get loose. We want to help you is all. Can you tell me your name? Don't you have a name?"

He heard a door shut, like the door to the freezer in Gran's pantry, and he gave up screaming, worked instead to catch his breath. As long as he didn't open his eyes he wouldn't have to see the faces of strangers. These people were definitely strangers, and it was becoming obvious why they should be avoided. Their voices were as sweet as pudding, but their hands were poisonous snakes. So much made sense after the upside-down confusion: whatever had happened to him back there happened because of these strangers. They wanted to get at him and so had hurt him, then tried to comfort him, and now that they'd succeeded in separating him from his mama the hurt would only get worse. They squeezed and pressed and stabbed him in his elbow with pins, pricked the back of one hand and then the other, swore and cooed — "Damn it what a good brave boy you are so ah for Christ's sake come on this kid has no veins" — still trying to pretend that they were going to help him when in fact they were going to do those things that couldn't be named and so couldn't be imagined, actions as awful and mysterious as the sea creatures living at the bottom of the ocean.

Mama's sweet Hobo was sinking into the realm of the unimaginable, sinking to a place beyond calling distance, beyond help. It had to be just so — everything that happened to him now happened for a reason beyond his control, and Bo understood that it would be useless to resist. An unfamiliar calm replaced the fear. It was easy to surrender, to give up hope of ever again seeing anyone he knew and to get used to this bright-dark world, where whirs and clicks signaled a forward motion so smooth it was almost unnoticeable, where voices said one thing and hands did another, where no one knew his name, where he couldn't have told his name even if he'd wanted to, for after all that had happened he'd completely forgotten how to speak.

Welcome to the world of strangers, Bo. Welcome to the bottom of the sea.

They traveled along Route 62 at an even fifty miles per hour, lights churning, sirens silent except for a short clamor of sound at every intersection. A rabbit hunched in a nearby ditch, waiting for the cold drops of light to fall like hail upon its head. Budding forsythia scratched at a stone wall. A raccoon in a driveway caught the glare in its eyes and darted behind a parked car. A line of poplars watched from the edge of a small field, surprised by nothing.

Above the treetops to the north, the darkness was fringed with the city's glow, and at the intersection with Route 103 the ambulance turned right and continued steadily in this direction, pulled like a splinter of iron toward a magnet. Cars slowed obediently and moved to the right lane. A dog on the porch of a decrepit farmhouse started barking. Behind the plate glass of a diner, a waitress with no one to serve looked up from her magazine, glanced at the clock, and continued reading. The ambulance drove on through the drizzle past a nursery, a gas station, a lot full of new tractors and backhoes, a warehouse, a stretch of freshly plowed fields, a block of brick ranch houses, another stretch of fields, more houses, a kennel, an old barn with a side wall collapsed, an office building, a parking lot, a stretch of woods and a playground. As the ambulance approached a traffic light at the bottom of a hill it slowed again, announcing its presence with a wail, and turned left, climbing up a ramp onto a highway, where it settled into its motion like a canoe on a river, drifting toward the left lane while other cars veered away from it. After five miles or so the ambulance moved to the right again, sliding down the ramp of the next exit as though down a small cataract, slowing, turning left and then right beyond the overpass, right at the next light, left and left and right and left in a series of short, sharp turns, traveling straight on for the last stretch along the avenue that bordered the huge parking lots of the hospital, turning right down a side road, right again into the drive of the emergency department, and coming to a halt at last.

The lights stopped spinning, and the engine clicked to silence. Nothing moved; no activity interrupted the stillness. For the briefest of moments, before the paramedic flung open the rear doors, the scene was made up of concrete, glass, and metal, without a living thing in sight.

Marjory Gantz, Jenny Templin's mother, did what she normally did that evening: made dinner for herself and her husband, Eddie, ate dinner with Eddie, rinsed dishes with Eddie, and watched television. Long afterward, thinking back to the night of the accident, she would wonder at her tendency to take for granted the ability of life to sustain itself. Although she didn't learn about the accident until close to midnight, she would never understand her complacency. Shouldn't she have sensed what had happened without having to be told?

Marge lived with Eddie and her younger daughter, Ann, on Hanks Lane in Hadleyville, a village on the northern slope above Hadley Lake. She'd moved here from Albany thirty years earlier with her first husband, Tony Templin, and had stayed in the house after Tony moved out. She and Eddie had married four years ago, when Jenny was fifteen and Ann twelve. Now Jenny was going on twenty — yes, *going on,* Marge still assumed shortly after seven o'clock on that rainy April evening — and with a child of her own, a little boy whom Marge had never met.

Never met him?

Not yet, Marge would tell her friends whenever they raised their inked eyebrows in wonder. What can you do with such a hothead for a daughter, eh? There was nothing else Marge could do but wait for Jenny to cool off after the falling out they'd had and in the meanwhile send Ann over to Jenny's place in Arcade with a money order twice a year. A money order, not a check, so Eddie wouldn't find out.

But Marge wasn't thinking about any of this when she sat down to dinner that night. She was thinking about how fine it all looked — roast chicken with mashed potatoes, homemade gravy and green beans, apple cobbler for dessert. She had no pretensions as a cook, though she had a director's instinct for timing and combination, and she enjoyed basking in the glow of Eddie's appreciation, which more than made up for Ann's absence. All the effort Marge put into a meal and Ann would only grab snacks and soda and an occasional slice of processed cheese snatched at odd hours so she wouldn't have to eat with the grown-ups. Just another phase, and Marge had resigned herself to wait it out, as she did any other phase, having mastered long ago a great talent for patience.

Now she was more patient than ever, for she had all the time in the world. She was fifty-seven years old, a grandmother already yet still fit for many kinds of work. But Eddie worked hard so Marge wouldn't have to work. A husband should support his wife, he believed, and though Marge wouldn't have minded a job that took her out of the house, she was content with the arrangement and found that she loved Eddie most when she pleased him.

Mashed potatoes and roast chicken pleased him. So did the cobbler, with its apple slices as thin as fingernails but still crisp, topped with a sugary crust that rose up in dark peaks. He ate slowly, suspending each forkful in the air and examining it to be certain of its perfection. He didn't demand perfection — he simply expected it, and Marge could satisfy him as long as she let him think of her as an extension of himself. He measured the world against his own formidable strength of character and impeccable decency. Such a man could only have a perfect wife.

The kitchen was perfect — so clean, so neatly cut into white planes and shadows by the track lighting. The cobbler was perfect, Marge agreed between her first bite and her second, smiling with closed lips at her ridiculous pride as she watched Eddie eat.

Marge had two living daughters to complain about, and in the next moment, *tickatick,* she had only one. She lifted a second heaping forkful of apple cobbler to her mouth, Eddie chewed with a deliberate grinding motion, upstairs sixteen-year-old Ann Templin listened through headphones to music, the wind rattled a window loose in its frame, and a crumpled cigarette pack scooted ahead of a gust across Hanks Lane, the pack having been emptied of its last smoke by Marge's former husband, Tony, who a day earlier had visited as he did without warning every couple of years, midmorning on a weekday in order to catch Marge alone in the house. She'd given him a cup of coffee and all the cash she had on hand and without telling him anything that mattered had shown him the door. Then she'd gone upstairs to put on earrings and get ready for her dentist appointment, and while she'd watched herself in the mirror maneuver the clip around her right earlobe she had felt Tony staring at her, or staring at the tidy sky-blue vinyl siding of the front of the house, which instead of hiding her revealed her all too clearly to anyone who cared enough to look. Tony shouldn't have cared as much as he did, which made him pathetic to Marge, and as she watched herself in the mirror she whispered what she'd shouted at him in the past — *go away!* He'd gone away eventually, he always did, but first he'd fished in his pocket for a cigarette, crushed the empty pack in his hand, and dropped it on the side of the lane.

So now the pack slid and skittered across the wet road, the rain fell lightly, and Marge opened her mouth to receive the sweet burst of apple and cinnamon sugar and butter, encouraging herself with some chagrin — *forget the calories* — and at the same time wishing she'd invited her next-door neighbors, the Jelilians, to come share the cobbler, an impulse that prompted in her a sudden urge to wince, for the thought of Dorrie Jelilian reminded Marge that Dorrie disapproved of Marge's girls, especially of Jenny. When Dorrie learned that Jenny's son had been fathered by a black man she'd made her repugnance explicit: How could Marge and Eddie have let it happen? But Eddie could always one-up Dorrie Jelilian when it came to the subject of Jenny. No one was a sharper and more pervasive critic of moral shortcoming than Eddie, a fact that made Marge vaguely aware as she lifted her fork that the guilt she felt was in some way connected to Eddie and his impressive capacity for indignation. Even before the mound of cobbler reached her mouth she raked her eyes across Eddie's face in an effort to understand his role in the abrupt shift in her mood and at the same time thought without quite knowing what she was thinking that time would make forgiveness possible. And so with her teeth she scraped the cobbler off the fork and welcomed the feeling of inexpressible relief, believing that her conflicting emotions had to do only with the perfect dessert she'd made, the pleasure of taste, too many calories, and the undeniable success of her effort.

While Marge was about to enjoy her second bite of apple cobbler, Sam and Erma Gilbert were sitting beside each other on their couch, concentrating too intently on the game show to allow the intrusion of random thoughts. Rain coated the windows with a fine glaze, and a swell of wind broke against the front of the house, causing the clapboard to creak softly. Sycamore Street was deserted except for a gaunt yellow dog that loped along, bounding for a couple of strides, then cowering, scrambling forward with its belly close to the wet road, then bounding again and disappearing around the corner onto Field Street.

The television screen in the Gilberts' living room was filled with the blur of a spinning wheel. Erma settled deeper into the cushions. Sam's stomach gurgled, and he belched into his fist. Together, Sam and Erma were working to solve the puzzle of a word, both of them thinking hard to fill in the blanks with letters and beat the contestants to the answer.

The Gilberts would have been Jenny's in-laws if Jenny and Kamon had married. Instead they were just Bo's grandparents and Jenny's good friends. Erma had worked for thirty years as a librarian in the public schools; Sam had been an electrician until his knee gave out. Now they lived comfortably enough off their pensions and Sam's disability, and they took care of Jenny's little boy five days a week. Jenny had been late picking Bo up this evening, though at least she'd called from the store where she worked to let them know, and Erma had given Bo his supper and was getting ready to dress him in the extra pair of pajamas she kept handy when Jenny had arrived to fetch him.

Then Erma had called her daughter Merry to check in, Sam had turned on the television to watch the news, and after ten minutes or so Erma had settled in beside him, dousing a tea bag in her cup of hot water and chattering over the newscaster's voice about Merry's daughter, Miraja, who had won a prize in school for her artwork. They'd gone on to watch the game show as they sometimes did on weeknights, grateful for the peace of the hour when they could sit back and enjoy each other's company — *just an old married couple, sure, luckier than most,* that's the way they saw themselves, though a certain rigidity in their tired bodies betrayed something besides gratitude. You could see from the way they leaned against each other, like two wide boards propped at a slant, that they weren't fooled by a day's routine. No, these were two people who knew the worst could happen and who were determined to stay wary.

They'd been hit hard before — they'd lost Kamon, their youngest boy, and not a day went by without one of them somehow acknowledging that loss to the other through a glance or a touch. Each breath they took was a kind of preparation — and every exhalation a relief. *Phew* — they'd been through it and survived, *wouldn't you know, life will play some dirty tricks and you just got to stand fast, spit in the eye of the devil, do good work, and come out singing your victory song at the end of the day.*

Wouldn't you know, everything adds up once you do the figuring, nine letters still missing in a five-word phrase, b *or* d *or* s, *no,* n *or* o *or maybe* g, k, p . . .

The wheel turned, the arrow bounced past meager sums and finally tripped across the last section to six hundred dollars. All you had to do was guess the phrase, a phrase now worth a grand prize of six hundred dollars added to thirty-five hundred, a fifteen-letter phrase with an *r*, an *l*, two *a*'s, and three *t*'s.

Four thousand dollars plus some, Sam was thinking.

Tale, Erma tried, *taps, tank . . .*

Shoulders rubbing. Breathe in, breathe out. Erma had a flash of an idea, a phrase made up of five words, *tack or tame or take . . .*

"Take it or leave it!"

Sam grinned and took her hand in his, telling her with the pressure of his squeeze that he still loved her even though she'd beaten him to the answer. Beaten everyone else as well. And to think she could have won them a fortune if she'd been a contestant on the show. *Wouldn't you know the way luck works,* Erma thought, returning Sam's squeeze. She yawned, looked absently around the room, and rested her gaze on the boxes of books stacked against the wall — dozens and dozens of books needing to be sorted by subject for the church sale, enough work to fill a few empty hours, a task that would occupy her more usefully than the game show. She'd better get to it if she hoped to be done by midnight.

"Take it or leave it," Sam echoed. The rain softened all at once to a feathery mist, and the yellow dog ran along the sidewalk up Field Street. At a bus stop on East Main a teenage boy ripped a purse from a woman's arm, over at the high school an intramural basketball team ran through drills, people across the city ate spaghetti, dumplings, buffalo wings, tacos, red hots, french fries, sauerkraut, snap peas, flounder, chicken pot pie, and anything else available, a truck idled along the shoulder of the inner loop highway, radio deejays shrieked, children laughed, keyboards clicked, men eyed women in aerobic gear, women eyed men lifting weights, men and women heaved together, somebody wept, somebody crapped or talked on the telephone to a relative in LA or nodded off, and just as the odds would have it, everyone within the city limits kept right on breathing for at least another minute.

The examination should be as formal and complete as time permits. Inspect the abdomen for distention, contusion, abrasions, or lacerations. Consider the possibility of cardiac, pulmonary, hepatic, and splenic injury. Auscultation is helpful, along with palpitation to search for signs of peritoneal irritation. Pelvic fracture can be assessed by bi-iliac compression. Check for the presence of blood in the rectum, subcutaneous emphysema, and sphincter tone. Remember that severe pain at extraperitoneal sites can obscure clinical manifestations. Unexplained hypotension may suggest the disruption of the thoracic great vessels. The standard upright posteroanterior chest film is often recommended. Look for obliterations of the medical aspect of the left or right paraspinous stripe, opacification of the aortic pulmonary window, and deviations of the nasogastric tube. Bear in mind that plain radiography is limited in the evaluation of blunt abdominal trauma in children. Special diagnostic studies, including DPL and CT scans, must be considered in pediatric patients with suspected intra-abdominal injury.

Hey you, Bo! They want you to wiggle your toes!

Of course he could wiggle his toes, but even if he'd understood what they wanted him to do he would have refused. *Leave me alone!* The words were hidden inside him, but he let out one shriek again just so he could hear himself and fill the air with something other than the voices of strangers. *Mama!* What was the word for *mama?* He could remember the idea of her, the smell of smoke and lemons, the green flecks in her gray eyes, the taste of chocolate milk, the click of the spoon against the side of the cup as she stirred in the syrup, the sound of her humming voice, the thousand different browns of her hair, her face slippery like wet clay when she came to pick him up at Gran and Pop's after work. He could remember the sharp slap of her hand on his ass. Who was she? The same person she'd always been, except that she had no name. Nor did Bo. Nor did anyone or anything.

What if he opened his eyes? He couldn't keep pretending that the strangers didn't exist as long as he couldn't see them. They were stealing his clothes and digging the tip of a little rubber ice pick into the soles of his feet. So what if he opened his eyes just a little? What if he peeked between his lashes and tried to see out without letting the strangers see in? Then he'd catch a glimpse of a woman's arm emerging from a green sleeve like Play-Doh pressed through a tower mold. And then, of course, he'd get scared and close his eyes again.

It didn't occur to him to ask what they were doing. This was their world, not his. They would use him for their pleasure and he would stay here forever. But he still had a private world, a world of old memories that belonged only to him, that could comfort him, even if he couldn't remember the words. What use did he have for words? He'd given up on the telling part. Not the looking, though. Careful, Bo! He squinted again, saw instead of the woman's arm and shirt a dirty white wall about ten feet away. No windows and no blue sky. Just a wall with a thermometer and bag attached to it, and white cabinet doors — closed. A metal counter. Another green shirt. A woman's neck, cream-colored like his mama's. The tip of a woman's chin, like a little cup on a platter of flesh. A woman's fish lips moving close to him. Whispering. A woman whispering.

He shut his eyes, fled from the woman who'd caught him looking and who had looked back, though not in. She hadn't had time to look in and see Bo and all his thoughts. He'd escaped this time, and he wouldn't try looking again, not if he could help it. He would keep his eyes shut forever, he would —

— Would not! The woman with the teacup chin was lifting the lid of his right eye, separating it so she could see what, exactly, Bo wanted to hide. She even shone a little flashlight into his eye so she could find his secrets in the shadows. He heard laughter. He wondered what they considered so funny. Even without words to describe it he recognized the expression of relief in the sound of their voices, but he could not connect that relief to their concern and never suspected that these strangers meant to help him. He was far too convinced of their cruelty to change his mind and blamed them not only for bringing him here and pulling off his stinking pants and cutting away his shirt with scissors but for leaving his mama behind.

Behind where? He couldn't remember where he'd just come from. His mama had been dancing — he'd been somewhere standing on his head and watching his mama dance. No, that was all wrong! He'd been catching rivers of quarters in his cupped hands as they fell from the mouth of the slot machine. No! He'd been curled up in a barrel and was bobbing along a river toward the edge of the earth. No! He'd been sleeping, dreaming a terrible dream. Now that would be a fine explanation, and it meant he'd wake up and find his mama sleeping in her own room, and oh would she sure be angry when she saw how late it was. She'd grab his shoes and clothes and stuff him in the car like a pillow into a pillowcase, and he wouldn't dare complain, not with Mama in one of her monster moods; he'd have to wait until she picked him up from Gran and Pop's after supper, then he could tell her about the strangers and what they'd done to him, or hadn't done to him *because it was just a dream, Mama, and dreams aren't real*.

What is the word for dream, Bo?

He didn't need to know the word to know that he wasn't dreaming. No matter how much he wished it, he couldn't turn what was happening into a dream, just as he couldn't turn a dream into something he could feel and smell and touch. Even if he couldn't remember how he'd come to be here, he was here, no getting around it, and his mama wasn't here and never would be here. How could he be so sure? He knew it because the walls were white and voices spoke nonsense and he was naked and smelled of piss. To have come this far from his mama meant that she could never, never catch up to him, no matter how much she wanted to, no matter how many people she asked for directions, no matter how mad she got or how much she wanted him, no matter how loud he shrieked.

He couldn't even remember her name. Her name, his name, or the word that described what he felt when he thought of her. He couldn't remember what had happened back on Route 62 and didn't know what was going on and couldn't find any sense in all the nonsense — "no tamponade, no pneumo—"

"Maintain trac— that's right — let me have a . . ."

"— no dyspnea, adequate urine output, no hypotension, no local swelling, no tachycardia . . ."

"Keep those handy, will you?"

"Anybody seen . . ."

"No deterioration so far."

"Lucky son of a gun . . ."

So once they'd sewn up the gashes on his face and had taken a set of X rays to ensure that his body wasn't hiding any terrible secrets, they could take him off the board. *Hear that, Bo! You comedian you, Mr. Macaroni, number 7153 on the chart, insurance carrier unknown, you're going to be all right!* He couldn't remember any of the names he'd ever been called, but he could remember how he'd laughed when he heard some of them. He remembered the ache of laughter and how Pop pressed a smooth knuckle into his side to make him laugh even when he was feeling angry. He didn't know that the doctors and nurses working on him couldn't have guessed his name even if he'd given them three tries. He didn't know that strangers had their own names, and if he'd been able to read and willing to open his eyes he would have learned what they were called from their name tags.

Dr. Amy Ratigan

Dr. Gordon Metzger

R.N. Carlie Fitzwilliams

R.N. Marianne Walsh

Bartholomew Kowalski the respiratory technician, who called himself Bart. He was waiting to tell his name to Bo, waiting for a chance to tell a joke or sing a song, waiting for the smile that would start to tug at Bo's lips sooner or later, sooner, hopefully, because Bart's shift ended at eleven, and it was already half past nine.

Nor did Bo know this: that the nurse Marianne, who planned to change her name to Mercy someday, was silently praying for Bo as she washed the dried blood from his face with wet gauze pads, asking God to give him a good home after he was released from the hospital, a better home than the one he'd had, judging from the unkempt clothes he'd been wearing.

Or that Carlie Fitzwilliams with the teacup chin was thinking about how hungry she was — she'd been working since three P.M. and hadn't yet taken her break.

Or that Gordon, the resident, was making up his mind that the child's condition indicated X rays but in all likelihood a CT scan would not be necessary.

Or that Amy Ratigan, the attending physician, would have insisted on a CT no matter what the X rays turned up, but at that moment a triage nurse leaned in the door and asked if she could borrow Dr. Ratigan for a walk-in diagnosis. Since the patient, though disoriented, had been stabilized and the team was working well together, Amy saw no reason not to go.

What did it matter? Bo was just a baby and couldn't have cared less who stayed or who went or where they took him, wouldn't have minded if they spit in his face, and had stopped wanting anything except to be left alone to think his thoughts.

"My . . . dog . . . Blue . . ."

"No ID yet."

Of course, years later, when he was all grown up, *if* he were allowed to grow up, Bo might care that Amy Ratigan had left Gordon Metzger in charge, and Gordon Metzger had been trained to avoid expensive tests when there was no specific indication, a sentiment shared by the resident radiologist, Bruce McDonald, who detected no abnormalities in the films.

"Any deterioration run a CT, otherwise . . ."

Otherwise, Bo need not be tested. A nameless kid without any form of health insurance, thanks to his happy-go-lucky mama, who'd chosen to gamble on the health and well-being of herself and her child rather than sign over a hefty portion of her salary for services they'd probably never use.

Otherwise . . .

Just leave him alone! That's what he wanted. Except when they did finally leave him alone, when they wheeled him out of radiology and into an ED cubicle and pulled the curtain around his bed, he started to remember what he'd been feeling earlier. A hurting in his belly. What was the word for *pain?* It hurt a little, not a lot, no reason for a big brave boy to cry. But the more he thought about it, the more it hurt. Like someone was grinding a fist into his belly. *Stop!* How do you say *stop?*

"I've got a dog and his name is Blue."

What?

"Bet you five dollars he's a good dog, too. My . . . dog . . . Blue . . ."

Bo made a deal with himself. He'd open his eyes first, and then the hurting would stop. Okay —

"Hello there, little man."

Who are you?

"My name is Bart. That's *B* as in *banana.* They call me Mr. O$_2$ Man. You can call me that, too. What's your name?"

B as in *banana.* BBBBBB. Bo remembered that part of his name began with *B.* But then he became aware of the hurting and felt so betrayed he started crying as loud as he could.

"Oh no, I didn't scare you, did I? I didn't say something wrong? Oh no, I'm just Bart, everybody's friend, you shouldn't be scared of Bart, I help kids, I like kids, I may be funny looking but I'm not a bad guy. Gordon — I'll get Gordon, he'll give you something to calm you down, he'll make you feel all better."

Don't go! He wanted the B-man to come back and sing to him again. He didn't want to be alone anymore. Maybe if he held in the crying. . . . Yes, this worked, for soon the B-man returned with two of the strangers. They were going to make the hurting go away, they were going to help him, they were going to give him —

"Something to relax you, sonny."

"Poor little angel. Still no ID. Won't you tell us your name, angel?"

He could not tell them anything, though he wanted to now. He wanted to tell them his name and to thank them for making the hurting go away. He wanted the B-man to stay and sing to him. He wanted to tell them that whatever else they did, they mustn't make his mama angry. He wanted to sing them the song she'd been singing before everything went upside down. Now that the pain was relenting he began to understand what had happened, the turning, everything turning one way while he turned another, turning and turning, and all at once he realized that his mama was gone. Not pretend gone. Not playing-like-on-TV gone. Just gone. He understood the fact even if he couldn't describe it. She was lying somewhere in a ditch, her mouth open, her eyes tiny suckers flecked with green. Gone was gone, and if one morning he got out of bed and snuck downstairs and left the house and kept walking up the street, past Mrs. Kelper's house to the bus stop and beyond, Mama wouldn't come after him, she wouldn't slap him and then cover him with kisses, she wouldn't say, *What a bad boy, bad!* She was gone, and there was nothing else for Bo to do except lie quietly and wait for a miracle.

Drifting. Dozing. Remembering things like how spiders and ants and birds and chipmunks and cats and squirrels and inchworms preferred him to other people. Inchworms dropped from low branches into his hair, squirrels hopped right across his sneakers, chipmunks snatched peanuts from his hand, and all the birds in the world nested in the trees around his house. No one had to tell Hobo Templin that the birds cheeped and chucked and scratched at the rainspout just to get his attention. *Don't wake Mama!* Back in his own bedroom he would lift his window a notch higher and stick out his head to see the brown weave of a sparrow nest jutting over the gutter. *Psss!* That shut them up every time, and Mama had gone on sleeping in her room next door like the robins slept, coiled deep in their own nest in the lilac bush beneath Bo's window, though sooner or later the baby birds would wake and spend the rest of the day with their mouths wide trying to gulp the blue of the sky.

What would happen if he dropped pebbles from the window into their open mouths? *Plunk plunk plunk.*

What would happen if he jumped out his bedroom window and flapped his arms?

What would happen if he clicked his mama's cigarette lighter?

What would happen if he never took another bath?

What would happen if he straightened the hook of a hanger and stuck the tip into an electric outlet?

What would happen if he climbed the chain-link fence, into the Harwoods' yard? The Harwoods had a big black dog that ate whatever it could catch — rabbits, beetles, stray cats.

What would happen if he shook a branch of the lilac bush? *Wake up!* One morning not so long ago Bo had reached down from his window and grabbed the tip of the highest branch, making the whole bush tremble, and the mama robin burst in a great flutter from the nest and hid in a tree in Pat and Sonny's yard next door. The baby birds squirmed like fat red worms, which made Bo want to hold them in his fist. He couldn't reach them so instead he threw a stale cracker into the nest, but it disappeared into the thicket of the bush.

Have you ever tossed a handful of glass beads across a room?

Have you ever put your whole head underwater?

Have you ever floated in a soap bubble high above the trees?

In a few weeks the lilacs would bloom and fill Bo's room with the smell of soap bubbles, and his mama would take him to ride a merry-go-round in the mall. He liked to ride the dancing pig that didn't dance at all, just grinned its pig grin and stood nice and still. Mama rode a horse that reared up to the ceiling and dove down, up and down, yet somehow Mama managed to stay on and could even balance no-handed — *look at me!* — while she drew circles in the air with her unlit cigarette.

Remember?

From his crayon box Bo collected four crayons — emerald, rose, sky blue, and black — and rolled his rug halfway up, starting at one corner. He always drew the pictures that he wanted to save on the wood floor. So far he'd drawn his house, his gran and pop, his mama, Josie the cat, the lilac bush, and a dinosaur. He added a picture of the merry-go-round with his mama on the horse and Bo on the dancing pig. The dancing pig didn't really look like a dancing pig once he was through with it, he had to admit, so he took a black crayon and darkened the line of the grinning mouth to make it easier to recognize. When he was through he felt hungry for ice cream, since his mama always took him for a vanilla fudge twist after riding three times on the merry-go-round. He'd be happy with a vanilla fudge twist for breakfast. He padded into his mama's room and stood at the side of her bed, staring at her sleeping face. In sleep, her face stretched lengthwise, and her lips formed a little oval. Bo put the tip of his finger between her lips to feel the breath escape, but she pushed his hand away and told him to get out of there. So he got out of there and went downstairs to the kitchen, where he made himself his own vanilla fudge twist with ice cream and a squirt of ketchup because he couldn't find the chocolate sauce. Even without a taste he knew he wouldn't like it. He filled another bowl with three different kinds of cereal, and since he didn't want to risk spilling milk on the floor he ate the cereal dry. Then he turned on the television and watched cartoons until Mama came down. She made a fuss about his ice cream, so he went outside and sat at the top of the porch steps in his pajamas and watched the older kids waiting up at the corner for the school bus. For fun they threw handfuls of dirt at each other. Bo decided right then and there that he didn't want to get any older than four, maybe five at the oldest. He didn't want to ride a bus to school, he didn't want to feel the sting of gravel against his back, and he always wanted to be small enough to fit on Gran's pillowy lap.

Blue morning sky. *Hello, sky!* He tilted his head back and opened his mouth to taste the blue, and his mama leaned over from behind him and kissed him right on the tip of his nose. Then she gathered him into her arms, carried him inside and upstairs, tugged down his pajama bottoms, and sat him on the toilet like he was *nothing but a shit-in-the-pants little baby, Mama, he was plenty old enough to do it standing up!* But he sat and frowned and pissed, he couldn't help it, and when he was done he kicked his feet free and threw his pajamas at his mama, who caught them with one hand while she brushed her teeth and twirled them above her head like a lasso, making Bo laugh. He didn't mind that his mama was his mama or that his daddy was just a name on a stone stuck in the ground or that he hadn't drawn the dancing pig so clearly or that there was no chocolate sauce in the refrigerator or that he couldn't see the sparrow's nest or that inchworms got tangled in his hair or that his sheets hadn't been washed in three hundred years or that Mama wouldn't kiss him after she put her lipstick on or that the kitchen sink was full of dirty dishes or that he had five videos but the VCR was broken and would always be broken or that once when he wasn't yet two he'd stepped on a piece of glass and the blood that ran from the cut had filled up the gutter, the street, the whole town, and he'd floated to safety on a kickboard.

Bye-bye bahbahbahbah-Bo.

Remember how Gran wanted to check out the sale at TJ's? She buckled him in the backseat — she wouldn't let him ride in the front like Mama did — and drove to the shopping plaza. When she opened the door and unbuckled him Bo dashed off, thinking it would be a fun game to make Gran chase him. He was just three big leaps from the sidewalk when he heard a squeal of tires and saw out of the corner of his eyes what reminded him of the silver buckle of Uncle Danny's fanciest belt but was really the front bumper of a truck. Bo looked up and saw the driver staring at him, jaw hanging, and then Gran caught Bo by the arm, pulled him to the sidewalk, and gave him a shaking that made him dizzy. The driver drove off without even a friendly toot of his horn, and Bo covered his ears with his hands so he wouldn't have to listen to Gran tell him that he'd been very bad, though what he'd done, exactly, he didn't know and wasn't about to ask and a moment later didn't even care.

Inside the store he ran between the aisles of dresses, opened and closed snap purses, tried on dark glasses, and danced on the platform in front of the plate-glass window with the mannequins, flew like an airplane around one long-lashed plastic missus, then hopped off the platform because he thought he heard Gran's voice behind the rack of raincoats. Peekaboo! But it turned out to be someone else's grandma standing there, and Bo realized that he'd lost his own, lost her maybe forever, all because he'd done something bad out in the parking lot. What a bad boy, bad! How would he ever get home?

Gran!

He must mind her now. No shouting.

She pinched the fabric of a shiny purple blouse between her fingers. To prove that he was a big brave boy he wandered off again, sat on the platform, kicked his legs, thump thump thump, against the wood until a store clerk told him that he'd have to leave the store if he kept that up. So he wandered with his hands in his pockets all the way to the other side of the store, bending down now and then to look below the hemlines and make sure he could still see Gran's sneakers and brown legs, wondering what he could do to get in a little trouble but not a lot, wondering what would happen if he gave that stack of shoe boxes a nudge, discovering to his amazement that the whole stack would come tumbling down in a loud avalanche of cardboard.

He ran back to Gran, found her just as she was passing between velvet curtains into the changing area. When she had on nothing but her bra and underpants he poked his fingers in the wrinkles of her knees, which caused Gran to reach down and give him such a strong hug he couldn't breathe, so he squirmed out of her arms while she laughed at him, and the half-dressed red-haired lady beside her laughed and two other ladies laughed across the room, *heedyheedyhaw,* and Bo wondered if he really was what his pop called him sometimes — a regular comedian. He rolled his eyes, then hid behind the wide trunks of Gran's legs, leaned out, played peekaboo with the pretty red-haired lady, who *boo'd* him right back and slipped off her store blouse so Bo could see her titties and smooth belly skin that looked so soft he wanted to rub his cheek against it.

Gran bought one blouse and a pair of felt-button earrings. Afterward they went to the grocery store at the other end of the plaza and ate pizza slices, and then they filled a shopping basket with a carton of milk, chicken drumsticks, Fudgsicles, green beans, Coke, and Pop's favorite — barbecue potato chips.

He lay in Pop's bed because he had a fever, and Pop told him a story about a hungry fox.

He sat on Gran's lap and watched game shows on TV until they both fell asleep.

He dreamed that he could breathe underwater.

He dreamed that a crab crawled out from the pocket of his baseball mitt.

He stood on a chair behind his mama and watched her face in the mirror as she brushed her wet hair.

He found three bottle caps, a pencil, and a garden snail.

He counted to five.

He counted to ten.

He let his cousin Miraja push him on the swing.

He taught himself to wink.

He wondered what, exactly, he wasn't supposed to know.

He stirred his orange juice into his milk and poured it into the kitchen sink when Gran wasn't looking.

It had rained during the night, and when Bo leaned out his window to check on the birds he saw only shreds of mud-caked grass where the nest used to be. He went downstairs and outside by himself, looked all around the grass strip beside the house, and finally found the birds in the hole beside the cellar window. The babies were lying with their beaks open, and the mama was sliced down the middle, with her insides and cords of white bird shit spilled out into the dirt. He knew that the birds were dead — he had seen dead bugs and dead moles and mice and once Ellie Toomer showed him a dead kitten wrapped in a striped rag — but he wasn't sure what being dead involved. Bo poked at the baby birds with a stick and rolled them from side to side like little sausages in a frying pan.

Was Mama ticked when she saw how late it was, ten o'clock by the time she woke: she'd be lucky if she kept her job! She stuffed Bo's clothes into a plastic bag and took him in his bare feet and pajamas to his grandparents' house, trying to inhale her cigarette in one big suck as she drove. Later, when she drove off to work, Bo watched her from the living room window and knew then that her life would have been much easier if he'd never been born, and he was mad at her for making him think that. He was mad the whole morning, until Gran made pancakes and let him spread the peanut butter himself.

He was mad when his cousins came over and Gran had to make pancakes for everyone. He was mad when he tried to skip two porch steps and fell and scraped his chin. He was mad when it rained. Rain was like a door that wouldn't open.

Did Mama have a surprise for Bo! She bundled him in his parka and rain boots, and they drove on the highway for such a long time that Bo fell back to sleep. When he woke they were in a parking lot like the parking lot by TJ's. Mama unbuckled him and led him by the hand down a path, around a garden terrace, down another path, through a building, onto an elevator with a few other people, and they went up and up to the top of a tower and out into the open air.

At first Bo couldn't tell what he was looking at from the top of the tower. Something so hot it was steaming. Hot lava, maybe. But then through the barrier he saw the river pouring over the precipice, and he realized that they were high above a waterfall. Mama stared the way she sometimes watched television, as though the show were her own dream and she could not wake up from it. Bo tugged her wrist when he saw the speck of a boat far below heading straight for the foamy center. The next thing he knew she'd dropped to her knees and buried her face in his shoulder and started to cry. When a policeman tried to lift her to her feet she jerked her arm free. Bo thought the policeman was reaching for his gun then but instead he pulled out his radio, and Bo forgot his mama and the people around them and watched enviously as the policeman whispered into the box.

Mama stopped crying on her own, and the people turned away, turned back to the steam pit and the tumbling water. Bo peeled his mama's hands off his arms. She sagged cross-legged onto the concrete floor and sat there looking as though life had been switched off inside her. A second policeman arrived and the two lifted her by the elbows and led her onto the elevator. Bo knew enough to follow. On the elevator Mama said she was sorry for causing so much trouble, explained that her little boy's daddy and the love of her life had recently died, which wasn't true at all — he had died long, long ago, but Bo knew better than to correct her. In an office in the basement the policemen asked questions that Bo didn't understand, but

Mama answered calmly, and after a few minutes they were allowed to leave together.

They walked through the parking lot, across a street, down the sidewalk, then Mama carried him piggyback across a long bridge that spanned the river. They strolled through empty gardens and window-shopped along the street, and then they climbed up steps into a buzzing, binging circular lobby lined with windows — what else could it be but a toy store! Bo was about to rush through the open set of red doors but was stopped by his mama, who told him that there wasn't anything for kids. It was a party place for grown-ups, she said, and the party never stopped. Bo looked inside and saw people descending on an escalator, some with drinks in their hands, others with cigarettes, one lady holding a fistful of dollars.

On the floors above, folks tried to guess what number would come up when a man threw the dice. You could win enough money to buy yourself a new car, maybe even a house with a swimming pool. And people could win money playing cards at the tables, like Mama did three games in a row while Bo waited in the lobby next to the coat check. She'd warned him not to wander off and under no circumstances to talk to strangers, oh he'd be in for it if she found him talking to strangers! Bo sat in an armchair and counted his fingers, and after not quite forever she came back looking as if she'd just stepped from a warm shower. She let Bo touch three crackly twenty-dollar bills and even shared a hot dog with him for lunch. Later she let him sneak around the corner and watch as she put quarters in a slot machine. He tried to predict what pictures would show up at the end, and sometimes silver coins came tumbling out like the water of Niagara Falls, and Mama clapped her hands, as happy as Bo had ever seen her.

They were rich, rich, rich! Mama sang when she buckled him back into the car for the ride home. Her little Hobo was her good-luck charm!

He drew a new picture beneath his rug of the machine with little windows and pictures that whirled round — lemons, grapes, bananas. What color were lemons? He colored them green, then realized that he'd made a mistake and threw the crayon across the room in a rage. But he found that with some effort he could scrape away the green with his thumbnail, and he colored the lemons yellow like the sun.

Listen!

Buzzing and binging, one thousand people talking at the same time, the sputter of wheels spinning, the clink of coins. Bo leaped out of bed and pulled a corner of the rug back to reveal his pictures. The windows of the slot machine were a blur of whirling shapes, the carousel was turning, the pig was dancing, Josie flicked her tail and hissed, and the dinosaur thudded across the floor and into the shadows beneath the bed, its huge tail burning a groove in the wood. Bo wanted to smash the pictures with his bare feet, but he resisted and instead squatted on the floor and watched the colors swishing and swaying, knowing even as he stared that no one would believe him when he tried to describe what he'd seen. *You and your imagination,* Gran would say. *Go back to sleep,* Mama would say, which reminded him that he'd better keep those pictures quiet or Mama would wake up and blame him for the noise. He unrolled the rug, smoothed it back into place with his palms, and when he still heard the sounds he lay on top of the rug and tried to quiet the pictures with his body but failed even to muffle the clamor. The next thing he knew he felt the floor begin to shake beneath him like the lid of a pot about to boil over, and he could do nothing but clutch the fibers to steady himself against the trembling of the house and the raucous laughter of one thousand strangers, the clatter of a river of coins tumbling over the edge of a cliff, the beeping and hissing of machines, the cheeping of birds, the plock plock of rain, a truck shifting gears uphill, the distant hum of a lawn mower, and a sportscaster shouting something incomprehensible into his microphone.

But what if they hadn't driven home after Mama won a million dollars at the casino? What if they'd walked past the parking lot to the edge of the river above the falls? The sky was dark as he imagined it, heavy with black clouds, and spotlights shone on the white water, illuminating the smooth swell of the river as it curled over the lip of the cliff. Without warning, Mama unzipped her purse, pulled out fistfuls of dollar bills, and threw them into the air, squealing happily as the dollars fluttered and spiraled like a flock of parrots toward the foamy water. Then Mama stepped out of her shoes and climbed over the rail and down the rocks toward the water. Bo watched as she lowered herself into the river. She gave Bo a thumbs-up before she turned and disappeared beneath the surface.

Bo tried to go after her, managed to curl his fingers around the top rail, pressed his feet against the lower rail, and just hung there. If he let go he would have fallen back onto the concrete, not into the foamy water. So he held on, thought *maybe if I swing a leg around,* and had just decided that the easiest way to the other side was to crawl under the lower rail when a policeman grabbed him from behind, wrapped his thick arms around Bo's waist, and pulled him away. Bo kicked and squirmed in the policeman's arms but the man held him fast.

So that was how he lost his mama.

Oh!

Not what he'd seen but the dream of what he thought he'd seen took his breath away. His mama stepping into the water, disappearing.

And here they were making it worse by prying open his lips to look inside and discover his secrets.

Get your hands out of my mouth!

"Are you in?"

"You're overextended — you're occluded — you're, what the fuck, using a cuff! No no no, get the tube without the cuff, the seal will be fine without the cuff, you idiot!"

"Two milliliters, put it in the jugular."

"Epinephrine ready?"

"Don't you want atro—"

"Yes, atropine, get it ready, now are you in?"

"I think I think I think I can't tell."

"We're okay, folks, hold the atropine. We're reading 170. Any-one know who's on in surgery? Carlie, you call, tell them we need a consult. Any family yet? Anyone here to claim the boy? Anyone know anything, or did this child fall out of the sky?"

Did you say something, Sam?"

"Nope."

"Do you want to say something, Sam?"

"Nope."

He had planted himself back on the couch and held a bag of chips on his lap while he thought about nothing, a talent Erma Gilbert envied. With the books sorted for the sale she had a chance to relax beside him again. But now that the television was off and her eyes were too tired to focus on print, she couldn't help but think about her firstborn, Alcinder: Would he keep his job with Park and Rec, what with all the cutbacks? And would Danny and Meredith stay married? Would her nephew Taft stay clean through his probation? And why did Kamon have to go out to the grocery store that night? Eleven-thirty at night stepping out for cigarettes, the foolish boy. And what would become of her four grandkids — Jeffrey, Joseph, Miraja, and Bo? And why did Jenny insist on living out in the suburbs, forty minutes each way when the traffic was light, but in the rain . . . And what could she do with Bo tomorrow? Another rainy day promised by the weatherman. She was tired of the mall but Sam's birthday was coming up and two weeks after that Miraja would turn seven, which meant a trip to the toy store, where Bo would want to choose something for himself. Why not? Her children thought she spoiled him but she spoiled them all and favored no one over the others. She loved her grandkids equally just as she loved her own children equally or almost, almost . . . all right, she had to admit, Kamon had been her baby and had a smile that said

Here I am! She couldn't resist giving him a hug even when he was all greased up after a day at the garage. He never pushed her away, not once, never was embarrassed by love. No wonder Jenny gave up everything for him, no wonder she left behind her own blood relations to start a new family, no wonder. . . .

Sam took a bite out of a potato chip. He examined the jagged border left by his teeth, finished the chip in one more bite, and licked the oily salt from his fingers. He reached for another chip, held it beneath the lamp shade so he could admire the waves and folds and red barbecue dust, hardly more substantial than . . . what? Than a compliment. *Why, Sam Gilbert, how handsome you are!* He broke off a piece of the chip between his teeth, chewed it into fine crumbs, and swallowed.

A communion of past and present. The pleasure of every chip he'd ever tasted relived with this new bag of chips. He took a deep breath and blew out with a whistle. Then and now. *How handsome you are.* Luck of the draw, ma'am. He'd been born handsome and would die handsome. White soft hair, smile lines around his eyes, brown skin as smooth as the skin of an apple no matter how many potato chips he consumed over the course of the —

"Telephone, Sam. You answer it."

"Me?"

"Yeah, you."

"Why me?"

"I'm busy."

"You're just sitting there."

"Well so are you. And I'm sitting here thinking about something but you're sitting there thinking about nothing. So you answer it, Sam."

"Okay then, okay, just hold on, I'm coming, you keep ringing, you damn ear-buster, I'm coming fast as I can so don't you give up on me now, I'll be there before you can say . . . Hey-low!"

"Mr. Gilbert?"

"Yeah?"

"Mr. Sam Gilbert?"

It should have been Bo on the line. It should have been Bo announcing, *Pop, it's me,* so Sam could wonder, *Where are you calling from, child? Where is your mama?* and Bo could answer, *I don't know* and Sam could try to find out whether Bo had gone wandering again, and Bo could insist that he wasn't lost, he just didn't know where he was, which would have left Sam to figure it out — *Now let me get this straight. You're somewhere, you've got to be somewhere. You don't know exactly where you are, but you know you aren't lost.*

But it wasn't Bo. Not Bo saying, *I want to go home,* and not Sam replying, *Course you do, you belong at home. You stay right there, wherever there is, do you hear? Your granny and me are coming straightaway, so you stay put. We're coming to fetch you, so don't wander off again, you hear? Bo!*

Instead, it was an Officer Tinney calling for Mr. Samuel Gilbert.

"What's that? Speak up, will you? There's static on the line. Officer who? Someone in trouble?"

It was Officer Tinney, Arcade Police Department. He'd been given this number by a Mrs. Kelper.

"I don't know any Mrs. Kelper."

"Jennifer Tow . . . let me see, Templer, or Templin . . . I can't quite . . ."

"Jenny — what about her?"

"We are trying to contact her family. If you could tell —"

— tell Bo a story, which was what he would have wanted most right then, if only he could have said it: *one of my pop's stories.* What kind of story? Something that would make him listen, keep him hanging on his grandfather's words from beginning to end.

Now I'm going to tell you a story about rain, about a fat raindrop that landed on the head of a little boy and turned him into a fish, and everyone thought the boy had drowned.

That's a sad story.

Hold on, Bo, there's more to come. I haven't even gotten to the part about the fisherman.

— Make it really scary.

— *I'll scare the living daylights out of you, if that's what you want! I'll make it hell for that boy-fish and you'll be thinking he's done for, but don't be so sure 'cause this is one story full of surprises, it's going to twist and turn every which way, and you've got to stay with me, you hear? I'm telling it to nobody except you, so you got to stay with me until I say, And they all lived happily ever after the end. You with me, child? You still there? Bo! Bo!*

"There's been an accident, Mr. Gilbert, and we're trying to contact the family of Miss Templin. If you could help us out. . . ."

"We are her family, officer. Now you tell me —"

"What's going on, Sam?" Erma had come into the kitchen and in her eagerness to find out what was wrong tried to grab the phone. Sam rotated in a heavy step and put his back toward her.

"No other relatives?"

"None willing to admit it."

"We're required to contact —"

"Her mother lives in Hadleyville. That's all I know."

"Sam, who are you talking to? Who's there? What's wrong? I got to know, Sam!"

"Hadleyville, you say?"

"That's what I said. Now you tell me what's happened. You tell me that Jenny and Bo are fine. You tell me that much and give me my peace of mind back, you hear, officer?"

For those few minutes while Sam was listening to the details, Erma figured that after losing Kamon three years earlier she'd lost Bo as well and Jenny, too, that the Lord had decided to call back to His side those who were too good for this debased world. Well, she knew how to mourn. She knew how to howl and curse Heaven for its separateness, and she was just summoning the strength to begin when Sam got off the phone and told her Jenny was dead but Bo was alive, though apparently he'd been knocked around some and was over at the city hospital. Erma's first thought when she heard the news was not *thank God* or *poor Jenny* but *Now that white girl is gone Bo is mine to raise properly.* She gulped down the realization to hide it from herself. Then she began to cry for Jenny.

* * *

Sounds of the night on West Lake Road off of Main Street in Hadleyville: the distant growl of a truck engine, the clack clack clack of a neighbor hammering a nail into plywood, the whine of a dog chained on a back porch, the broken *what did you . . . hahahah!* of a television show, the buzz of a twin-engine plane, the click and fizz of a man opening a soda can, the suck of rubber against rubber as the refrigerator door closed, a girl muttering into the phone, *it's out of the goddamn question is all he said to me!* — the rip of tires on wet asphalt, mice scraping through plaster behind the wall, the shush of a man's fingernails scratching his chin stubble, water running in the pipes, the refrigerator whirring, warm air whooshing through the grate in the floor, lashes sticky with mascara clicking faintly when Marge blinked, the surf of blood when she cupped her hands over her ears, the gurgle at the back of her throat when she swallowed, the irregular puffs of her own breathing as she thought about the cigarette she was denying herself, the whisper of nylon against wood when she rubbed her heel against the leg of the chair, the meow of a stray cat she'd been feeding on and off for three days, the man's sudden cough, the girl's *fuck you* and the slam of the phone back onto its cradle, the music of a television commercial, the rattle of a car, the remnant of rain dripping from a stopped-up gutter at the corner of the roof.

The only thing Marge couldn't hear was the sound of her satisfaction. Another day behind her and she could look around and calculate the sum of it. No more than this? To be alive and secure, with a house of her own, a yard big enough for a vegetable garden, sunflowers, and a bed of roses, a husband who didn't mind hard work, and children who were mostly grown. Soon Ann would leave, just like her older sister, Jenny. Sure, someday prodigal Jenny would come home, though not to stay — Jenny had her own life to lead and a child in tow and Marge herself had finished with all that. She was like a traveler who had arrived at her destination and found everything in place in her modest hotel room, everything just so, and though she'd never have more than what she had now, well, flip the coin around and consider this: she didn't have much to lose.

She wouldn't deny that she'd made her share of mistakes, nor that Tony Templin had been her worst mistake. Tony and his whiskey. Tony promising her this and that. If it had been up to him they would have had eight children together. He'd wanted to fill the house with the voices of children, with Christmas presents piled to the ceiling, with little bodies in pajamas, with little shoes lined up the side of the stairs, with little hands holding little spoons, with little mouths shouting, crying, screaming — and then off he'd go to Gifferton one town over, to the Jubilee Lounge or the Rabbit Hole or Romeo's, and maybe he'd drag himself home a few days later or maybe he'd wait a few months. An old story, Marge would be the first to admit, and why she hadn't known better than to agree to marry such a man and throw away her love on him, she couldn't explain.

It had taken far too long for her to recognize her mistake, but when she finally did she had no trouble turning love into cold indifference. She divorced Tony, spent a decade raising her children on her own, and then Eddie came along, Eddie Gantz, without promises, Eddie, the most honest and to-the-point man she'd ever met. For more than thirty years he'd been employed as a service technician and manager for Worthco Appliances and hadn't once skipped out. And he'd proved as reliable at marriage as he'd always been at his job. He paid the utilities, he took Marge to dinner every Saturday, and he covered all expenses for their annual vacation. Last year they'd gone to Miami Beach. Marge wouldn't mind a repeat trip, along with five hundred dollars of spending money, which Eddie would give her without any strings attached, not even asking for affection in return. He didn't need Marge to display her love and never demanded favors from her; truthfully, he didn't show much interest in sex, a relief to Marge, who had given up desire when she gave up Tony and who had let herself *thicken,* as she liked to describe it, for the word *thick,* unlike the word *fat,* was compatible with vanity. Thin women suffered during the winter, but thick women thrived, she'd tell her thickening friends, who all agreed. It was better to have padding to protect you against the blow to your buttocks when you slipped on the ice, better to have blubber to seal in the body's heat. It was simply better to be thick than thin.

Marge smiled at the thought of her friends at lunch, the fun they had, the sense of secret power, these thick old broads who had managed to arrange their lives in such a way that now they could do just as they pleased. When she was with her girlfriends Marge didn't lament the paucity of her accumulations, no more than she lamented her dimpled flesh. The girls made her laugh, and when she was in the midst of a crowd there was no better defense than laughter. Laughter was evidence of a person's value, the hiccups of pleasure as significant as one's appearance, and since Marge's wardrobe came from discount outlet shops and her hair and nails were done by Tessie on Main Street rather than by any Monsieur Couture, she enjoyed flaunting herself inexpensively, over a cheeseburger and Coke, laughing so loudly that everyone else in the diner would look at her and wonder what she found so funny.

Eddie rarely laughed. He was such a steady man that the inconsistencies of others aroused in him an unyielding indignation. How could people be so crass, so stupid, so decadent, so selfish? He would have made a fine judge, Marge liked to tell her friends, and she took care not to act in ways that might invite his disapproval, though it would have been difficult to do so, for just by being married to Eddie, Marge enjoyed in his eyes an angelic disposition. She could do no wrong as long as she remained his wife, and she'd remain his wife as long as he held himself up to the highest moral standards. So what if he didn't like to laugh? Marge could depend on him — this, she'd learned after the mistake of Tony, was all that mattered.

And whether her life added up to a glass half empty or half full, what she had was enough simply because she'd grown tired of wanting more. No more, please. The scene of her old age was set, the props carefully arranged, nothing of value to speak of but she was snug — almost. If only Ann would go back upstairs and Eddie would switch off the television and the rain would fall hard to drown out the other noises, Marge would be content. The time she liked even better than her cheeseburger noons with her friends was midnight, when her home was as quiet as an empty theater and she sat alone in the living room, no longer performing the role of herself, no longer weighing her value against others, when solitude erased vanity and Marge could enjoy the silence of night.

There, Ann had folded a slice of white bread around a piece of cheese and left the kitchen. And soon enough Eddie came in to rinse his soda can. He tossed it into the recycling bin, kissed Marge on the back of her head, and then returned to the living room to turn off the television and a table lamp, leaving the other lamp for Marge to turn off when she came up later. An evening routine — and both he and Marge preferred routine to improvisation. How compatible they were. How perfectly suited. Through the doorway Marge watched his shoulder blades shift under his green turtleneck as he started to climb the stairs, felt proud of his reliable companionship and let herself feel another stab of regret at having wasted so many years on Tony, years of pounding music, squealing children, Tony howling lyrics to one indecent song after another. Sometimes the neighbors called Marge to complain, and sometimes they just called the police.

Wasn't it understandable, then, that when all was said and done, Marge should love silence even more than laughter? And here she was, melting into the quiet of an April night. She looked through the kitchen out the dining room window — she couldn't hear or see the lake but she felt it there inside the darkness. For thirty-five years of her life Hadley Lake had been just a few hundred yards away, down the slope and across the road. Marge hadn't had much chance to swim as a child and as an adult had felt no inclination to learn; instead, she preferred to watch the water as she would have watched a wolf in a zoo. There it lay, its great heart beating so forcefully that the beating of her own heart was no more than a weak imitation.

She was settling at last, just as she had night after night for years now. There was nothing but the routine of solitude, the drift of wind through the trees, the sound of the rain and of her own breathing — lovely quiet sounds in this pocket of time. Precious little to fill the emptiness, and that was as it should be. Adding up to no more and no less than this, everything in place, the furnishings adequate, the circumstances uncomplicated.

Marge meant to keep out all disturbances. She would not watch the news or even read a magazine. So when Joe Simmons, who happened to be the Hadleyville sheriff as well as Eddie's hunting buddy, rang the bell, Marge answered the door and before he could speak she said, only half joking, "We don't want any."

"Marge, there's been an accident."

She looked past him and saw that he'd come in the patrol car rather than in his Buick. She couldn't have said how long she stood there listening, but at some point Eddie came up behind her and draped his arm over her shoulder. He wore the navy blue terry-cloth bathrobe she'd given him for Christmas, and he'd tied the belt in a bow. His breath smelled of peppermint mouthwash. Joe stopped explaining what had happened long enough to say, "Heya, Eddie," and Eddie answered, "Hi, Joe," in the familiar tone of voice born from a long history of cahoots. Marge decided then and there that everything Joe had told her was a lie.

And then what happened?

Well, right around midnight the cold spring drizzle that had made the roads slick and tempers short changed to a steady rain. It rained in the city and straight on across the countryside. It rained in the valleys and in the mountains. It rained on plowed fields and gathered in thick brown streams between the mounds of wet earth. The rain fell through the trees and onto the surface of the dark lake.

What about the boy?

The boy snuck from his house while his mama napped in front of the TV, and he ran between the raindrops to the shore. He sat beneath the canopy of an old willow tree and watched the rain hit the lake.

Why?

Because raindrops hitting dark water is a fine sight, that's why. So fine that boy decided he wanted to taste the rain. So he squatted on a willow root jutting out from shore, leaned over, and caught a sweet raindrop on his tongue. But he hadn't realized how slick a willow root becomes after it's been rained on for a while, and the boy slid right off and into the water.

And then what?

He sank straight to the bottom of that lake, and when he tried to push himself up his hands got stuck in the mud. He just held his breath and waited for someone to come help him. But no one came. So he gave up and took in a good lungful of water. He tried to pull his hands out of the mud and discovered that he had no hands. And wouldn't you know, he could push himself forward by wriggling his tail. He sipped that murky water, glided forward, and headed for the river that would take him to the seaway. He thought he heard his mama calling for him, but he kept going.

Why?

Because heroes and heroines have to endure a terrible loneliness in order to prove themselves worthy. And I'll tell you, that little boy hadn't been sure what loneliness was until this moment. Now he knew. It was the taste of lake water in his mouth. It was the body of a fish. It was the voice of his mama calling in the distance.

PART TWO

Here's what happened the first time Jenny Templin's father was fired from a job: at about noon Dorrie Jelilian came by with a box of tulip bulbs, and Marge ended up chatting with her for half an hour in the living room, leaving Jenny alone in the kitchen with the flour bin and the flour and sifter. She made magic North Pole snow that would never melt. She dumped cupfuls of flour onto the kitchen floor and left a serpentine trail of footprints. She dusted her hair and eyelashes with flour. She clapped and sneezed and threw handfuls of flour in the air. She rolled her teddy in the flour, she rolled her sister's bottle in the flour, she rolled herself in the flour. She was building a little snowman out of the ball of sticky pie dough Marge had left on the table when she heard a tapping on the glass pane of the kitchen door.

Oh no! It was Tony to give it to her good. *Crack crack crack* of the wooden spoon against her bottom. Jenny had better run for her life, but the best she could do was clamber under the kitchen table and hug her knees to her chest and hide her face so she wouldn't have to see the spoon descending, *crack crack crack!*

Now Tony was inside, slipping his arms around her waist and pulling her out from beneath the table like a bucket of sloshing water, lifting her up and whispering in her ear, "Quiet, girl!" while he hopped through the magic snow and ran out the back door.

"Put me down!"

"Come on, Jenny-Benny, let's go have some fun."

Sure, but first he'd hit her with a wooden spoon. Jenny knew the usual order of things. Except Tony wasn't his usual self. When had he ever before grabbed Jenny and run with her out the back door and across the yard, through the patch of woods, down the old logging road all the way to Goram Creek? Never! Until today, Tony would appear around suppertime and heap his plate with food, eat his meal, take turns tossing Jenny and Ann high in the air, then disappear again. Tony was lots of fun when he wasn't in a temper, but you couldn't count on him to stay around for long or to take you with him when he left.

Yet now Tony was different, and Jenny felt an urge to call him by something other than his name. But Tony had always liked to be called Tony, and the rest followed — Marge was Marge and Jenny was Jenny and Ann was Ann. Nothing could change any of that, not even the surprise of a trip to the creek. So Jenny called, "Tony!" between hiccups of laughter and clung tightly to him so she wouldn't jiggle quite so much as he bounced along the trail.

It was early fall, a glittering blue day, and the creek was as cold as the air inside a refrigerator, Jenny discovered, combing her fingers through the water after Tony had set her down. Yellow birch leaves floating between the rocks looked like paper-thin sheets of gold. "Look what I found!" she called, lifting a leaf, but Tony didn't bother to look. He was examining pebbles he'd dredged from the bottom of the creek.

"Gold, Tony!" That got his attention. He looked at Jenny with panic in his eyes, as though he'd been caught stealing, and she wanted to say, "Don't worry," but right then her foot slipped off the rock into the water. She cried until Tony took off both her sneakers and let her go barefoot.

Oh how wonderful the icy moss on the rocks, the yellow leaves, the blue sky mottled by treetops, the glinting mica. And look — a fish! Two dragonflies! A yellow bird flashing like a falling star! Jenny climbed onto a boulder, cupped her red toes in her hands to warm them, and decided that she'd wait a little while before she complained. Tony needed to find whatever he was looking for and would get angry if she interrupted him. She sucked her lower lip beneath her front teeth. She listened to the coo of a mourning dove and the distant rattle of a woodpecker. Her feet ached from the cold. A cloud shadow darkened the woods, and Jenny wondered if there were bears around. She started to ask Tony if he'd ever seen a bear at the creek but he suddenly found what he'd been looking for and shouted, "Come here, Jenny! You won't believe it."

He'd finally found gold. And was it a coincidence or had Tony arranged to have more than just Jenny for an audience? At the clearing where the trail led to the edge of the creek stood a fancy brass-buttoned trooper and another man wearing gray slacks and a navy sweater. And then Mrs. Jelilian of all people huffed up beside them, fixed her hands on her hips, and shook her head at Tony as if to say, *You have no right to that gold!*

Jenny wanted to clap for her father but sensed that she should keep quiet. She waited for Tony to say something. He just stood there hiding his treasure in the bowl of his dripping hands.

Then Mrs. Jelilian broke the silence. "Tony!" she said sharply.

"What's wrong?" he asked.

"What's wrong? What the hell is wrong with you?" She stomped her foot at the edge of the water, splashing the hem of her skirt. Tony made his way over the slippery stones back toward Jenny, who eased down from the boulder and stood shivering in the shallow water, causing Mrs. Jelilian to cry, "And the poor child with no shoes! Taking her out of the house with no shoes!"

So that was the problem — she wasn't wearing shoes. "Here are my sneakers." Jenny lifted a soggy sneaker as proof.

"Her shoes!" Mrs. Jelilian cried, ignoring her.

"But what's wrong?" Tony said again, smirking now, Jenny could see. As he lifted her by the waist and carried her back to shore he secretly pressed his treasure into her hand. "Don't tell," he whispered.

Don't tell what? Jenny wondered even as she closed her fist around the secret. Tony just handed her across the last spread of water to the trooper and shielded himself with his hands from Mrs. Jelilian's screaming accusation that he had the whole county looking for him and Jenny. He started laughing, so Jenny laughed, too, and the trooper laughed, and the man in the navy sweater said what Jenny wished she had thought to say — "Just a lot of fuss over nothing."

It turned out that the treasure was not gold. It was just a dull gray slab of shale. But Jenny kept the stone anyway, kept it all her life. She discovered only years later, when she was packing her things to move out of the house, that etched into the hard surface was a finely detailed fossil about the size of a marble — the spiral of a prehistoric snail, a relic that would last almost forever.

The next time Tony lost his job Jenny was in second grade. He didn't come home for six days, and when he did pull up in his truck at dinnertime the next Monday, Marge locked the doors against him. To Jenny's disappointment he didn't even try to bust in through a window. As she liked to remember it, Tony walked in his sad, slouched fashion down the porch steps and turned in the rain and stood looking up at the house, not caring about the drenching, caring only about the melancholy girl who stood at the living room window looking out. But the truth, Jenny knew, was that her father had tried the door handle, knocked, and when no one answered he simply stomped back out to his truck, lit a cigarette as he stood by the cab, then climbed in and drove away. A gray cloud bed hung low to the ground, but in fact it wasn't raining and hadn't rained all that day.

What happened later, however, was just what Jenny would have wanted to remember:

"Jenny-opolis."

"What?"

"Shhh. Be quiet. Come with me."

"Where are we going?"

"I have no one to dance with. Will you dance with me?" And with that the light burst from an invisible balloon, loud music filled the room, and she was spinning in her pink ballerina nightgown around the pole of Tony's arm, twisting her forefinger inside his hand while Tony sang a song about love. Ann was there, bouncing across the floor — *Badump, badump, badump!* And then Marge, no-nonsense Marge, her arms folded to prop up her bosom beneath the plaid robe that Tony had left behind, Marge frowning, Marge crying, Marge being kissed by Tony, Marge dancing and laughing until the phone rang and she stopped to answer it.

"That's it," she announced, clicking off the stereo after she hung up the phone. "Dorrie has promised to call the police if we don't settle down. Girls — up to bed. March!"

And so they marched, Jenny singing softly as she followed her little sister: "The ants go marching one by one, hurrah, hurrah," leaving Tony and Marge to a tense new privacy, enabling them to renew their marriage, if that's what they wanted, and how could they have wanted anything else? That was Jenny's thought as she drifted back to sleep. *How could they want anything else? Hurrah, hurrah.*

The third time her father lost his job Jenny was nine years old, and Tony came home so drunk that Marge couldn't risk sending him away. So she let him sleep on the sofa, and the next morning when she left for work he was still sleeping. Ann hit him across the head with a pillow to wake him up because she and Jenny wanted breakfast. So Tony made them a breakfast of French toast and bacon, then he ordered them to change their clothes, to put on their pretty Easter dresses. Hadn't they been told? It was a holiday — *Happy Racetrack Day!* He drove them to the track an hour east of Hadleyville, he gave them each an amazing fifty dollars, and he bet it for them at the window in increments over the course of the day, winning nothing back, nothing but the fun they had losing it, screaming for their picks to run faster, faster, not caring when their horses came in fourth or fifth or even last because Tony didn't seem to care. He just loved being with his girls. Loved them more than any other girls in the whole wide world, he said, draping his arms over their shoulders and leaning against the empty bench behind him. Did they say their prayers at night? Did they listen to their teachers? They must not let themselves get fat like their mom, he said — fat as an old sow. The boys wouldn't like them if they let themselves get fat. But they shouldn't even be thinking about boys, not at their age. They should be thinking about dollars — "Dolls, I mean dolls," he said, correcting himself and breaking up in laughter that provoked in the girls an uncertain echo. Were they supposed to laugh? Probably, so they laughed with faint *tee-hees*, until Ann stopped abruptly and announced that she had a stomachache and wanted to go home. Jenny certainly wasn't going to be the one to mention that they hadn't even eaten lunch, and Tony thought only to buy two Cokes and a beer on the way out.

He dropped them at home just after three o'clock, and when Marge came home two hours later she didn't ask any questions and so she never found out where the girls had gone. At the supper table Jenny sat in silence, wondering how such a strange and memorable day, the one and only Racetrack Day, could have no consequence.

Six years later, Jenny would have been able to pick him out of a crowd. She knew that faded red baseball cap and the curve of his neck as he walked along. Even after six years of not seeing him she would have recognized him. Even after smoking a joint with her friends. Even after piling into Stephie Johnson's mother's red Datsun. Seven fifteen-year-old girls packed into the two-door sports car. Three in the front, four in the back. Oh the giddy feeling of danger! Gina had a learner's permit — none of the others did — but it was Mrs. Johnson's car so Stephie drove. Brit doled out cigarettes and Carrie held the lighter. Stephie drove up North Lake and onto Route 62. Fifty-five, sixty, seventy miles per hour. *Don't worry.* There were never speed traps along Route 62. A twisting, neglected country road, a striped, pocked ribbon of tar. If you knew what to look for you'd see wild asparagus growing along the side of the road. Honeysuckle, buckthorn, spicebush, mountain holly, patches of blooming charlock and peppergrass. Two-thirty on a May afternoon, a half day for the Hadleyville schools, and the girls were having the time of their lives.

"Just don't drive into a tree, Stephie!"

But they liked to picture it — seven coffins in a row, all of Hadleyville in black, weeping, weeping. Front-page news from Buffalo to Syracuse. The adults deserved a good tragedy.

"You can drive a car but you can't vote George Bush out of office, that shithead!"

"Stephie can't drive a car!"

"Then what's she doing now?"

"I'm not sure. But I wouldn't call it driving!"

"Stop it, Gina. You're making Stephie laugh!"

"Be careful, Stephie!"

"Watch out!" It was Erin's loud voice that Stephie finally acknowledged. She veered away from the shoulder of the road back into her lane.

"Still alive to tell the tale," Gina said.

"The young get old," Stephie piped. "The old get sick. And the sick die."

Had they ever laughed so hard before? They were young, not yet old and sick and dead, and had found in themselves the capacity for revolution. Except that Gina suddenly remembered she had to baby-sit at three o'clock, so they'd better turn around and head back to Hadleyville.

Not back along Route 62, Stephie decided. No — they'd drive right through the center of Gifferton.

"Are you crazy?" Carrie shouted as Stephie speeded up after a turn.

"Crazy as a loon!" Stephie cried, zipping along Main Street while the girls covered their faces so they wouldn't see the horrified residents of Gifferton jumping out of the way. But crazy Stephie managed to obey the traffic laws, and no one looked twice at the red Datsun.

On their way out of town, the girls grew bolder. They unrolled their windows and *yeehawed* at the top of their voices, laughed and sang as Stephie drove them beneath the highway overpass. Jenny reached from the back window to the front, tried to grab Gina's cigarette, tried to sing through her laughter. Hilarious, dangerous life. They loved the boys! They loved each other! They loved driving without a license!

Of course Jenny recognized him: the bum stumbling along the sidewalk in the gloom of the overpass just a couple of arm lengths away. The girls didn't call such men bums. They called them *hobos*. The drunken hobo in the red baseball cap. At that moment his foot slipped off the edge of the sidewalk, he lurched to the left, steadied himself, and took another step forward, though by then he was behind the car, and Jenny somehow managed to keep herself from turning in her seat to watch him, pretended to be watching the scenery instead, pretended to agree with the common assumption that the drunk, the bum, the hobo beneath the overpass, was worthy of no more than a passing glance.

So here was a treasure to add to the fossil Tony had pressed into her hand long ago. She knew that she would never tell her friends what she'd seen back there, what they'd missed. She could not tell them anything that mattered. Honesty was a well-kept secret — to last almost forever.

In a car again, this time her mother's car, smoking a cigarette. Sixteen years old and she could go anywhere, do anything. She could skip her afternoon classes, browse in thrift stores and costume shops, engage in conversation with the clerks and pretend to be someone else. She could watch people waiting at a corner for the light to change. She could page through magazines in a drugstore and drink coffee from a Styrofoam cup. She could create a commotion and steal a woman's purse. She could sell her mother's car and buy a bus ticket to the West Coast. She could lean against the doorway of an office building. She could lie down on a park bench. She could pretend to belong here. She could pretend to care about nothing.

There appeared to be no end to this freedom beyond her capacity to savor it. But as she turned the car onto East Main, the clutch refused to engage — Jenny fought with the handle, pumped her foot against the pedal, let the car drift, and finally managed to return to second gear.

And that should have been that — the end of the afternoon's potential, the recognition of limit.

You wouldn't have guessed it, looking at him thrust his grimy hands under the hood of the car, but Kamon Gilbert didn't let any piece of information slip past him. If there was something to be learned, he'd learn it. He knew the difference between fission and fusion. He could explain how a blast furnace worked. He could tell you about the flaps on an airplane wing and show you why the clutch in your mother's car had trouble engaging.

But the thing he knew best was light. His daddy was an electrician, Jenny learned later. And besides that, his mother used to drill him with this simple question —

What should you do when you leave the room?

Turn off the light, Ma!

— the exchange repeated over and over until Kamon couldn't enter a room without reminding himself to leave it in darkness. Light, however necessary, was expensive. Light was a treasure that mustn't be wasted on an empty room. Between his father's work and his mother's prudence, Kamon learned to appreciate all kinds of light and made no secret of the fact that he planned to earn his living as a photographer, manipulating high-frequency photons in order to illuminate the material expression of personality and the colors dependent upon light, the colors in Jenny's hair, for instance, glinting in the sunlight as she watched Kamon work. Of course he didn't speak about any of this, not yet. Instead he tried to draw her into a conversation about the weather, the hint of winter in the air, and her name . . . ?

"Jenny," she said, and clamped her mouth shut while she listened to him tell her what she didn't care to know: that his name was Kamon Gilbert and this was only a part-time job. He was a junior and would head off to college in a year. So what did Jenny do?

Look, she had to go. If he couldn't fix the car right away she'd bring it back later. But in truth she didn't intend to bring it back. Why drive all the way to the city for repair work that could be done in her hometown of Hadleyville? The only reason she'd stopped in at the garage where Kamon worked was because she'd come up to the city to shop for a Halloween costume to wear to Stephie's party next week. At least she'd succeeded in finding a costume — a pillowy white cube with black dots, a giant die propped on the backseat of the car.

"No, I can't fix it right away. You'll have to leave it. What's that?"

"My Halloween costume. I can't leave the car here overnight. I'll bring it back another time."

Kamon closed the hood while Jenny slid behind the wheel. He took a few steps back, folded his arms across his chest, and waited as she turned the key.

"See you, Kamon Gilbert."

"You remembered my name."

"Why shouldn't I?"

"Why? Because most folks don't listen."

"I know how that is."

"You do, huh?"

"I'll be seeing you, Kamon."

"Hope so, Jenny."

And that would have been that, except Jenny on her way out managed the extraordinary feat of backing her car up against a fire hydrant near the edge of the lot, maneuvering the wheel in such a way that the spout of the hydrant lodged between the rear tire and the bumper, preventing her from backing up further or going forward without tearing the bumper from the car.

She shifted into first gear and back into reverse, rolled and lurched while the clutch protested shrilly. Kamon just stood with his hands in his back pockets and watched. Jenny tried not to look at him but sensed his eyes on her and was surprised to find herself feeling as pleased with his attention as she was irritated by the upturned corners of his closed lips, the hint of a smug grin. *Go ahead, laugh!* She tried turning the steering wheel and accelerating forward, succeeded only in drawing from the torn bumper an exclamation of despair. She tried reverse again, but the rear tire spun in place, stripping the grass from the muddy ground. Finally she gave up, let the engine idle, and leaned back against the headrest.

"Whatcha doing?" Kamon finally asked.

"Me?"

"Yeah."

"What am I doing?"

"Yeah."

"You mean, why am I sitting here in the car?"

"Yeah."

"No reason," Jenny said with her eyes closed.

"Oh."

A minute or so passed before Kamon broke the silence again.

"Anything I can do?"

"Nope."

"I'll be seeing you then." He didn't move. The other three me-chanics had come out of the garage and were standing together watching Kamon, who was watching Jenny, who was looking up at the sky darkened by the tinted edge of the windshield.

"I got to get back to work," he said, circling the toe of his sneaker on the sidewalk.

"Sure. Go ahead." Kamon just stood there. "Go on!" Jenny insisted.

As he headed back to the group of mechanics, Jenny studied his slack, dirty jeans, the cap of dark hair, the plaid shirttail tucked messily into his pants, the flannel crumpled at his narrow waist. *Wait!* Jenny Templin had gotten herself into a ridiculous predica-ment, she had to admit it. But she was just a hick girl who had come up to the city looking for trouble.

"Kamon Gilbert," she called out the window, "I need you."

"You sure do."

Now if she put the car in drive and eased forward, Kamon could lift the bumper up and over the hydrant spout. Amazing Ka-mon. What had he wanted to ask earlier?

"Maybe I could find another one of those costumes . . ."

"You want to be a pair of dice with me?" What a hoot! Except that Jenny couldn't show up at Stephie's party with a black guy from the city. But they didn't have to show up anywhere, did they? Where could they be alone together? Jenny thought about it while Kamon spoke.

"How about I come by tomorrow? I'll fix your car for free."

"It's my mother's car."

"Whatever."

"I don't think so."

"Okay, okay."

"How about we go for a drive?"

"Just drive around some?"

"I live way out in Hadleyville."

"By Hadley Lake?"

"We can just drive around."

"Sounds fine with me."

It wouldn't be fine with Jenny's mom and stepfather. So Jenny asked Kamon to meet her at the corner of North Lake and Route 62. Kamon's eyes glittered with the anger he couldn't speak of. "I get it," he murmured. "See you there." Jenny said with her own eyes, *Maybe we can fool around.*

Maybe. As she drove away she swallowed the one word, leaving the rest to consider: *We can fool around.* This was just the kind of trouble she'd come looking for.

Waiting for him to arrive, certain that he'd stay away and then certain that the next car would be his and immediately feeling embarrassed by just about everything: her silver loop earrings, her baseball cap, the birding guide left by her mother in the backseat along with a *berry finder* book — "a guide to native plants with fleshy fruits." Oh my god, she'd forgotten to shave her armpits. And in this light you could see the grape jelly stain on the sleeve of her blouse. And what was *that* hanging from her nose? Oh my god.

"Hiya."

"Hi."

"What's up?"

"Not much. I don't know."

"What?"

"I don't know. What's up with you?"

"Not much. . . . Well, so . . ."

"So what?"

"So you want to drive around?"

"Sure."

"Okay."

"Okay then. Fine."

"Good."

"Yeah, good. Great."

"Great."

"Great."

"Just don't get caught," said Jenny's sister, Ann, after Jenny told her she was going to see Kamon Gilbert again.

She watched his teeth close around the outer rim of the burger, seize the bun and meat and draw the mouthful in between his lips. He chewed slowly, his eyes locked on hers. She clamped her own lips around her straw, sucked until a thick clump of milk shake oozed free and spread across her tongue. He continued to chew. She continued to suck. She lowered her gaze so the fringe of her lashes nearly covered her eyes. He shifted in his seat, tore another mouthful from his hamburger, and as he chewed explored the area beneath the table with his right sneaker, stopped when he bumped against her ankle, pressed his toes gently against her shin, rubbed softly and managed to lift the cuff of her jeans up over her sock. She stared down at her glass full of strawberry milk shake and sucked. He stared at her and chewed. She reached over to his plate, closed her thumb and forefinger around the tip of a curly french fry, lifted slowly, separating the one curl without jostling the others, pulled her arm back and dropped the fry whole in her mouth, like a pelican swallowing a fish. She smiled. He hooked a finger around the base of her glass, slid it toward him, and without looking down caught the straw between his lips. He sucked. She chewed. He rubbed. She smiled. She sucked. He chewed. And so on.

* * *

"Jenny, phone!"

"I got it. Hello?"

"Hey."

"Hey."

"It's me."

"I know it's you."

"I'm watching the game right now."

"So am I!"

"Go figure."

"So you saw that loose-ball foul?"

"Wasn't that something!"

"You watching, me watching . . ."

"We might as well be an old married couple."

"Might as well."

"Yeah."

"Yeah."

What she realized then, reclined on the backseat of his parents' Pontiac, feeling the torn upholstery against her skin, feeling the tingling as his hand explored her body, was that love, or just this love, conjured with its minute and breathtaking pleasures the opposite of love. Not hate but loss. How was it possible that her life would lead to nothing, that the cold autumn sun would eventually burn itself out, that love would draw to a close? She would have chosen not to love him if she could have helped it. Not because he was black and she was white, not because her mother wouldn't have understood why she'd fallen for Kamon, not because Eddie would have killed them both if he'd found out. She would have chosen not to love him because to love him as she already did meant she had to face the absolute loss of him.

She huffed aloud at the silly, inadequate word. *Love.* Who named it? Who dared to give the feeling a single name?

"What?" murmured Kamon.

"Love," said Jenny.

"This now, you mean?"

"Yeah" — without doubt or hesitation. Yeah. This now.

Or in the movie theater, with Kamon's arm around her. Knowing that Kamon was watching her instead of the movie. Watching the play of light on her face, like beams diverging on the flat surface of a hologram and giving the image uncanny dimension.

Or in the bedroom of Miraja, Kamon's little niece. Feeling the mattress bubble and sag while Miraja held Kamon's hands and hopped in place on the bed: "One fell off and bumped his head. Mama called the doctor and the doctor said —"

Or lying alone on her own bed in the dark, thinking of him, certain that such intensity of thought could be felt by Kamon miles away.

Tuesday the fourteenth . . . Wednesday the fifteenth . . . Thursday the sixteenth . . . Friday the seventeenth . . .

Here's a picture of Kamon walking up the steps from a basement exit at his high school, his hands in the front pocket of his jeans, the sides of his open parka tucked beneath his arms and creased by the straps of his backpack, his face cast in meditation. He hasn't yet seen Jenny standing with his camera.

Here's a picture of Jenny at the lake, Jenny hanging by her knees from a tree branch, Jenny nearly overcome with laughter while Kamon recites behind the camera, Oh blessed, blessed night! I am afraid this is all a dream, too flattering-sweet to be substantial.

Here's Jenny with her arms folded, frowning at Kamon for snatching her image before she's had a chance to brush her hair.

Look carefully at this one and you'll see that they've tied the laces of their sneakers together in a knot.

Here you can see Kamon's arm extended across the lens as he holds a lit match at the tip of Jenny's cigarette.

Here Jenny leans against the bumper of Kamon's car.

Or feeling him slide into her, feeling him inside her, feeling more amazed than she'd anticipated by the possibility of making a child together. An intoxicating, defiant proposition. Her own secret treasure.

"You're kidding!"

"Sure I'm kidding. Hahaha. Why aren't you laughing, Kamon?"

"You're sixteen years old, Jenny. Have you thought about it? Think, girl!"

"I don't need you. I don't need anybody."

"Think about it. You have to think about what it means."

It meant that she needed something. What? A future? A place in the future? A fullness? Value? Morning sickness? Something that belonged to her? Something unknown becoming known? Love made visible? The attention of doctors at the clinic? The repetition of her own childhood? Something instead of school? Something instead of adolescence? Something instead of a cramped bedroom in her mother's house? The extension of nothing into something? Kamon's child? Kamon's love? The consolidation of love? All the prohibitions, warnings, guidelines, and concern? The surprise? The rebellion? The admission of mistake? The insistence of desire? A possession? A pet? A crib and stroller and high chair and five thousand disposable diapers? The worry? The dissolution? The fevers and teething and colic? A playmate? A trophy? A happy ending?

* * *

Here's what Jenny's sister, Ann, thought: whatever drew Kamon to Jenny and Jenny to Kamon was something like a gust of wind that catches a leaf as it falls from a tree and sends it spiraling upward.

Or in the tub feeling her skin turn elastic and stretch. The bliss of fatigue. The sour taste beneath her tongue. Feathery, shifting motion. A kick and nudge. Seeing the mound in her belly formed by a restless limb. *Cool!* Body inside a body. Nothing cooler.

Jenny's stepfather wouldn't have her in the house anymore, so she moved with Kamon into the extra room at Taft's place. Taft was Kamon's twenty-two-year-old cousin. Kamon's parents gave Kamon money each month so he only had to work part-time at the garage and could finish school and go to college. They all agreed that Kamon must go to college no matter what, though Jenny didn't see the need and believed that Kamon could have prospered as a photographer without a college education. But she didn't want to spoil his vision of the future any more than she already had. She sensed that she could never win the family over. *White girl aiming to ruin Kamon's life.* They'd put up with her for Kamon's sake, but they weren't going to like her. White girl plopping herself down in their midst and asking them to take care of her. *You can stay. Just don't go bothering us.*

Saturday the twenty-second . . . Saturday the twenty-ninth . . . Saturday the fifth . . .

And then one winter night Taft wanted a pack of cigarettes. Taft — all two hundred and eighty pounds of him. He'd come from Buffalo to go to technical school, lived with Kamon and Sam and Erma for a while, but he took to petty dealing and was busted for possession right in the Gilberts' front yard. On probation now, he had his own apartment and had promised his family he'd stay out of trouble. He called Jenny *Hey bitch,* in light derision: *Hey bitch, you want some pizza? Hey bitch, you seen Kamon? Hey bitch, get your ass up here!*

"Hey bitch, you go out and buy me some cigarettes and I'll give you a big tip," Taft said out of the blue one night.

"It's almost midnight, Taft. I'm not going anywhere."

"Kamon, how about you? Come on, here's an extra ten, bird on a wing, take it or leave it."

"Make it twenty and you got yourself a deal."

"Twenty fucking dollars, cousin? You a ballbreaker! Fifteen."

"Twenty, you lazy shit."

So that's how much Kamon's life turned out to be worth. Twenty dollars. Twenty dollars and a carton of cigarettes. Jenny had wanted a cigarette, too. And twenty dollars wasn't nothing. The glance that she exchanged with Kamon before he left assured her that together they'd get rich off Taft's stupidity. Kamon wore Taft's parka and a bright orange knit hat, but he didn't bother with boots. Jenny knew how he liked to walk on new snow in his sneakers, how he liked the silence of the streets, the light dancing in the salt puddles, cigarette smoke mixing with winter air, the taste of cold, the taste of Jenny's tongue when he kissed her good-bye.

She watched the basketball game with Taft while Kamon was at the store. She'd played on her own junior varsity team and had a special talent for stealing the ball from her opponent. She'd taught herself to use her left hand as a paddle and could sweep the ball away and take off downcourt, running free from the pack and leaping into the layup. As she watched the players on the television, she flattened her fingers and remembered the rough surface of the ball against her palm.

The shots in the distance sounded like the popping noise of corn inside a microwave. Jenny wasn't sure what she'd heard, but her heart went pop-pop-pop because she felt the force of it before she knew the truth, felt it as the beginning of the end of the world. Hadn't she somehow known what would happen, as though she'd read through the book first a long time ago and when the movie started had a vague recollection of how it would turn out?

The baby did a jig inside her, roused by Jenny's fear. Taft kept watching the basketball game. Jenny wanted to tell him to go find Kamon and bring him home. She wanted to rip Taft's chest open with a knife. She wanted Taft to take her in his arms while she wept. She wanted to go down the street and find out for herself what had happened, but she couldn't rise from her chair.

Funny how her intuition flagged, and she started to think, *what if?* What if those really were shots she'd heard? What if Kamon had been hurt? And gradually the *what if* changed to *if.* If Kamon had been hurt . . . if Kamon had been shot . . . if Jenny lost Kamon now. . . . For a long minute the street outside remained silent, and the silence reassured Jenny, transformed the *if* of catastrophe to *maybe.* Maybe nothing had happened and Kamon would be bouncing up the steps soon, one of Taft's cigarettes hanging from his lips. Maybe Jenny was stirring herself up just so she'd experience the pleasure of relief. Maybe everything was perfectly fine. *Maybe* — she swallowed the word and waited for Kamon to hurry up and come home.

Because Kamon had been killed on a city street Jenny moved out of the city a month before her son was born, and because she couldn't afford to rent a house of her own she had to settle for half of a double in a run-down neighborhood in the town of Arcade. Because she lived way out in Arcade she bought a used Ford Escort with the money her mother had sent her, and because she had a car she could take a job at the mall. Because she worked at the mall she had to drive a total of twenty-eight miles to get home — from the mall to the fourteenth ward in the city to pick up Bo and back to Arcade. Because she had such a long, boring drive ahead of her she liked to relax at a bar with some friends before she set off, and by the time she got home she'd be feeling so tired that when she settled down beside Bo to sing him a good-night song she'd often fade into sleep herself. She'd sleep for a few hours, and then she'd wake with groggy surprise to find herself still in her clothes. Usually it would take her an hour or more to fall back to sleep in her own bed, and during that time she was good for nothing but some middle-of-the-night B movie on television. While she watched she'd get to thinking about the shambles of her life and how her sister, Ann, who tried to help out with baby-sitting now and then, blamed her for the mess. Once Ann had even tried to prove her point by dumping all of Jenny's beer down the drain of the kitchen sink. Seven dollars' worth of beer!

You're a goddamn drunk, Jenny! You're gonna end up like Tony!

But Ann didn't know what she was talking about, since she had no idea what happened to Tony. She remembered him only as a giddy, celebrating drunk, a ridiculous clown whom you had to beat over the head with a pillow to wake up. But Jenny remembered Tony beneath the overpass — Tony the hobo, the vagrant, the wanderer. And Jenny would lie awake imagining the satisfaction she'd feel if she could really fulfill her little sister's expectations. Okay, so she'd end up just like Tony: penniless and drunk and nobody's fool, free as the wind.

Just watch me! Bo, pack up your suitcase, we're going on a trip.
I want to go to Disney World!

We'll go there and everywhere else. Now you be a good kid and hang out over at Ashley's until I get back. Mama has to do something.

She'd drive the twenty miles southeast to her mother's house in Hadleyville, sneak in through the back door, and slip Marge's wallet from the purse hanging in the vestibule. Then she'd drive back to Arcade and bring Bo back to their side of the house and set to work packing his bag and hers. Oh, she'd be in an ugly mood by then, one of her monster moods, she called them, and Bo wouldn't dare open his mouth to ask her what she was doing. He'd just sit on his bed and watch her, and the silence would be tense with anticipation.

But nothing happened without incident, Jenny knew. Sooner or later there'd be a knock on the door, a knock that meant she'd have to postpone her plans.

And then the knocking would turn to pounding, pounding, pounding, hammering against the door, as though someone were firing a cannon, or driving a backhoe into the side of the house. Bo would watch Jenny, and Jenny would pretend to hear nothing.

Jenny, open up! You're in there, I know you're there. Open the door. I said open the damn door!

She'd let him go on for a long five minutes, and then she'd open an upstairs window and throw an empty beer bottle onto the sidewalk. She'd return to her bedroom and continue stuffing clothes into the suitcase, cursing all the while — *you fucking Eddie, you leave us alone!*

Bo had never met Eddie, *fucking Eddie,* Jenny called him, the

only thing she ever called him. If Jenny really ever did steal her
mother's wallet, fucking Eddie would leap into his car and drive to
Arcade and try to force his way into Jenny's house. Eventually he
would succeed. He would grab Jenny and tear her head from her
neck and without even wiping the blood from his hands he would
come searching for Bo to do the same to him. That's what happened
on the television at three A.M. That's what would happen to Jenny
and Bo, unless Jenny had the prescience to whisper between her
teeth, *run, Bo, go on, run!* and maybe threaten him with a hairbrush
so he'd do what she told him to do. He'd hop down the stairs with
his head turned to make sure his mama was following, he'd run
ahead of her through the kitchen and out the back door, and he'd
leap from the top step into the open arms of the man waiting for
him, that fucking Eddie, who would stagger against Bo's weight,
steady himself, and stand there looking like a long-lost husband returning home with a huge turkey in his arms, like Tony Templin
would have looked if he'd ever attempted a reconciliation, all traces
of humility lost to his sense of triumph. *Aren't I something, appear-
ing on the doorstep with a turkey after all these years . . .*

  Give him back to me, Eddie!

  *Nothing doing. You just sauntered into our house, stole your
mother's purse, and sauntered out three hundred dollars richer. I say
that's about the cost of this plump little rascal here. Three hundred
buckaroos. See you later, Missy.*

  You let him go!

  Eddie would keep on clutching her little boy in his arms, and
Jenny would just stand there on the threshold, knowing that she
should give Eddie's arms a tug, maybe kick him in the groin and
wrench Bo free. All she had to do was fight for her son. But she
wouldn't fight. Instead she'd just stand there whining like the Harwoods' dog when he'd gotten his leash tangled around the trunk of
a tree, whining for Eddie to give Bo back while she watched him
carry Bo down the couple of steps to the concrete path.

  Here, Eddie, here's your money!

  She'd throw greenbacks over the rail, though you didn't have to know Eddie well to know that money meant little to him. He'd rather have Bo than three hundred dollars. Who wouldn't? Too late to change your mind now, Jenny.

What would happen next? Would Eddie take Bo to Candyland or to the Worm King's dungeon?

Caught in the trap of cause and effect, Jenny would try to comfort herself thinking about how Aunt Ann would be waiting at the end of the driveway on Hanks Lane, ready to welcome Bo. And Marge would be there beside her. Marge, after all, was the kid's grandma. She'd lift him out of the car and give him such a big hug that Jenny would feel comforted by the scene as she imagined it. And it was only imagined, wasn't it? Selling her son to Eddie so she could head off alone to Disney World? Jenny would never do that, but even if she did, Ann would keep him company and take him to look for rocks down by the lake, Grandma Marge would cook him macaroni and cheese, and the next day Eddie would get to work building him a tree house. He'd make sure no nails were sticking out of the boards, then he'd lift Bo into the tree house, hand him up a bag full of red licorice, and leave him there while he went to work. Maybe he'd leave him there all day. Yes, that's what would happen and Jenny couldn't change it: no one would come for Bo no matter how hard he cried, no one except Grandma Marge, who would pass him up a blanket and maybe a peanut butter sandwich and say she loved Bo but couldn't help him. They didn't want to make Eddie angry, did they? *No, you don't want to see Eddie get angry. He's a good man, except when he's angry. No matter what, you don't want to make him angry, for Eddie doesn't hold back and has been known to pick up a cat that scratched him and throw it against the wall.*

Stop!

What's wrong, Ho-bo-bo?

It's too scary.

You keep listening to this story, listen to how the sparrows bring you bottle caps and snail shells, and the spiders spin their webs into thick silk sheets to keep you warm, and the raccoons bring you choco-late chip cookies, and the squirrels take turns lying still so you can hold one against you while you sleep. Spring turns into blazing summer, and from the fort Eddie made you can see the lake, you can watch the sailboats while you eat wild strawberries that the crows bring you, buckets of strawberries, then peaches and plums, then the first wind-fall apples and it is fall, the nights grow cold again, and —

I'm not listening.

— *the snow comes, soft as sifted flour falling through the open window of your little tree fort, then* —

I'm not listening.

— *sleet, a blizzard of ice, so the next morning you wake up to find the trees around you all shimmery. Remember that ice storm, Bo, when the world turned to glass? Well, this will be just like then* —

I don't want to hear anymore!

— *and the squirrels will come out of their nests and puff their warm breath to thaw the walls and warm you.*

Stop!

You're a lucky kid, you were born lucky and will always be lucky, Bo, for you are your mama's baby and will be taken care of no matter what. Even though Grandma Marge and fucking Eddie stop taking care of you. Even though Aunt Ann moves away because she can't bear living in that goddamn house anymore. Don't cry, Bo. One day you'll look across the snow-covered yard and see, standing by the back door of the house, a scrawny old man in a red baseball cap staring at you, just staring, and even though he doesn't make a move to help, try to re-member that when he disappears he will go to find someone who can help you, he will walk for days through the snow, his toes will freeze and turn gray inside his worn-out shoes but still he'll keep walking, and you'll wait for him, you'll know that he'll return with someone who can save you, your very own gran, and Pop, too, he'll track them down and lead them back to you and everything, I promise you, everything will be all right.

Everything will be all right.

"Bo, sweetie."

Face as shiny as a leaf of myrtle, eyes like huge painted pearls, brown irises surrounding targets of black.

"Everything's going to be all right."

"Do you know us, Bo?"

Another face beside the first. Faces like two rubber balls he'd lost so long ago — and finally found again.

"You rest up now. Gran's gonna stay here night and day until you're ready to come home. I'm not leaving this room, child. Not without you."

Didn't I always tell you everything would be all right, Bo?

Yes you did. You did.

PART THREE

For practical purposes we could say that Bo liked to change his position with respect to a stable surface — e.g., the floor, any floor, first the one in his hospital room, then in the corridors, then in the parking lot, then in Gran and Pop's living room. Aristotle would have described it as a violent motion, since it involved change produced by human agency. Galileo would have applied his law of inertia and described the transition from motion into rest, from rest into motion. Newton would have pointed out that Bo's action and reaction were equal and opposite. Einstein would have introduced the notion of relative time. And the one and only Mr. O_2 Man, the B-man, Bart Kowalski, would simply have used the word *hop* to describe the motion, did in fact say on Bo's last morning in the hospital, "You sure like to hop, don't you?" and Bo proved the accuracy of the word by hopping, hopping, hopping until the spectators in the room, including Bart, and Bo's gran and pop — Erma and Sam — were worn out just from watching.

Just don't hop on Pop!

And off Bo hopped into a better world, nothing to show for the trauma that nearly cost him his life but a butterfly bandage on his cheek and a little pink seam down his middle, where the surgeon, Dr. Platt, had cut him open to repair his lacerated spleen. Bo was whole again, though missing a mother, it was true. Who didn't feel sorry for him now? Who didn't want to reach down and pat him on the head and let out a whistling sigh of sympathy?

He'd had so many visitors back in his hospital room — the

B-man, Gran, Pop, his aunts and uncles and cousins and doctors, nurses who arrived laden with pudding and apple juice, gray-haired women who brought him picture books. But despite the attention Bo was glad to put the hospital behind him and hop hop hop into the cozy future, the *real* future, and see what he could see. Everything would be all right in the real future, even though his mama had gone off without him, leaving behind only Bo's idea of what she would have wanted him to do.

She would have wanted him to mind his gran and pop. So when they said, *Wake up!* he woke up and saw the basket hanging from his bedpost. A basket full of purple grass and hollow chocolate eggs and a windup bunny that went hop hop hop across the floor. This was only the first morning of Bo's future and everything was already all right, simultaneously strange and familiar, new and old, just like Bo himself.

Bunny hop, bunny hop, bunny bunny bunny hop.

He'd get around to talking again one of these days. Not quite yet. He enjoyed hiding behind the stamp of a silent face, preferred not to tell what had happened, all that had happened. What he really wanted was to go to the toy store as soon as possible. *Please?* He practiced the expression with his eyes, climbed onto the rim of the bathroom sink to check the success of his efforts, decided that as long as he raised his eyebrows just so, in a high arc, and plumped his cheeks with a smile, no one would be able to resist him.

Gran was downstairs in the kitchen, busily filling the house with the smell of fresh coffee and bacon. Pop rattled the windows with his snores. Bo hopped down two stairs, then three to the landing, then hopped stair by stair to the ground floor, hopped across the living room, and froze.

There on the windowsill behind the couch, sitting between the gauzy white curtain and the glass, was the image of all that he wanted to ignore, a shadow, form without substance, a cat, an ordinary cat, his cat, Josie, back like Bo from the land of the dead. How did he know from the outline that it was Josie? From her stillness.

She'd always liked to do just that: to play statue. And there she was on the windowsill, Josie the Statue, Josie gazing proudly at the world, believing that it all belonged to her, waiting for Bo to approach.

He climbed onto the couch, lifted one knee from the crevice between the cushions, steadied himself against the back of the couch, and hissed. That's how he'd always been able to stir Josie into motion. He'd hiss, she'd dash off, and he'd chase her. *Sssss!* But Josie did no more than flick her tail, causing the curtain to billow lightly. Bo reached forward and drew the curtain away so he could see the cat clearly. She refused to look at him, so he hissed again. She didn't budge. Bo prodded her in the haunches with the knuckles of his fist, and Josie did what she'd never done before — she swiped her paw, treacherous claws extended, across the back of his hand, leaving fine pink lines that filled momentarily with tiny pearls of blood.

Oh, after all Bo had been through — and now this! Betrayed by the creature that should have loved him most. It was an outrage worthy of a howl, so Bo indulged himself, shrieked until it felt like Josie was scratching inside his throat, then he pressed his face against his grandmother, who suddenly appeared and drew him into the tight circle of her arms. He sobbed in fury because not only had Josie betrayed him but Gran had no right trying to hush him up. He deserved to wake the whole world with his clamor and felt no remorse when Pop came limping down the stairs leaning heavily on the banister and wearing only his polka-dot boxers. Pop could run down the street naked for all Bo cared. His grandmother and grandfather had no right trying to calm him. They had no right stealing Josie's love. They had no right to Josie or to Bo, and if Gran wanted to let Bo feel the warm pad of her skin against his body, if she wanted to coo softly in his ear while he cried, she could go ahead and waste her breath. Under no circumstances would Bo stop crying. He'd cry until nightfall. He'd cry for a year, for ten years, forever. He'd cry until he fell asleep.

When he woke he was covered with a quilt, bathed in midday

sunlight, and the bundle of fur tucked between the top of his head and the arm of the sofa was Josie, purring lightly as she dozed. Bo ran two fingers along the back of her neck. He had a vague taste of unhappiness in his mouth and then remembered all at once the important fact: everything would be all right. Another fact occurred to him: he was hungry, and Gran, it turned out, had left Pop in charge of Bo and a ham baking in the oven while she went on her own to the late-morning service at the Mount Olive Baptist Church.

There was plenty to eat to tide Bo over until dinner was ready, bacon and pancakes, orange juice, chocolate milk, and along with the chocolate Easter eggs in Bo's basket Pop gave him a bag of peanut M&M's. When Miraja arrived she laughed at the chocolate ring around Bo's lips, and her daddy, Uncle Danny, clamped his hand over her mouth, a reproach that was obviously meant in jest but that left Miraja huffing angrily in a corner. Soon the house was full of people Bo remembered knowing, though he couldn't remember their names or why they mattered to him. And just when he was starting to miss Gran, she came home, catching Bo by the hand and drawing him through the crowd like a pull toy. While she peeled potatoes she went through the list of names all over again: Uncle Danny, Uncle Alcinder, Aunt Meredith, and the cousins Miraja, Jeffrey, Joseph, and others connected in some indistinct way, Taft, Johnny, P.J. — and last but not least, Bo. She included Bo's name as though he were out there in the living room laughing with the others, throwing playing cards in the air and pushing Miraja onto the beanbag chair instead of sitting on the kitchen counter, kicking his legs against the cupboard doors, and listening to anything Gran had to tell.

The rest of the day was all talk and food and poker in the background. Bo didn't do much more than trade Gran's lap for Pop's, Pop's lap for Gran's, clambering back and forth while the grown-ups laughed and shouted and even slammed fists against the table in order to attract attention, though nothing of importance was said, as far as Bo could tell — no part of the conversation, even when it included such phrases as *I sure as hell am* . . . or *Come see for yourself,* led to any action, not until Uncle Alcinder finally announced that he had to get home and stood up from his chair and headed for the door.

That was the first day of Bo's future.

On the fifth and sixth and twelfth, thirteenth, and fourteenth day, it rained. On the eighth day Gran took Bo to the park to see the tulips with their yawning red and purple petals. On the night of the fourth day Bo had a dream about his mama, and he spent the whole next morning thinking that she would be coming to pick him up in the evening. On the twenty-first day he vomited after lunch, and Gran rushed him to the clinic. By the time they got back home four hours later Bo felt fine. On the fifteenth day Pop made up a song about a tree. Tree was the only word of the song. Tree tree tree, tree tree tree. He dared Bo to sing along, but Bo refused. On the twenty-second day Josie didn't appear to eat her supper, and Bo wouldn't go up to his own bed without her and finally fell asleep on the sofa. At about noon on the twenty-third day, Josie came back. On the thirtieth day Bo asked Gran for some milk, and Pop called from the living room, "You got your voice back, eh?" Bo kept his mouth shut until the thirty-third day, when Pop asked him if he wanted one of those plastic sand-and-water play sets advertised on television, and Bo said, "Yeah." This time Pop didn't question Bo about his long-lost voice, and by the thirty-seventh day Bo had forgotten his resolution to keep quiet and answered any question addressed to him.

"Want to go up to the big lake, Bo?"

"Yeah yeah yeah yeah yeah!"

Idle May light dancing on the water. Fleas leaping across pockets of sand. Driftwood logs, the refuse from winter storms. Wishing stones. Blue forget-me-nots and lily of the valley blooming on the wooded slope. Mud and sand. So this was how it felt to be up to your ankles in liquid ice! Hop hop, bunny hop. What happened to London Bridge? And was it just a lie or was Bo really getting older? Surely Gran and Pop had always been as old as they were now, no older, no younger. Bo had known them for a long, long time, from way back when all the way to now, and they hadn't changed at all. Neither had Bo himself. Josie had been a kitten once, that was true. But nothing else changed except by accident. Bunny hop hop bunny hop. When you're really happy for the first time in a while there's nothing else to do but take off all your clothes, so he slid his arms out of his T-shirt and struggled to free his head from the tight neck. "Help!" Gran helped lift the shirt off and went on to read Bo's mind and help him out of his shorts and underpants, warning him not to go into the water over his knees.

Here was his fine pisser that could spray in a glistening arc. Here was the skin on his arms raised in goose bumps, and the pink scar that made him special. There was the lake as wide as the sky, and the warm sun and the wisps of clouds. Here were the icy droplets rising when he clapped his hands against the surface of the water. There was the disappearing world.

He was happy through the end of spring and into the summer. He stayed happy even when Gran and Pop sat in chairs on their porch drinking iced tea and blotting sweat from their foreheads, even when he ran smack into the gate leading to the side yard, even when Miraja threw a water balloon at him and it broke and soaked his shirt, even when the man named Taft called him stupid-shit and dropped a cigarette butt on the sidewalk in front of Bo and ordered Bo to spit on it to put it out. Taft could have ripped Bo's head off his neck, so Bo did as he was told, got down on his hands and knees and spit on the cigarette until it stopped smoking. He didn't understand why after he did exactly what Taft wanted him to do Taft called him stupidshit again and proclaimed him useless. So what? While Bo had crouched on the sidewalk he'd found a woolly bear caterpillar and had slipped it into his pocket. Later that day he set the caterpillar free beneath the porch, where no one would step on it.

He dreamed that he stood still, his arms extended, and a swarm of honeybees blanketed him head to toe, but not a single one stung him.

He was, amazingly, who he'd always been, even though *Mama's little* had been dropped from his name, leaving just Hobo, alone and wonderfully alive.

The weeks passed. Pop changed his tree song to a star song — star star star, star star star — and made up a story about a little girl who fell from a star and landed on a trampoline over on Edgewood Street, bounced up over the trees, and landed with a thud on the sidewalk in front of Gran and Pop's house on Sycamore. She smelled, Pop said, of cinnamon and sugar. He was describing the sound of her laugh when he heard the phone ring. A while later he heard the snap of plastic against plastic as Gran rammed the phone into its cradle. Pop called, "Erma?" Bo said, "She's boiling like a pot of water." Pop called Bo *a little comedian* and reminded him that when he made his first million in show business he must treat Gran and Pop to banana splits. Gran came in and began plucking toys from the floor of the dining room like they were dandelions gone to seed. "That was Jenny's mom on the phone," she said in an icy voice. "She's passing along a hospital bill. Seems we're gonna have to come up with eleven thousand dollars. That's how much it costs to patch up a little boy. Now did Miz Marjory offer to help us out? What do you think? Did she offer to give us a dime?"

"Not here, Erma."

"He belongs to us — that's the way she sees it, and she don't want anything to do with him."

Who was *he*? Who was *she*? Josie the cat was a she. Maybe Gran was confused. Bo wondered if she'd been on the phone with Giantman Taft. Only someone that big and mean could have riled her so.

"Erma . . ."

"Eleven thousand dollars. We'll have to cash in a bond —"

"Erma!"

"You'd think maybe since she's related she'd see fit to help us out with the cost of his medical —"

"Stop it!"

Pop was shouting. Gran was seething. Something had gone

wrong, and happiness was just a story like any story Pop told, but this time Bo had mistaken the story for a fact. Star star star, tree tree tree. Or else everything would be all right. Yes, everything would be all right . . . see? Indeed, it took his grandparents just a few minutes to settle their differences and press on with the undeniably true story of happiness.

The girl who fell from a star could make wishes come true — three wishes altogether. Bo wished he could fly. What else? He wished he could breathe underwater. What else? He wished for three more wishes. *You little comedian, you!* Wasn't he too cute? Even when he picked his nose; even when he announced that he'd deposited a fine turd in the potty; even when he screamed in thrilling fury.

But Gran kept falling *into a temper,* as Pop said, which made Bo realize that despite all that had happened he couldn't name anyone he actually hated. Even the worst of them, Giantman Taft, had his good moods as well as his bad. But the strength of hatred was a source of power, apparently, for whenever Pop tried to talk Gran out of her temper, she snapped back in such a vigorous defense of herself that Pop could only grunt and shake his head. And Gran snapped more and more as the week wore on. She was mad at someone out there, a stranger living out beyond the neighborhood. Whomever she hated had started something that would culminate in a final bloody scene of terror. Bo dreamed of it one hot still night later in the week — he saw a wild man crash through the front door, grab Gran, and tear her head from her neck. Bo hid in the closet in his dream and watched through the keyhole but by then he could make out nothing beyond the explosion of red, no faces, no expressions, only the bursting cartoon blood, and he knew at once that the scene wasn't real. Yet when he awoke he couldn't shake his fear, and for this reason he respected Gran's new temper, learned to avoid her when she was snapping and to keep quiet when she wanted to make her point to Pop by thumping her fist against the table. There was an enemy somewhere out there, an enemy no one was willing to name, and life was suddenly dangerous.

So what? Bo jumped into the Park and Rec pool, jumped right through the loop of Uncle Danny's arms, went under, kicked to the surface, and was greeted by applause. *Thank you, thank you.* A pigeon landed on his arm and ate crumbs from the palm of his hand. A billy goat at the petting zoo tried to eat the tail of his shirt. Bo picked a ripe tomato off the vine, and Gran laughed so hard drops of maple syrup fell from her eyes and left sticky lines on her cheeks. Pop ate barbecue potato chips straight from the bag. The kids in the neighborhood sat on the porch steps and ate Fudgsicles. Dogs fought in the street until Giantman Taft came along and kicked them both in the ribs and sent them howling. Pop told a story about a little girl who fell asleep in a pile of laundry and was sent to the cleaners. Gran said, "Tell him something he needs to know." So Pop made up a story about a Mandingo boy captured and sold into slavery, where he was beaten with a whip by cruel overseers and forced to pick worms off cotton plants until he couldn't take it any longer and ran away. He ran through the night, tore through brambles, swam across rivers, hid in trees, and finally reached freedom. Bo was too embarrassed to ask for the meaning of *freedom* — one of those words, he sensed, that he should have already known. So he made up his own meaning, which had to do with breaking the surface of the water after he'd put his head under for the first time. The cold water turned his red scar yellowish. Bo ate buttery popcorn. He rode a neighbor's Newfoundland dog as though it were a horse. He went with Miraja and Aunt Meredith to see the trout in the hatchery, as many trout in a single tank, Miraja said on the way there, as there were stars in the sky. And every one of those fish seemed to be looking at Bo, searching his face for something. The dark gleam in the eye of a fish. Whom should Bo learn to hate?

He peed in his bed. He tried to cry for help in his dream but couldn't make a sound. He pulled Josie's tail, daring her to scratch him again, but she just flicked her tail loose and scampered off. He chased the pigeons. He climbed out of the grocery cart while Gran was selecting a carton of eggs from the shelf. "I hate eggs!" he screamed, pleased to remember that he did hate something after all. He tried to catch the first leaves as they fell. He kissed the maple syrup on Gran's cheek. He grew older by the hour but remained, in everyone's estimation, too cute for words. He turned his face up, yawned as wide as he could, and took a big bite out of the sky.

Eddie Gantz bought a hot dog and Pepsi from a vendor in front of the federal building and sat on a bench to eat. With an extra napkin he wiped the sweat from his face. He chewed slowly, thoughtfully. He'd been coming up to the city for the past three days to serve as a juror on a civil trial, a whiplash case. Eddie Gantz was an opinionated man, he wouldn't deny it, and if anyone bothered to ask him his opinion about this trial he'd tell him that it was a plain waste of taxpayer dollars. Consider that the plaintiff offered as proof of her extreme pain and suffering a myopic doctor who threw Valium at her without performing any tests, and the defense countered with an eyewitness who testified that the defendant couldn't have been traveling at more than eight miles per hour at the time of the accident. A minor fender bender that left the plaintiff incapacitated for three months? A bump in a traffic jam that made it impossible for the woman, a housewife already on disability for chronic depression, to pop a frozen dinner into the microwave? How absurd! The lengths people will go for money!

Eddie tore a piece off his hot dog bun and threw it into a clutch of filthy pigeons, then watched the flurry of competition that followed, just as he'd watched the trial, fascinated by the contradictions in testimony, the distortions, the self-pity, the moral blindness. He had never been able to fathom moral blindness. The sinner who commits a sin with full awareness — now this he could understand, for morality makes itself known with sharp contrasts. Yet there were criminals who refused to recognize their culpability, sinners who considered themselves saints, individuals who lied under oath, women who believed they had the right to take the life of their unborn child. It was the role of belief that puzzled Eddie so. Such people managed to convince themselves that night was day and wrong was right, and they couldn't be budged, no matter how obvious their error of judgment. In the name of *choice*, women had gone so far as to insist that they should be allowed to have a viable baby's brains sucked out of its skull so it wouldn't be born alive. And just last Sunday a fellow usher at Eddie's church had passed along a copy of a magazine article in which the author set out to explain the increasing practice of infanticide among American mothers and came damn close to declaring the atrocity a necessary evolutionary development and therefore worthy of judicial leniency!

It was this kind of thinking that aroused in Eddie a deeply private panic, never to be spoken of or revealed in any way. You wouldn't have seen any change in the attentive expression on his face as he sat on the bench and watched the traffic on the street. His sharp blue eyes followed a police car turning right on red at the intersection. His jaw remained set, his lips closed in a straight, earnest line. The skin of his cheeks had a red hue, not from too much drinking but from chronic eczema. He kept his white hair, what was left of it, cropped close to his scalp so from a distance he appeared entirely bald. And though he carried thirty pounds more than an average man his height, he looked fit, like a professional football coach or a retired military officer, certainly not like a man in danger of losing his sanity. But this was how he felt sometimes. The idiocy of civilized people shook him to the core — not because he considered himself superior but because he appreciated the innate intelligence of the common man. He was common. Born into a family of dairy farmers in Herkimer County, educated at a community college, living in a fine little cape with a view of Hadley Lake, managing an appliance store, taking care of his wife. He was sixty-seven years old — he'd had plenty of time to choose wrong over right, plenty of time to commit a crime or to politic for Satan. But with a little guidance from his church and the experience of his parents' common goodness to remember, he had found it easy to lead a life of steady virtue. Why wasn't it easy for everyone else? Why wasn't it easy for the woman — a common woman, a black woman, a Christian — sitting in a state supreme court on the fourth floor of the federal building to distinguish between right and wrong?

Maybe the attorneys were the ones to blame. Their interpolations, their third degrees, their siftings and calculations, their dissections and disputes and discord spun out of nothing so that they could bill their clients two hundred dollars an hour and drive away, whether they won or lost, it hardly mattered, in their black Mercedes. And what about the judge? Why had he permitted this matter to come to a head in his courtroom? So he'd have something to keep him busy. A respectable man must keep himself busy. The busier you are, the more you have your ear glued to your cell phone and your calendar filled with appointments, the more respectable you seem — a deception designed to give meaning to empty lives.

The problem, in plain words, was *a crisis of faith*. Americans had lost their faith and struggled to find something, anything — ambition, hatred, licentiousness — to replace it. As Eddie sat on the bench in front of the federal building, he considered this crisis as an explanation for his own panic. Not that his faith ever wavered. But his deep ability to sympathize with others made him feel what they were afraid of feeling — panic in the absence of God.

He felt calmer at this thought, his panic subdued by understanding. He pried open the tab on his Pepsi can and sipped. A school bus pulled up to the curb in front of him. The children stared out the windows at Eddie and Eddie stared at them. They were city kids, seven- and eight-year-olds, doomed children who would one day be standing before a judge in this same federal building pleading not guilty to charges of theft, prostitution, drug possession, or worse. Eddie watched as the doors opened and the youngsters bounced down the steps of the bus and followed their teacher into the temple of justice, the city's own temple that might as well have housed the altar of Baal. Turning his face to the sun to soak up the last heat of summer, Eddie daydreamed of Gideon, himself as Gideon marching up those stairs, tearing down the altar with his bare hands, and building an altar to the Lord, laying the stones in due order. He would give the children back their faith. He would save them — in his idle dreams, not in reality, for Eddie Gantz was a quiet man who attended to his own affairs and didn't interfere in public matters. He would continue to mind his own business, take care of his wife, serve, when called, as a fair and impartial juror in a court of law, and pay his bills on schedule.

The afternoon session would begin in twenty minutes. Eddie decided to take a short walk. He didn't much like the noise and smells of the city street, but he liked the feel of concrete beneath his shoes and the solidity of the buildings rising around him. He liked the visible, weighty evidence of hard work. Someday this city would lie in ruins, destroyed by years and years of neglect, but the ruins would tell of noble effort.

Neglect, Eddie would tell you, can be costly. Neglect can add up to eleven thousand five hundred and fifty-two dollars. He couldn't forget that number: eleven thousand five hundred and fifty-two dollars, which would have come out of his pocket if the medical establishment had had its way. Eleven thousand five hundred and fifty-two dollars.

That so?

On Monday evening, after his first long day of jury duty, he'd been eating supper and thinking about the trial while Marge prattled on. She'd returned to the subject of Jenny's accident, a subject Eddie preferred to avoid but which Marge kept bringing up out of the blue. Why had Jenny gone off the road? Why had Jenny been driving so fast? Why had Jenny been drinking? Marge was trying — and failing so far — to develop a paranoid plot to account for her daughter's death. Months had passed and so should have the paranoia, Eddie felt, but he couldn't dissuade his wife with logic and chose to stay silent while she spun unlikely fictions that even she didn't believe: Jenny had been run off the road by drug dealers; Jenny had been trying to escape; Jenny's death wasn't accidental, no, there were others involved, a stalker, perhaps, or gang members out for revenge — all false possibilities, Marge admitted, yet oddly comforting to consider.

But Monday night she wasn't talking about the cause of Jenny's death. She was talking, Eddie eventually realized, about an extraordinary hospital bill that had come in the mail. The bill had been sent to various wrong addresses, apparently, and had gone back to the hospital a number of times until someone finally figured out the Gantzes' correct address and had sent the bill certified.

"And you signed for it?" Eddie asked.

"What else could I do?"

"You could have refused."

"But I didn't know what it was. The postman told me to sign, so I signed."

A bill for eleven thousand five hundred and fifty-two dollars, with *overdue* highlighted in red. Eleven thousand five hundred and fifty-two dollars out of Eddie's pocket to pay for the care of a child he had never met? Jennifer Templin's illegitimate child?

Marge had promised to make phone calls Tuesday while Eddie was in court. On Tuesday evening she reported that Jenny had carried no insurance and hadn't been eligible for Medicaid. She'd spoken with child protective services, with various people in the hospital, and finally with the Gilberts, who had custody of Bo and would be the obvious "source for reimbursement," as the woman in patient accounts had put it.

As it turned out, the matter was swiftly resolved when Erma Gilbert agreed to cover the medical costs. No question about it, Mrs. Gilbert declared, the bill was their own responsibility, though she couldn't help adding that in a better world the money would have gone in the opposite direction, from the hospital to Bo, *compensation,* as she described it, for all the mistakes the doctors had made — coming in late with the diagnosis, letting the child go into shock, then subjecting him to surgery, major surgery that should have been avoided.

That so?

Marge couldn't recount the precise details from the conversation with Mrs. Gilbert. But she did know that the child, Jenny's child, had suffered needlessly. He shouldn't have suffered. Jenny shouldn't have died. Marge wouldn't rest until she identified the person to blame for what had happened. But she needed rest, and Eddie had helped her to rest. He'd stood behind her chair and massaged her shoulders, only half listening by then, luring Marge from her despair with sympathy expressed through the strength of his fingers. And he had succeeded eventually, drew the sorrow out of her and felt the muscles in her meaty arms relax into gratitude.

That was last night. Eddie had left this morning before Marge woke. He'd picked half a dozen black-eyed Susans from the garden and arranged them in a vase on the kitchen table for her to find when she came down for her breakfast. There was no pleasure keener to Eddie than the pleasure of giving comfort. He was sure he'd have felt this even if he hadn't been a Christian, for he knew in his bones, knew it without ever being told, or at least without remembering the lesson, that the gift of sympathy was its own reward.

He'd been walking for seven minutes, so he turned around and headed back. The light changed just before he reached the intersection of Main and South; as he waited for the traffic to pass he thought about the strength of virtue. He was a virtuous man, a strong man, a comfort to those in need. He saw himself in the policeman mounted on the hefty bay horse clip-clopping along the street. He saw himself in the stern, solid bricks of the office buildings. He saw himself in the sidewalk and in the laws governing the people. *Vindicate me, O Lord, for I have walked in my integrity, and I have trusted in the Lord without wavering. Prove me, O Lord, and try me; test my heart and my mind.*

The immediate test would be the decision he'd have to make about the liability of the defendant in courtroom 4A. But that would be an easy test. Eddie wanted a more difficult test, a test that would prove the strength of his faith, a test like, oh, say something like . . . like a bill for over eleven thousand dollars to cover the medical expenses of a child he'd never met. That would be a challenge, certainly. He had been reluctant to pay the bill not because he couldn't afford to but because he wasn't responsible for the child. Yet what if the bill had been a test of his compassion? How would he know? *Prove me, O Lord, and try me.* If the bill had been a test, he'd failed it. The scope of his compassion did not exceed his greed. Had he committed a sin by declining to fork out eleven thousand five hundred and fifty-two hard-earned dollars for the care of a child who did not belong to him?

He continued walking along the last couple of blocks toward the federal building. He lifted the sleeve of his jacket to glance at his wristwatch. With the napkin he wiped the film of sweat from his forehead.

The child is not responsible for the sins of the parents. The child is not responsible. The child is not responsible.

He ran his tongue along the inside of his teeth. He brushed his palm against the side of his head. He felt the constriction of his full bladder and hurried up the steps of the building two at a time.

Prove me, O Lord, and try me. Eleven thousand five hundred and fifty-two dollars. A series of mistakes. Extravagant care. Why did Marge sign for the letter? Overdue! Why did Jenny drive off the road? Why did she have relations with a black man? What color is the child? The court would be in session in six minutes. As for me, I walk in my integrity. My foot stands on level ground. Clip-clop clip-clop. Sturdy resoled shoes. The child is not responsible. The child is not responsible. The child is not responsible.

There was right and wrong, white and black, day and night, and Eddie knew the difference. He would always choose right when offered a choice, even at the cost of eleven thousand five hundred and fifty-two dollars. Marge and Eddie had done right by redirecting the bill to the appropriate party, in this case the Gilberts. The boy belonged to the Gilberts now, who were being tested by this sudden expense to demonstrate the depths of their faith.

In the men's room he turned on the faucet, tested the temperature of the tap water with his index finger, and jammed the palm of his other hand against the box above the sink to force out the last remnant of liquid soap. He scrubbed rapidly to build up sufficient lather and watched as the tap water flattened the soap bubbles against the back of his hands. Soap and water. He'd spent most of his adult life counseling consumers on soap and water, demonstrating with his plastic models the elegance of rotor blades and the perfection of worm gears in order to convince people to buy their washing machines and dishwashers at Worthco rather than at some other appliance store. Prices were higher at Worthco, but so was the quality. And you couldn't beat the store's service contract. Eddie had stayed on at Worthco all these years because he believed in its ability to honor its promises. He was a man of infallible honor, whatever the circumstances. He'd lived a steady, quiet life, and though he'd had his fair share of suffering and had lost his first wife to cancer when she was just thirty-eight years old, he wasn't one to complain.

The woman in courtroom 4A hoped to make a bundle of money by complaining. On the witness stand she'd complained about the pain in her neck radiating down her left arm, the pain in her head, the pain in her upper back and lower back and sometimes in her hip joint and even in her left buttock and leg — all because a businessman in an Infiniti had bumped into her Ford Escort in a traffic jam.

Eddie watched the warm tap water spill out of the bowl of his palms, form a transparent cylinder, then splash against the dirty white enamel. He liked to notice things and over time had learned to slow down fast-moving images simply by looking carefully at them, as though his mind somehow controlled external motion, as though the world were a film he could manipulate by pressing a button or turning a dial. The drops from the water scattered, splashed against the sides of the sink, and slid toward the drain.

He turned off the tap and shook his hands. As he dried them with a brown paper towel he examined his reflection in the mirror and let his mind drift slowly through a chain of associations that would eventually bring him back to the thought he'd been thinking when he entered the men's room — from the fact of his white skin to black skin, to the fact of Jenny Templin's stupidity and the consequences of her errors, to the fact of her innocent child. An expensive child, as things had turned out. He wondered if the Gilberts had the means to pay for Bo's medical expenses. He wondered if they'd contest the bill, seeing as how, according to Erma Gilbert, the doctors had made so many mistakes. If the trial about to conclude in courtroom 4A was any indication, all accusations no matter how outrageous were valid and deserved to be heard before a judge and jury.

Eddie examined his mouth to make certain that none of his lunch remained stuck between his teeth, then he returned to the courtroom, where the parties of the plaintiff and the defendant had already taken their seats. He walked slowly down the aisle toward the rear door and the deliberation room, feeling the eyes of strangers on him, feeling privately the scope of his power, a juror's power to rule for or against the accused. It occurred to Eddie that every person present in that courtroom wanted to know what he was thinking. They'd find out soon enough, but for the time being it gave him more than the usual pleasure to keep his thoughts to himself. He was not a wealthy man; he did not hold an official position; he had no title. He held strong opinions, but he had no illusions about the importance of his opinions and accepted the fact that no one but his wife, his few friends, and the more courteous shoppers at his store cared to hear what he thought.

The people in the courtroom were far from indifferent. As Eddie walked past the defendant's table he imagined the attorney, a sharp young blonde, slipping a bribe of five hundred dollars into his pocket. He imagined refusing it. And as he crossed the area in front of the plaintiff he felt an almost physical sensation as she peered through squinting eyes at him. His thoughts mattered. They had never mattered this much to anyone. Seven other jurors had listened along with Eddie to the testimony, and their individual opinions would have immense consequence. This was a sacred democratic power, a power bestowed upon ordinary citizens to separate truth from lies.

Intoxicating power. Eddie could keep his eyes focused on the door ahead and think whatever he pleased. *Liar!* he could think without glancing at the plaintiff. *Nigger bitch!* he could think if he were debased. *I'm gonna kill you all!* he could think if he were inclined toward violence. He could think terrible and terrifying thoughts that everyone would want desperately to know.

The thrill would be over too soon — this was his thought as he stepped past the bailiff and through the doorway to join the other jurors waiting in the back room.

He drove home through the soft blue light of the September dusk. He kept the driver's-side window cracked to let in the warm evening air and cued in the local country music station on the car stereo. For no apparent reason he felt an indistinct dream from the previous night press close to his consciousness, though not so close that he could remember any details beyond a lingering sensation of defeat. He directed his mind back toward the day's work and felt instead the sharp pleasure of pride.

The jury had delivered their verdict against the plaintiff, a fair verdict — they'd saved an innocent man from fifty thousand dollars' worth of damages. That they'd done the right thing was as clear as the sky with the evening star already visible in the fading light. Fifty thousand dollars the defendant did not have to pay thanks to Eddie Gantz and his fellow jurors.

How satisfying it was to act on behalf of an innocent man, to do right, to pronounce judgment against a false accusation. Eddie had passed today's test of character, undoubtedly. But what about the other test, the eleven-thousand-five-hundred-and-fifty-two-dollar test?

He kept his eyes locked on the stretch of highway ahead and in his peripheral vision watched the land fall away as though off a sharp precipice. He considered the possibility of a malpractice suit as if it were an algebraic equation. He isolated the factors, identified the unknowns, imagined possible scenarios, and calculated a final sum. How much had the child suffered? How much was he worth? Marge's daughter Jenny had proven herself a fool, but her child hadn't proven anything yet and could very well prove himself deserving if given the chance.

The horizontal light of the setting sun caused the shadow of the truck in the right lane ahead of Eddie to stretch out like spilled tar across the highway. In the left lane a sleek red sports car sped past. Eddie drove a black Ford Bronco with tinted windows. He preferred to travel in the middle lane between seventy and seventy-five miles per hour, fast enough but not so fast that a state trooper would come after him. He shoved in the cigarette lighter to heat it, a habit he continued though he'd stopped smoking over a year ago after he developed some arrhythmia. When the lighter popped out he left it in place.

Thank you, members of the jury, for your time and effort. You are dismissed.

Eddie hadn't elected to receive the meager financial compensation offered to jurors for their time. Instead, his compensation was the knowledge that he'd helped to secure justice for an innocent man. On the highway between the city and the exit for Route 62 south he decided to do the same for Jenny Templin's child, the child he'd never met. Now Eddie wanted to meet him, to guide him, to help him find justice for whatever neglect he had suffered at the hands of people who lacked compassion as well as the insight to recognize their lack. Eddie wanted to treat the poor child to his compassion. This was a service he could perform in the name of God, an act of devotion, evidence to be submitted on his behalf in the highest court of all. Eleven thousand five hundred and fifty-two dollars. His heart, he once had calculated, beat on average thirty-one million five hundred and thirty-six thousand times in a single year. Eleven thousand five hundred and fifty-two dollars was nothing in comparison. He'd agree to a settlement that fell somewhere in between.

The judge would want to know why Eddie and Marge had taken no interest in the child until that point. Because, he'd explain, the situation being what it was, with Jenny blaming her family for her misfortune and teaching her son to despise anyone who had anything to do with Marge and Eddie Gantz, they had no choice but to leave Jenny alone. It broke Marge's heart, but that's the way it had to be as long as Jenny held on to her resentment. The situation being what it was, with Jenny loosening up to every young man who looked her way, no one could say for sure who had fathered the child, or that's what Marge had admitted to Eddie one Christmas Eve when she was swelled with wine and spite because Jenny had refused her holiday attempt at reconciliation.

That so?

Jenny had said the father was Kamon Gilbert, but Jenny said a lot of things.

That so?

She sure did. She'd open her mouth and out would come a curse, a foul exaggeration, a lie, an expression of contempt — at least that was Eddie's experience back in the days when Jenny was still part of the family. She'd said a lot of things she didn't mean. She sure did. Eddie had stopped trusting Jenny long before she stood in the kitchen and announced in a voice loud enough to be heard all the way across the lake that she hated Eddie Gantz, she hated him, she hated him!

She'd said a lot of things she didn't mean.

She loved Mike, she loved Randy, she loved Tom, she loved Bruce, she loved Kamon. She'd been right about this: Marge and Eddie just didn't understand her.

How could a nice girl . . . ? Marge wanted to believe that someone had killed Jenny. Eddie never spoke of his suspicion: that Jenny had killed herself.

That so?

Marge and Eddie had an obligation to bring their grandson back into the family, to raise him as one of their own, to provide for him, to teach him their values and secure for him a reasonable in-demnity to make up for medical negligence. They were late in ad-mitting their responsibility, guilty of their own brand of negligence, but they could make up for it, counter remorse with nurturing, and help the child to get past his early unhappy years.

With the possibility of astonishing success speeding far ahead of him, Eddie pressed his foot on the pedal in an effort to catch up.

As stipulated in Article 17 of the Surrogate Court Procedure Act, this Court is authorized to appoint a guardian of the person and/or property of an infant, and whether or not a written instrument of designation regarding custody exists, a petition for appointment of a guardian may be made by any person, including the child if he or she is over fourteen years old. The Act requires the court to consider whether the child, a person nominated to be the guardian of the child, or the petitioner is the subject of an indicated report filed with the statewide register of child abuse and maltreatment. The Act also states that letters of guardianship may not be issued to an infant, an incompetent, a felon, a non-domiciliary alien except in certain cases, and anyone else who is ineligible in the Court's discretion.

In the absence in the case before us of nomination by will, nomination by deed, or appointment, and given the limited anecdotal evidence permissible and lack of any non-testamentary document signed during the mother's life, also taking into consideration the material support provided by the litigants for the first three years of the child's life, the Court awards the deed of guardianship to Declarant 1 named in the Petition, one Marjory Gantz, also identified as the child's natural grandmother, designating the Declarant the child's standby guardian. . . .

This is what the judge would rule, or something along those lines, according to the optimistic lawyers, Paul Krull and Wilson Krull, who assured Marge that she had clear-cut rights to her grandson, despite the fact that the child did not know her, she'd only seen him once, asleep in a hospital bed, and she had willingly signed the form to release him to the Gilberts. The truth of the matter was, Marjory Gantz was the mother of the mother of the child and so could give him the love he deserved. Material proof was the money she'd sent Jenny, thirty thousand dollars total, unbeknownst to Eddie at the time, though now that he knew about the money he agreed that it was strong evidence of Marge's maternal devotion. Meaning that in no time at all Marge would have the powers and responsibilities of a parent regarding her ward's support, care, and education, she would take reasonable care of her ward's property, and she would maintain sufficient contact with her ward to know of his capacities, his limitations, his needs, his opportunities, and his health.

Meaning that there was shopping to be done, rooms to arrange, new toys to buy and old toys to be taken from boxes in the attic, pediatricians to call, appointments to schedule, luncheons to cancel, and much, much more.

Marge stretched flat the pleats of the bedroom curtains to examine the cloth for dust, decided that instead of washing them she'd leave them up and in the spring buy new, cheerier curtains. Same with the wallpaper — tumbling roses wouldn't suit a growing boy. The rug, a powder-blue soft pile, would last for a good long while, along with the bureau, a four-drawer unit high enough so that the boy wouldn't be able to reach the metal frames that held photos of his mother: Jenny as a baby, Jenny on a tricycle, Jenny missing her front teeth, and Jenny at sixteen wearing a cardboard die for Halloween. That was the Halloween Jenny had staggered into the house at two A.M. in nothing but her leotards and a black turtleneck, having thrown her costume into Hadley Lake, she'd reported to Marge with an odd, hiccupping laugh, the laugh of a drunk. That was the Halloween Marge gave up any hope of disciplining Jenny. From then on she could do no more than wait up through the night for Jenny to come home, night after night, until Eddie convinced her that they would serve her better by ordering her to get out of the house and to stay out until she pulled herself back together.

Jenny had never tried to keep her pregnancy a secret; rather, she'd used it as a wedge, a taunt, a sign of her independence, and though she'd gone ahead and spent the money Marge sent, she never so much as thanked her. But Eddie kept assuring Marge that her prodigal daughter would come around, and she believed him because she wanted to believe him. So she went on waiting for Jenny to provide the opportunity to forgive her, and though it never happened, she couldn't bring herself to stop waiting.

Now she was waiting to become the guardian of Jenny's child. He would sleep in Jenny's bed someday, or that's what was supposed to happen; Marge would touch her lips to his forehead and kiss him good night, a scene far less believable to her than the imagined scene of Jenny's contrition. This child she didn't know, her own grandson, Kamon Michael Templin. He belonged here, Eddie had insisted, right here, in their home on Hanks Lane. Now it was just a matter of gaining legal guardianship. And as soon as they'd done this, they could commence proceedings on behalf of their ward to seek compensation for medical malpractice, a necessary suit given how the poor child had suffered, though the exact details of the case — what was done, what was said and by whom, the child's current medical condition, his prognosis, the estimated medical expenses — whatever they'd need to know in order to file a claim against the hospital was not yet known and may never be known. But Marge hardly cared about all that, for what mattered was the flesh-and-blood child, the child in person occupying space in their house, the child, Bo, lying one day soon in Jenny's place on Jenny's bed.

Marge pulled the fitted sheet tight. She'd already thought to put a plastic sheet over the mattress in case the boy was a bed wetter. And she'd found the metal rail in the attic to secure against the bed so the boy wouldn't roll out during the night. It was the same metal rail she'd used when she'd moved her own children from crib to bed. She had saved many of the children's clothes as well, their stuffed animals, their pull toys and Wiffle balls and board games, all arranged neatly up in the attic.

She prided herself on her ability to keep things in order,

though she had no illusions about her limit. Jenny's death had been beyond the limit, and Marge would have fallen apart completely if it hadn't been for Eddie.

What would I do without you, Eddie?

But Eddie Gantz didn't like anyone to feel beholden to him, so Marge kept her gratitude to herself. She trusted Eddie as if he had no private self, as if he were always on display, like a mannequin behind glass, always reliably *there*, without secrets, solid and unchanging, inspiring Marge to pull herself back together with his own example. When she couldn't do it on her own, he'd stepped in to help, providing for Marge just what she needed most: a child to replace the one she'd lost.

Marge hadn't even considered the possibility. That Jenny's child should be raised by Kamon Gilbert's parents had seemed right at the time, since the Gilberts had been involved in the child's life from the start. Besides, Marge had lost her common sense when she lost her daughter, and she'd spent her waking hours thinking up nonsense to explain Jenny's accident, *nonsense* in hindsight, though at the time it had all seemed logical, beginning with this obvious proposition: Jenny could have been involved with drugs. And if that was true, then Jenny would have known drug dealers. And maybe she hadn't liked what she'd seen and had made a point of telling someone, who told the dealers, who labeled Jenny a threat and killed her to silence her forever, almost killing Bo along with her. Jenny had been run off the road on a rainy April night, forced by another vehicle to careen into a tree. Such things happened. If such things happened to others, they could have happened to Jenny. Why didn't the police investigate the matter properly? Because they must have had something they, too, wanted to keep hidden. Drugs, illegal weapons, conspiracy, corruption. What couldn't happen these days? The unimaginable was possible, and nothing terrible happened accidentally. *There was no such thing as an accident —* life could not end violently without the propulsion of evil.

Or such had been the tenor of Marge's thoughts during the months following Jenny's death. Crazy thoughts. She might as well have been wishing for Jenny to rise from the dead. But now she had something better than an angel. She had — would have — a flesh-and-blood grandson to raise.

"I don't think you should be doing this." Ann stood in the doorway, her tight-jeaned, stocky figure backlit by the sunlight shining through the hall window. Ann in Jenny's place, Ann wearing a black sweatshirt that had once belonged to her sister, Ann standing where Jenny once stood when she was sixteen years old and had arrived home at five in the morning to find Marge waiting for her in her room.

"So would you have him raised by strangers?"

"They're not strangers to him. Listen, Marge, I've spent time with Bo, I know the kid, I —"

"Yes, and you will help him to adjust. A familiar face — he'll need you."

"Marge, listen."

"I'm no fool. I know your sister hated me."

"She didn't hate —"

"She would have come around eventually. Forgiven me. Until then . . . Jenny would have wanted Bo here, at home, her own home. The child belongs with us."

"The Gilberts are family to him. They're all he knows."

"Sit here. Come over here, sit. Now tell me: Did your sister ever say to you something like *in the event . . . in the event . . .* ? Did she ever indicate her desire regarding —?"

"She didn't think she was gonna . . . oh, come on, Marge. The last thing she was thinking about would be leaving him to someone else. But you just don't go grab him by the collar and say, *You're coming with us, buddy.* He won't want to stay here."

"Of course he won't. He'll have to get used to us, over time, and with your help. He'll be fine, Ann, soon as he stops and takes a good look at us, at you and me. He'll see his mother in us. The blood in his veins — that's our blood. My only regret is that I did not take him in at once. Such indifference . . . well, there's cause for condemnation. I'm to be blamed, I offer myself for blame, for your hard judgment, but not because I'm bringing home my flesh-and-blood grandson. You may blame me for waiting so long to do it."

"I don't blame you, Marge, and to tell the truth, I want Bo here as much as you do. I can't say whether or not Jenny would have wanted it. But the kid won't want it. He's better off where he is, with the family he knows. *Family*, Marge, flesh and blood. Kamon was his father."

"How can you be so sure? Jenny did a lot of things we never knew about. And now she's left her boy behind for us to raise."

"Whatever. You can think whatever. But promise me this, Marge. If he doesn't want to stay, you won't keep him here."

"He won't want to stay, you've said so yourself. Our job will be to convince him —"

"Over time, okay, but think of him, I don't know, think of him like, like, like a cutting from one of your rosebushes, you know, transplanted, and if he doesn't take, if we're not right for him, then we bring him back, okay? Okay, Marge?"

"Yes, if he doesn't take. But we must give him time."

"Enough time, but not so much that, you know what I mean? Now let me give you a hand with the bed."

Sorrow had made Ann kinder. She would grow kinder still with the arrival of her sister's child. Ann, with her cropped hair dyed ink black, her square face, purple lipstick fattening her lips, her boxy arms and legs — yes, she was calmer than she'd been before Jenny's death, more attentive, less eager to move out, less available to the boys who tried to lure her away. When Ann wasn't in school she hung around the house and stayed close enough to Marge to keep her within hearing, reminding Marge of both her daughters when they were small, the way they used to clutch her skirt or sleeve, the way they'd follow her with their eyes, fearful of losing sight of her and therefore losing her forever.

Although in this way she hadn't changed: whenever the phone rang, as it did when Ann was tucking the crease of the bedspread underneath the pillow, she'd dash for it.

Leaving Marge to smooth the spread flat while she thought

about how some night soon she'd be smoothing it over the warm mound of a child. The rise of the bony knees. The soft belly. The eyes searching her face. Here in this room, the room with a sloped ceiling and a single window looking over the backyard, the room where Marge could still hear, if she listened carefully, and if the rest of the house were completely silent, the sound of Jenny humming. Residue of life, the sound of a voice still hanging in the air, sensation lingering on, still real enough, apprehensible — such was the power of memory.

See how it can be done: the indentation of Jenny's head recreated in her pillow, the scent clinging to Tiny Monkey, pieces missing from a puzzle, the plaster showing through where she'd peeled back the wallpaper, rocks in a shoe box, Ann waking up from a late nap crying, the kitchen door snapping back into place and Tony calling, "I'm home!" and still the dishes from lunch had to be washed and oh how Marge's chest ached from bronchitis and she couldn't stop thinking about the magazine article, the one written by a mother about the death of her young child from leukemia, the photograph of the smiling girl and words like *courage, fortitude,* and *hope* strewn messily about. See how it's done: sinking onto the bed, lying in the place where your daughter used to sleep, feeling the warmth she left behind seep through the sheets and the bedspread and your blouse, feeling yourself sinking — *Jenny!* — sinking — *Jenny, come clean up your room!* — sinking happily because you knew you were the luckiest woman in the whole wide world.

Oh, but what kind of luck was she remembering? Fisherman's luck, lady luck, a stroke of luck, good luck, a lucky streak, a lucky break, collector's luck, happenstance, or fortune? Was it new luck or luck that had been previously overlooked, the force of cunning, scorned luck, luck dispensed by a divinity, shared luck, impossible luck? Was it luck that can be invoked with a rabbit's foot or luck that springs from the shards of a broken mirror?

Maybe it was the kind of luck understood as the given condition of things. Maybe Marge's idea of luck could best be compared to a large body of water that defines and sustains the land — an ocean dotted with islands, the water invisible behind the horizon, a place where storms are born, where chance is spun into experience.

Luck is not something that can stand in for faith, and Marge wouldn't have pretended otherwise. But later that day, when she was stepping out onto the dock shared by all the houses along the lane, having come for no other reason than to gaze at the gray water and consider the vital changes about to occur in her life, she made a dangerous mistake: she'd taken a single rock from the old shoe box full of rocks, a dull piece of shale, a perfect wishing stone, and instead of keeping it to give to her grandson she wished aloud that he would learn to love her, and she tossed the stone into the lake.

And to think what we've done for this boy all his life long, making sure he had everything he needed, watching out for him from the get-go, Jenny on the birthing table cursing Kamon, our Kamon, while a nurse held one leg and I held the other and said, *Give your lungs a rest, girl, save your strength.* I was there. Where was her own mama? Sitting at the hairdresser, I bet you, having her hair dyed pinky blond, happy to forget she had a daughter who was having a child of her own, a no-good daughter who couldn't keep her hands out of the pants of no-good black boys, and look where she landed, in a hospital room up in the city with black ladies on either side holding her legs apart while she howled, hating our Kamon because he wasn't there, hating him with all her might because he was already dead and she was lit up inside, burning out of control, hating him, damning him to hell, not knowing what she was saying and forgetting it soon as her son slid out, slippery as a kitten still in its sack, and there she is loving both Kamons like her life depended on it, crying because she'd lost one and gained another, while I'm trying to get used to the fact that the baby's not his daddy all over again, not fat and red and bellowing like Kamon had been when he came out of me, not bright-eyed, no, Kamon Junior was scrawny, color of a lemon, and he wouldn't open his eyes for three days, wouldn't even take his mama's titty in his mouth right away, like he didn't much care for things as he found them, reminding me of you, Sam, when I got to wake you early for one reason or another, you in your drowsy mood, too tired to care about anything except being tired. But just like you, Sam, our second Kamon bided time for a while, gathered his strength while he grew brown and one day announced to the world, *HERE I AM AND I'M GLAD OF IT!* rattling Jenny with his roar, those gums clamping like he was trying to suck the blood from her along with her sweet milk. And that's just like you, I got to say, so strong in your wanting, chock-full of happiness when you get it and taking for granted the getting, like every barbecue potato chip had been made exclusively for you."

"Aw, now when you put it that way I got to argue with you and say I know the difference between appreciation and foolishness as well as you, Erma, and when you remember how I was short on the getting for all of my early years, you'll paint a kinder picture of me, coming up from the bottom of the heap as I did, hauling scrap metal with my daddy, missing out on school and smashing my kneecap when I slipped and fell carrying a rusty old iron auger, and then no money to pay the doctor so we went back into debt, we gave up our sugar and coffee and even our vitamin A. But you know how I stayed good as gold, Erma, and how when the next war came around I spent it working on equipment heading out to Korea, I learned my trade, and I came out ready to get some of the things I'd been wanting, you most of all, Erma, far as I can tell God made us a perfect fit, and as for my barbecue chips, well, they are exactly to my liking, it's true, and maybe it's a coincidence, or maybe the manufacturers keep me in mind when they're writing their recipes, who can say?"

"And every planked steak and every pineapple and every turnip and potato and beet, and every chicken wing with dipping sauce, every bottled beer and all the greens I heap on your plate, the TV shows, the magazines, the books I bring home, they're all absolutely to your liking, eh, the stars are winking right at you, the sun is shining for your sake, the whole planet is to your liking because you're living on it!"

"I can't help it if I know how to turn even the bad times inside out and wear them with pride. I can't help my good nature."

"Just like you can't help your good looks."

"Nope. Can't help that either."

"Then I'm going to have to kick you to wake you up to the fact of what's happening. Since September Jenny's folks have been closing in on us. Now time is running out, there's a court date set, and that caseworker has been sizing us up. You've seen the way she smiled, like she had reason to feel sorry for us. We're going to lose Bo like we lost Kamon, all of it happening right here on this good planet while Heaven stands by watching and waiting for us to take charge, Sam Gilbert, waiting for us to think a thought or take a step!"

"You're not starting on that again, are you? I thought that evaluator was plenty nice. And I'll remind you we got Sue Bruno working on the case for us, and when you consider how she's a woman who's used to winning, why then you can believe she's going to win us our boy. Trouble is it takes time, like anything else. When you consider how the light from the sun takes more than eight minutes to reach my appreciating face, why then you'll understand about time. We are just going to have to be patient, Erma, that's what we can do, we can be patient and wait for Sue to put together a case on our behalf."

"I'll tell you what she'll put together! Smoke in the air, that's what, and nothing she'll say will make any difference, the judge will see white versus black and have no trouble deciding against us. We'll lose soon as we walk into his courtroom, Sam, soon as we show our appreciating faces. So we're not going to that courtroom, you hear? We're going to turn and head in the opposite direction and make up a new story to take the place of the other, the one Jenny's folks are planning to tell to all their friends and neighbors, how they went to court and got what's due them, pulled their grandson up out of the pit of nigger-hell and bundled him up in a soft white blanket and took him home. No, Sam, we're going to make up a new story, and if you just put your mind to it you'll come up with a razzly-dazzly start, something like —"

"On a cold January day the old grandma tucked her grandson under her arm and took off running, and the old granddaddy ran after her, they ran out of the city and across a field and into the woods, they kept running through the night, and when morning came they tucked themselves against the trunk of a tree and tried to sleep, holding the boy in the center of their huddle to keep him warm, thinking to themselves that they couldn't go on much longer like this, no ma'am, they were on their own and so stiff from the cold that they could hardly stand up and move on."

"You're taking too long to get to the happiness part, Sam, so it's my turn. You go fetch the canvas bag from the basement, the one Kamon used to take to scouts camp, and you start packing our clothes."

"Erma, you keep wanting to tell a different sort of story, the fact kind, the kind I can't tinker with."

"Let me spell it out for you, Sam: We're going to take a vacation, so you pack two outfits for winter and three warm-weather outfits for both of us. And then you go fill up the car with gas, a full tank, Sam, and stop at the machine for as much cash as it will spit out, and I'll pack up Bo's stuff along with enough food to last us a few days at least, we're going to be eating plenty of peanut butter sandwiches for a while so don't bother complaining. When you're ready you pull up behind the house and I'll meet you there."

"We run, they catch us, we might never see the boy again. Understand what you're suggesting."

"Listen to me, Sam — here's something that came to me last night. I figured out what's wrong. It's not just losing Bo. It's a hunch I got about those folks in Hadleyville. Now I know I've had hunches before, and most of them have been mighty ridiculous, but this one here won't let up. I've got a hunch things won't turn out well for Bo. Those folks don't want him. I know they're paying plenty in lawyer fees, I know they're working hard to steal him away from us, I know they will be pleased to win. But they didn't want Jenny around, and they won't want her son. I can't say why they've gone to all the trouble. But I got a hunch that once they bring him home they're going to want him even less. It's a hunch so close to the truth I wonder if an angel whispered it in my ear while I was sleeping."

"You know as well as I do the way a human mind works. You know how a human mind can pull amazing stunts and trick us into believing that the desert is an ocean and the devil is God. It could be — now don't be angry at me for saying this, Erma — but it could be your hunch comes from your own strong wanting. You want Bo to stay here where he belongs. So you come up with a hunch that suits the wanting —"

"It doesn't matter whether this hunch comes from outside or inside, it's making my heart beat fast right now, it's pumping blood into these stout old legs, it's telling me to pack up and go away for a while. Do you hear me, Sam. This isn't just talk now. No matter whether you choose to come along or stay behind, I'm going away for a time, and I'm taking the child with me. Sam, you hear? Sam!"

"That old canvas bag, the one Kamon used for scouts?"

"Yeah."

"Two winter outfits, three sets for summer?"

"Yeah."

"Then I'll fill up the tank and meet you out back?"

"That's what I said. Just don't go honking the horn and waking up the neighbors. Go on now. Get to work."

"I got my orders. See you in a bit."

"See ya. Bye-bye. Go on!"

I guess I finally wore him down then, all the chattering I've done these last months. You know he'd prefer to let others decide the matter for us. But I say our only hope is to get out of here, try out someplace new and see if we can make it work, put this mess behind us until Jenny's folks forget what they were wanting. Why? Because you belong to us, child, that's why. Wouldn't matter to that judge if you were Kamon's carbon copy. Jenny was her mother's daughter, and that mother wants you in her life and is ready to pay a load to get you. Easy as fitting the last piece in a puzzle. Trouble is, Bo, you don't fit. Won't matter to the judge. But it matters to me, so we're taking you away, snatching you right out of the arms of the law, and on the count of three we're going to vanish! Anyone else do such a thing I'd call them wicked. Then we're all going to be wicked together, singing and joking and eating peanut butter sandwiches as we head south, leaving the rest of our family to guess what we've done, leaving without kissing them good-bye so they won't be liable in any way. We've got to keep them innocent no matter how much they're going to miss us. You see they'd give up everything for us but we won't let them, we're going to sneak away tonight, Bo, that's why I'm packing these bags, we're going out into the cold and we're going for a drive, we'll keep driving until we find a proper summer and the flowers start blooming along the roadside and the ocean is warm as bathwater and nobody knows us from Adam.

Funny how it is, Erma with enough sense for both of us. But this job we're about to undertake makes all the sparking service panels I ever handled seem like cotton candy in comparison, all the hot wires and cracked caps, they're nothing to what's ahead of us, running away from the law, sixty-five years old, me with my bum knee and Erma with her asthma, and here we are running away from the law. Comes from having our third baby so late in life, Kamon taking us by surprise in our middle age and then hurrying up to Heaven ahead of us. He never got used to waiting, did he? He couldn't wait for tomorrow, always in a hurry, running up ahead of the rest of us when we were in an ambling mood, scampering around the curve of the park path, paying no mind when we called him, hiding in the branches of the magnolia, dropping soon as we spotted him and running on, leading us wherever. Now we're getting set to run wherever, just wish I were better at it, younger, richer, braver. Instead I'm so sick with worry I can't stop my hands from shaking long enough to zip up this duffel, wondering if I believe what I'm trying to tell myself, that everything is going to be all right, everything is going to be all right.

"How you making out, Sam?"

"I'm nearly set. I'll go ahead and take the bag down and go get us some money. I'll be seeing you, what, in about ten minutes, I'd say."

"Ten minutes, then."
"Round back."

*Now here's Sam's toothbrush and mine and Bo's, our Crest paste,
Sam's razor and blades, my perfume and lipstick, Sam's aftershave, my
skin lotion, Sam's aspirin, my Advil, our Ben-Gay, Sam's prescriptions,
my prescriptions, Children's Tylenol and cough syrup, our hair scissors
and nail clippers, my polish, my tweezers, Sam's comb, my brush and
pins, our antacid and fiber and vitamins, some tissues and towelettes,
my jewelry, Sam's reading glasses, my reading glasses, peanut butter, a
loaf of bread, cookies, chips, a knife, a roll of paper towels, my wristwatch, my pocket mirror, a pad of paper, a pillow, a blanket, a flashlight and batteries, a picture book for Bo, a book for me, another book
for me, a book for Sam, a book for both of us, another book for Bo,
maybe this other one here for me, and this one for Sam, maybe one or
two more, no harm in that, a magazine for the trip, this soapstone
heart Kamon gave me when he was ten, these photographs, old letters,
postcards, an extra set of keys, stamps, envelopes, pots and pans and
coffee cups and while I'm at it how about that old sitting chair Sam
likes so much along with the sofa, the dining table, the lamps, the
walls, here it comes, everything we own and every thought I've ever had
in this house, every feeling, every moment of surprise, all the worry, one
deep breath, come on, breathe, breathe, take the deepest breath you've
ever taken, draw it all inside.*

*Then breathe it out, let it go, the copper wires you put in, the extra
outlets, the fuses, all the washers on the faucets, the plastering and
sanding, the pipes, the bookcases, the storm windows — on and off, on
again and off, year after year — and all the snow I shoveled, the
garbage hauled out on Thursdays, leaves raked to the curb, house
scraped and painted, scraped and painted, scraped and painted, fence
repaired, gate set back on its hinges, bulbs planted up at the corner,
bushes trimmed around the street sign, driving away, driving home,*

driving away and home and away, driving home again one last time, home and away. Breathe it out now slow and easy, let it all go.

Moonlight lighting up the floor.

This gas station, this pump handle, this hose, this old Pontiac ready for the junkyard.

This telephone in its place, my voice.

This money in my hands.

My babies.

These streets.

This child.

These houses.

This child asleep in my arms.

"Hey there."

"Shhh, don't wake up Bo. Lift in that bag for me, will you, Sam? Just keep on sleeping, Bo, keep on dreaming. We're going for a ride."

"That everything?"

"Most everything we're going to need. You give us a full tank?"

"And checked the oil."

"Then we're ready."

"You sure?"

"Sure as I'll ever be."

Where are we going? he wanted to ask after he'd been awake for a while, but he understood just by studying the back of their heads that they didn't want to hear from him right then. Instead he breathed circles of fog on the window and then licked the glass to make curlicues. Cold, slick glass against his tongue reminded him that it was winter. And nighttime. If Gran and Pop had chosen to drive off late on a winter's night when snow was swirling in the air, then there must be something wrong. If Gran was holding her neck that straight and Pop was gripping the steering wheel with both hands and Bo wasn't asleep in his own bed, then there must be something wrong. They were running from trouble. Not wandering step by step down the street picking up acorns and bottle caps but speeding as fast as they could away from trouble. They were running away and taking Bo with them. They were running away from a huge rumbling monster with yellow eyes and rubbery paws. Look, he was gaining on them, opening his mouth to crunch their car in a single gulp. *Faster, Pop, faster!* But Pop didn't drive fast enough, so the monster pushed past them and barreled ahead in the left lane, disappearing around a bend in the highway.

They were surrounded by darkness again. Darkness tasted like canned pears that had been left for a week in the refrigerator. It is always better to head toward daytime. If you crawl through an old sewage tunnel beneath the road, you must hold your breath until you can breathe in the day. Never walk into the center of the night — walk away from it, up the steps onto the front porch lit by an overhead bulb.

What do you do when you leave a room?
Turn off the light, Gran.

As you slide into sleep, think about the morning. Drive toward the sun, though don't get so close that your wings melt and your hair catches on fire.

Miraja liked to tap him on the arm and declare, *You're it!* Pop and Gran were *it* now, and they were bringing Bo along for the ride. *It,* the thing you become when you've been left alone. Pop and Gran were alone together and were keeping Bo near for company, the way Bo kept Josie near when he was tired of being *it.*

"Josie!"

"Shhh, sweetie, that's all right, now try to sleep some more."

"I want Josie!"

"Hush."

"I want her!" If they were running away from home, and Josie was still at home, then they were running away from Josie.

"I want Josie!"

"Hey Mr. Macaroni." Pop glanced back at Bo in the rearview mirror. "You go back to sleep and I'll give you a dollar when you wake up."

Now that was tempting. "Two dollars!" Bo squealed.

"All right then, two dollars. Good night, you little comedian. And don't worry about Josie, she'll be fine."

Josie would be fine — that's as much as Bo understood, and he was trusting enough to believe that his grandparents would send for Josie once they were settled in their new home. Bo felt sorry for Josie but could comfort himself by looking forward to seeing her again. Where? If he spoke aloud Pop would know he wasn't asleep, and Bo would forfeit the two dollars. He shoved his thumb into his mouth to keep himself quiet and scissored two fingers of the same hand around the smooth hem of his blanket. He closed his eyes and pretended to sleep. He imagined that he was playing bubble basketball with Miraja, chasing a bubble as big as his fist, puffing to guide it through the air toward the empty bucket. Then he remembered that Uncle Al had promised to teach him the Morse code.

Then he thought that he'd like to build an obstacle course with string and paper and pillows. He leaned his cheek against the window, opened his eyes, and watched the blur of the guardrail, like a stream of water flowing backward into the night. The snow had stopped but Pop hadn't bothered to turn off the wipers, so they squeaked against the dry glass with every rise. Bo had the feeling that he was about to remember something he didn't want to remember. Whenever that happened he counted to himself, from one to one billion trillion infinity. One. Two. Three. Four. Five. Six.

"My money, please. You promised!"

Somehow the sky had turned the color of the rug in his old bedroom, wherever that was, and above the trees Bo could see a stripe of glitter-red fingernail polish, the kind worn by his mama, whoever she was. Gran once told him that because his mama and daddy were watching over him, Bo was never alone. So he couldn't get away with pouring his orange juice milk shake into the sink or drawing on the windows with a bar of soap or lighting a match without his mama knowing. Oh, he'd be in for it! For this reason he preferred to think of other things. Like the two dollars Pop owed him.

"Two dollars. Pay up, mister."

"Shhh, Bo. Let your granddaddy sleep." How could he be sleeping and driving at the same time? It couldn't be done, even Bo knew that! But the guardrail wasn't flowing past anymore, and the highway signs didn't look like green-winged birds darting away from the car. So the car had stopped. Through the far window Bo saw a strip of road, another guardrail, and the highway. Through the near window he could see dimples in the snow where pinecones had fallen from the trees. He smelled the pine smell and car exhaust and Gran's perfume. Pop slept in the front seat with his head tipped back, his breath making the sound of sneakered feet scampering down a staircase. Bo wanted him to wake up. He asked loudly, "Why's Pop sleeping?"

"Shhh!" There was that hiss of anger from Gran. Without another word she handed Bo an unwrapped chocolate cupcake, pinching the sides between her thumb and forefinger and setting it carefully on his accepting palm.

This is the way to eat a cupcake: first you loosen the firm round top of chocolate frosting to separate it from the cake. You hold the frosting by an edge like a wet piece of paper. Then you lay it back down on the cupcake and with great care you rip one chocolate half away from the vanilla zigzag seam. You hold this piece of frosting near your mouth, seize it between your teeth, and with a quick lift of your head you toss it in the air and catch the piece on your tongue, where you let it sit and melt while you tear the other half of the chocolate frosting away from the vanilla seam. You swallow the syrup, and what hasn't melted you chew slowly. Then you roll up the second piece of frosting between your hands, you pop it in your mouth like an M&M, you chew it twice and swallow it. You nibble the vanilla seam zig by zag.

When you're finished with the frosting you can go on to the cake itself. You hold it close to your lips and catch small pieces between your teeth, being careful not to break into the cream center. You can eat quickly now, nibbling away at the cake, reshaping the squat cylindrical cupcake into a ball the size of a walnut. At this point you must start licking to smooth the crumbs against the cream interior. As you lick you curl your tongue a little to draw the excess crumbs away. Soon the white cream will begin to show through the chocolate cake. Only when it is in danger of dripping from your fingers do you plop the cream filling into your mouth.

"I'm thirsty!"

"What's that, eh?"

"Now look what you've done, Bo. Woken up Sam . . ."

"Someone say . . ."

"Bo is asking for juice. You go back to sleep."

"What?"

"Nothing. Go back to sleep."

"Sorry, Pop."

"Mmm. That's fine."

"Don't forget my two dollars."

"Bo, let him sleep."

Pop yawned a yawn that seemed to lift Bo up and set him right down in the middle of the story of the three bears. Papa Bear was tired. Mama Bear was tired. But look — someone was sleeping in Baby Bear's bed!

"Morning," Pop growled.

"Take your juice, Bo. What do you say?"

"Thank you."

"You're welcome."

Here's what you shouldn't do with a juice box: you shouldn't press the sides with your fingers so that the juice shoots up like water from the spout of the whale.

"I spilled my juice."

"You sure did. Here's a paper towel. Now you be careful. We still have a long way to go."

Bo sipped through the straw. After a minute or so he tested the silence with a question: "When are we going to be there?" He thought silence would be his answer. But finally Pop said, "Not for a while."

Which reminded Bo that he had to pee. "I have to pee," he said softly.

"Figure we can drive for most of the day," Pop said to Gran, "and then stop at a motel for the night, get a good rest."

"I have to pee."

"Make it to Charlotte, you think?"

"We can try."

"I have to pee."

"Want me to drive now that it's light?"

"I'm fine for a while. Another cup of coffee would be nice."

"I have to pee!"

"Why didn't you say so, child!" Gran said. She got out and opened the rear door, unbuckled Bo and helped him on with his jacket. His sneakers made shallow prints in the snow. He walked in circles to make a figure-eight design. "Right in here." Gran held his hand as he mounted the steps, then she struggled with the door, yanked it open, and they were greeted with such a stink that Bo tried to back down the steps and nearly slid off. "I'm not going in there," he said.

"Oh, it's not so bad," Gran insisted, holding the door open. Bo pinched his nostrils between his two forefingers and stepped onto the sticky metal floor. The lid of the toilet was open, revealing below the brown stew of shit and paper and cigarette butts. Bo saw in an instant his fate: falling forward, headfirst, plummeting from his sweet life into stinking death.

"I don't have to go anymore."

"You don't?"

"No."

So Gran helped him down, though this time she nearly lost her footing. As she swayed backward she managed to steady herself with a hand on Bo's shoulder.

Just as they reached the rear bumper of the car he said, "I have to pee." There was the laughter peeking through Gran's angry eyes. "Here's just fine," she replied, bending down to unsnap his jeans. Bo, nearly bursting by then, peed into the fresh snow. He watched the stain splatter the white, then burn a hole to the grass beneath. He etched a zigzag line, dividing the snow in half. He smelled the faint heat of his own piss mixed in with the piney cold. He hoped Gran was watching him. He felt powerful, rugged, worthy of praise. But Gran was standing with her back toward him now as though to shield him. He was struggling to close his pants when Gran spoke. "You done?" she asked, bending down to help.

Only when he was climbing into the car did he notice that a police car had pulled up behind them. He wished the policeman would turn on his siren and lights. His eyes were hidden by the rim of his hat, but Bo could see his lips set in such a way that showed he was waiting for trouble. The policeman should have known that trouble was somewhere ahead of them now. Or behind. Or both.

"What did he say?" Pop asked as Gran buckled herself in.

"Nothing. Just nodded when I waved. Now what are you worried about? No one will be missing us for hours still."

Pop turned the ignition, the engine churned, vroomed, and died. He swore. Gran didn't tell him to watch his language. Pop made the engine vroom and sputter and knock. But it wasn't the engine knocking, it was the policeman. Pop unrolled his window enough to frame the policeman's face.

"You okay?" he asked.

"A little trouble getting going, that's all," Pop said. Bo could tell from the scratch of Pop's voice that he was trying to keep a secret. He started the car again and this time the engine sputtered, vroomed, and chugged steadily. "There we are," he said, more relieved than he needed to be. "Thanks for your help, officer."

"But he didn't help at all," Bo said as Pop rolled up the window.

"No he didn't, did he?" Gran answered.

They drove on. Bo wondered about Pop's secret and the policeman's curiosity. He blamed the policeman for *poking his nose into nobody's business* — whatever that meant. Because of the policeman Gran had been distracted and Pop had had a little trouble getting going. At least they were driving toward sunrise. On either side of the car wooded bundles of land reminded Bo of dollops of cream filling covered with chocolate crumbs.

"The Endless Mountains," Pop said, reading a sign aloud.

"The Endless Mountains," Gran echoed with a whistle. "Why don't we lose ourselves here? Take up in a little cabin in the Endless Mountains, spend our days eating peaches and fishing. . . ."

What were they talking about? The most Bo could make out was a hint of disappointment in their voices, as though they were remembering something they had lost, a favorite book, a picture, a jar they'd filled with pennies, four years' worth of pennies, a penny for every day that Bo had been alive.

What about his birthday? Tuesday was his birthday, and Uncle Al had promised to build him a sandbox. What about the sandbox? What about his army troop, his baseball mitt, his Matchbox cars? His grandparents were whispering now, and their voices were sand running through a crack in the sandbox Uncle Al had promised to build.

"What about my two dollars!" Bo sobbed.

"Oh, Mr. Macaroni, why are you, what's, what do you, oh sweetpie, little angel . . ." Now their voices were water running into the tub. Everything was going to be all right. Gran fished around in her wallet for two crisp bills. Pop sang a song about a red balloon. They all sang the ABC song. Then Pop started to tell a story about a puppy lost in the mountains. In the pocket of the door Bo found a paper clip. He straightened one side and chewed on the wire while he listened to the story. The puppy was lost in the Endless Mountains, it was winter, the puppy was hungry and cold and scared, and along came a grumpy old crow who said, *Go ahead, eat my lunch, you need it more than I do.*

"Bo, what's that in your mouth?" Gran had swiveled in the front seat and was trying to grab the end of the paper clip in her fingers.

"Nothing." Bo handed the paper clip to her, swishing his spit in his mouth so he wouldn't lose the taste of metal. Gran started to tell him what he already knew — that it was wrong to chew on a paper clip — but she stopped because right then the car sputtered and coughed like it had when his grandfather had tried to get it going a few miles back, except that this time the engine didn't settle into a steady chug. It simply stopped, and they glided out of the lane at an angle, Gran gripping the dashboard with both hands, Pop looking between the road ahead and the rearview mirror.

They came to a stop on the highway's gravel verge. For as long as it would have taken Bo to count to sixty three times, Pop kept turning the key in the ignition and nothing happened.

Finally Pop said, "I'll tell you, this whole journey is starting to seem doom—"

"Don't you say it!" Gran interrupted.

They discussed their predicament in low voices while Bo stared out the window at the steep slope of woods rising high above his head. He knew what his grandparents would do even before they'd made a decision — they'd walk together to the exit ramp up ahead, salt and pebbles crunching beneath their shoes, the cars shooshing past. Pop wanted to leave Gran and Bo in the car while he fetched help, but Gran wanted to stay together. Bo agreed with Gran, though for his own reasons — he wanted to make more footprints in the snow and climb to the top of the slope and surf back down on his belly. He concentrated hard, trying to influence the conversation with his thoughts. *Walk, walk, walk,* he thought.

"Let's walk then," Pop said.

So Gran let herself out of the car, opened Bo's door, and zipped his jacket again. She helped him push his thumbs into his blue mittens. She gripped his left hand tightly. Pop came around the side of the car, his weak leg dragging slightly, making a little furrow in the snow with each step. Bo walked ahead with his grandma and Pop followed a few steps behind. Once every half minute or so a car or truck sped past, sucking the fresh air along and leaving behind the stink of exhaust. No one stopped to offer them a ride.

The old crow fed the puppy with pickings from roadkill. The crow complained plenty about his charge, but really he was proud. And the way it was up there in the mountains, with just one strip of highway making fresh roadkill, there wasn't enough food to go around. The crow grew thin, the puppy grew fat. Then the other crows found out that the old crow had been sharing food with a dog. They didn't like this, let me tell you. So they roosted in the trees around the old crow's nest, and when the old crow flew out one morning to go check the highway, they came at him all at once, cawing and pecking something horrible.

Aw, cut it out now.

Think of this: people have walked barefoot through the snow. They have carried babies through the snow. They have bled to death in the snow. They have frozen to death in the snow. If only all of history could be told. . . .

Still no one stopped to offer them a ride.

Pop dragged his weak leg, Gran's lips were chapped, but Bo kept skipping along, happy to be leaving footprints on a mountainside in the middle of nowhere. What did he care about the people in passing cars? What did the people care about him?

They reached the exit ramp after half an hour of walking. It started to snow again, needle-sharp snow that blew at a slant into their faces. Luckily there was a gas station at the end of the ramp. Gran carried Bo for the last couple of hundred yards, then set him down in the empty lot of the gas station. The windows were covered with plywood, and the pumps had no hoses. Pop found a pay phone around the side of the station but the phone had been ripped from the box, leaving the metal cord to flop and shiver in the gusting wind.

Gran opened her shin-length wool coat, lifted Bo inside, and buttoned her coat back around him. He squeezed his legs around her waist and rested his chin on her shoulder. Through squinting eyes he watched the snow.

"If we hadn't . . ." Pop let his voice drift off until there was nothing but the gusting wind and the wet shoosh of traffic in the distance.

"Go ahead, blame me," Gran said stiffly.

"I'm not —"

"You're thinking it."

Their voices were as cold and sharp as the snow. *Stop it,* Bo thought.

"We keep on walking then."

"Walking where?"

Pop didn't answer. They started walking side by side across the parking lot, Bo still propped in the hammock of Gran's hands, still gripping her soft hips with his thighs. They walked and walked. The wind died, and the snowflakes turned thick and light, feathery puffs of white that sparkled when the sun found a band of clear sky between a ridge and the clouds. They walked close to the divider of the empty road. Gran sang, "You set me down, sweet Lord, on a pile of bones, we passed them round, sweet Lord, that pile of bones . . . dry bones . . . dry bones." After she finished the song they walked in silence. Finally they came to a ramshackle trailer with white siding streaked with rust and a thin stream of smoke rising from the stovepipe. A skinny calico cat leaped onto an overturned pail and perched there, staring at Bo with quizzical green eyes. Bo stared back. Pop went up to the door and knocked while Gran and Bo waited a few feet away. No one answered. Pop knocked again. A white sheet serving as a curtain was pulled back from the window, and a woman's face appeared. She shook her head, motioned to them to go away. Pop banged the side of his fist against the door.

"Stop it, Sam!" Gran shouted — "Get back here!" — in the voice she usually saved for children.

"Sweet Jesus," Pop said as they set off walking again. "Welcome to the heartland." They moved to the side of the road when a pickup truck drove past. The tip of Bo's nose was cold; his ears were cold inside his hood; he was tired just thinking about how tired his grandparents must have been. He had two dollars in his pocket — maybe this would help.

"I have two dollars," he offered. No one answered. He rested his chin back on his grandmother's shoulder and remembered the face of the woman in the trailer window. But his memories got mixed up, and what he remembered was the splotched face of the cat staring out from inside the trailer.

"Try this one, sweetpie," Gran said after a few minutes. "Say there's a narrow pipe that goes down about a foot into the ground. Say you drop a Ping-Pong ball into the pipe. You can see the ball at the bottom of the pipe but you can't reach it. Say all you got to work with is a piece of string, a magnet, a cardboard box, and a gallon of apple juice. Tell me how you're going to get that Ping-Pong ball out."

Bo thought hard, trying to imagine how he could make a hook with the string or fashion a little scoop with the cardboard to scoop up the Ping-Pong ball.

"Well?" Gran said.

"Call for help?" Bo proposed.

"Nope. There's no one around to hear you. You got to figure it out for yourself."

"I'm stumped," Pop said.

A magnet, a cardboard box, a piece of string, and apple juice. Bo kept reciting the list to himself as he stared over Gran's shoulder at the road. A magnet, a cardboard box, a piece of string, a car, and apple juice. A magnet, a police car, a piece of string. A policeman and a Ping-Pong ball.

"You in trouble, folks?" The policeman, the same one they'd met back at the rest stop, drove slowly along beside them.

"It looks that way, doesn't it?" By answering a question with a question, Pop was taking a risk — even Bo sensed this.

"I'd say so," the trooper replied flatly. "You want a lift?"

"That would suit us fine, officer," Gran said. "We've tired ourselves out in your hills here."

"So you have. Where you from?"

Inside the car Bo settled between his grandparents on the backseat. He listened to the crackle of voices, watched, delighted, as the trooper picked up his radio and spread the news of their adventure around the world, struggled to keep his one wish to himself, hugged himself to keep the wish inside, and then heard in astonishment his own voice burst, interrupting the grown-up conversation, "Can you do the siren?" He looked in fear at Gran, wondering what his punishment would be, but she was laughing, they were all laughing.

"Listen to this," the trooper said, clicking a switch on the dashboard. The wail came from far away, from outside the car and above the clouds, from another time, a time before. What Bo heard he'd heard before. He'd sat here in this police car between his grandparents; he'd listened to a siren and wondered what would happen next. Which meant that what would happen next had already happened before. He tried to remember the outcome of this adventure, squeezed his eyes shut in an attempt to squeeze the memory to the front of his mind, but all he could come up with was the feeling of the same thing happening twice. No, it was the feeling of forgetting. Having known something once, he'd forgotten it and could do no more than remember the forgetting.

The trooper shut off the siren and with a quick series of turns and back-ups pointed the car in the opposite direction. There was talk among the grown-ups about local garages and motels. Lies were told, deceptions spun with fancy words — *investigating some retirement communities* was the phrase Gran used to explain why they happened to be passing through the Endless Mountains. Pop tossed in terms like *fuel pump* and *spark plug* and tugged the lobe of Bo's ear as though to say, *You're in on this, too, Mr. Macaroni!* At some point he managed to throw in a story, the factual kind, that added up to this: in the town where Pop grew up a man named John Humphrey Noyes lived maybe one hundred or even two hundred years ago. Had the officer ever heard of him? No, the officer hadn't. Well, John Humphrey Noyes was a respected leader in the town. He was known for making changes, and the change he became famous for was abolishing money altogether — for five long years, the town carried on business without any money. For five long years, there was no private property (Pop tugged again on Bo's ear, but by this time in the story Bo's comprehension had fallen far behind) and no need for competition.

"That so?" the trooper said.

Gran whispered something to Pop, and Pop kept quiet for a while, though he winked secretly at Bo while Gran told the trooper just how much she appreciated his help. The trooper didn't reply, and they fell into a tense quiet.

"That was before there were any Negro folk living in town," Pop said out of the blue. "Way back when."

"Sam —"

"Here we are." The trooper drove into the lot of another gas station, this one with lights on inside and a man moving behind a desk. The man, like the woman back in the trailer, watched them through the window with an expression that said he wasn't inclined to let them come inside. The trooper held open the car door for his passengers, and as Bo slid off his seat behind Gran he caught sight of the leather holster strap and wanted desperately to see the gun that it contained, to know the gun's story, the robbers it had cut down, the people it had saved, the sound it made when it went off.

"Boom!" Bo shrieked and fell down dead in the snow.

"Ain't he a little comedian," Pop said, pulling himself out of the car. "Takes after his granddaddy."

"Get up, Kamon Junior," Gran ordered.

She hardly ever used his real name, and when she did, Bo wanted only to disappear. He didn't like being called the name of someone who was really dead, even if that someone happened to be his own daddy, whoever he was — letters on a gravestone, dry bones, a face in an old photograph, a subject of grown-up conversation, an angel watching him and reporting to his mama everything Bo did wrong while his mama was sleeping.

Bo rolled to his knees, hopped up, and skated through the snow toward the far side of the station. No one told him to come back, so he kept on going, glided around the corner, and pressed his back against the wall, waiting a minute to give Gran a chance to begin the chase, and then he'd pop out with a crackling *boo* and scare her plenty!

But what was that? A few old cars frosted with snow, broken-down cars like the one he and his grandparents had left behind on the highway, cars just waiting for him to clamber into and practice his driving. He skipped in long strides, stirring up the snow as he went, and pulled at the handle of the driver's door, balanced himself by pressing a knee against the side of the car, pulled at the door, which wouldn't budge, and was nearly ready to give up when all of a sudden —

What was that?

A flash of color caught his eye. Beside the rear bumper of the car stood a strange animal playing statue, too big to be a cat, too cat-like to be a dog, the fur on its body the color of Bo's own skin — reddish brown — with a blond mane framing its face and the black tip of its nose dabbed with snow. Bo didn't recognize it as a fox, wasn't even sure that what he saw existed in a reality outside his dream of this place — the snow, the abandoned cars, the silence. . . . He stared at the fox, asked it with his eyes, *Who are you?*

In the animal's eyes he saw the question thrown back at him: *Who are you?* A brazen strategy of evasion — animals were skilled at evasion, Bo knew in his own way, especially wild animals, so this creature must be wild.

Don't be afraid, Bo told himself and then directed the reassurance outward. *Don't be afraid,* he told the fox.

I'm not afraid.

Are you cold?

No.

Are you hungry?

Yes.

I'd give you a cupcake, but I already ate it. Do you like cupcakes?

Yes.

And popcorn? I feed popcorn to the squirrels. I live in the city now. Where do you live?

Up there, in the mountain.

Can you show me your home?

The fox leaned back slightly, reached forward with a fat paw as though it were going to approach Bo, then turned and darted off in the opposite direction. Bo ran alongside the car and into the clearing beyond. The fox sprang lightly off the ground with each stride, trotting forward so swiftly that it seemed to be flying, its belly grazing the smooth surface of the snow. Halfway across the clearing Bo stopped to catch his breath. The fox settled on its hind legs at the edge of the woods about twenty yards away and licked its shoulder as it waited. The tip of its tail and its legs were black. It stopped cleaning itself and stared at Bo. Bo stared back. How still everything was, and yet how alive. The gray cloud bed hung so low to the earth that some of the treetops were shrouded by mist. Bo had never experienced such a full silence before, and when his grandmother's voice broke the serenity, calling his name, he pretended not to hear, though he could see that the fox was listening, pricking its ears forward, cocking its head to make sure it had heard correctly.

Bo, the fox said.

What is your name? Bo asked, but the fox refused to tell him, as Bo knew it would, since wild animals never give up their names. They stared at each other. Bo wondered about its life, its family, its grandparents and cousins, the games it played, the foods it ate, the stories it knew. The trail of paw prints formed a single wavering line across the snow.

I wish I lived here, Bo said.

Do you still want to see my home?

Yeah.

The fox, sitting back, raised a front paw and jerked its head to the sides, then stepped forward again, preparing to turn. Its tail flicked against the snow, and behind the powder swept into the air Bo saw the animal's eyes narrow into a slant of suspicion, as though suddenly it had decided not to trust him and meant to flee. Before Bo could call out to it the animal crouched, preparing to spring, and then leaped off all fours, stopped in midair as though it had hit an invisible wall, and twisted around itself while a *boom* filled the air, a great *boom* that hurt Bo's ears and hurled the fox back into the snow, where it just lay there with nothing more to say to anyone, nothing left to tell.

Bo started to run toward the bloody mound but the trooper scooped him up from behind, grabbed him around the waist with a "No you don't," and carried him back to his grandma, who stood near the row of old cars holding her hand to her throat, trying to catch her breath and swallow away her terror.

"You okay, lady?"

She cleared her throat, tried to force her breath back to an even rhythm, insisted in a broken way that she was all right.

"Rabid foxes around," the trooper said as Sam appeared between the cars. And as he passed Bo over to Sam — "That wasn't no kitty cat, son."

Pop wanted an explanation, Bo couldn't stop crying, Gran was saying something about a fox, a rabid fox . . . the trooper . . . the gun . . . the crack of gunshot and Bo nowhere in sight . . . the gun . . . their baby . . . the fox.

"Go away." Bo sobbed, clutching the buttons of Pop's shirt, pressing against his chest and feeling on the surface of his cheek the vibrations of his grandfather's heart.

The trooper offered to drive them to a local motel, a decent place with its own restaurant. They might as well sit back and enjoy the scenery, he suggested, maybe watch a little TV and warm up with a hot meal while their car was being repaired.

Might as well, right? Right?

"Right," Pop whispered after a long silence. "That'll be fine."

The Gilberts and their grandson stayed one night at the Grotton Peak Motel in the Endless Mountains. The next day they picked up their car with its new fuel pump and drove home slowly, through a freezing rain, having *learned their lesson,* as Erma would tell her daughter, Merry, who had been waiting by her phone for them to call — *no use running.* They settled back into the routine of their life, celebrated Bo's fourth birthday on Tuesday, went out to eat on Friday, went to the movies on Saturday and to church on Sunday.

Down in Hadleyville, Marge and Eddie Gantz were biding time, waiting for the phone to ring with news from their lawyers. The court-appointed evaluator had visited twice and as soon as she'd seen the Gilbert household a second time she'd draft her report. The hearing was set for the fifth of March, but the lawyers, Paul Krull and Wilson Krull, were keeping in close touch with their clients at every stage. If they won the custody case, Eddie had promised to hire their firm for the malpractice suit.

Marge's daughter, Ann, turned down a part-time clerical job in Gifferton because she wanted to be available to baby-sit for her nephew in the afternoons. She watched television after school, talked on the phone, and took to making up crossword puzzles when she was bored. Across-1: hamburger and fabrication. Down-1: Fish with peas.

Marge, who had quit smoking three years earlier, found herself craving nicotine more than ever, so she busied herself in the kitchen, baking cookies for neighbors on North Lake Road whose basements had flooded during the January thaw.

On the third Saturday in January Eddie helped his hunting buddy, Sheriff Joe Simmons, break up a tile floor in Joe's house. While they were working they got to talking about the custody suit and Eddie's concern about the care the child, Marge's grandson, had received at the hospital. Joe remembered an acquaintance, an emergency medical technician named Jerry Cassada, who worked out of the city hospital.

A few days later, Jerry and an emergency department nurse, now named Mercy, formerly Marianne, *reborn in Christ's almighty love,* met for coffee in the hospital cafeteria. Jerry told her what he knew about the accident to spur her memory. Yes, she remembered the kid coming in from the motor vehicle accident on Route 62. A black boy wearing such sloppy clothes you had to feel sorry for him. She didn't remember much more about the case other than that Dr. Platt up in surgery had been furious with the trauma team for missing — what was it? — a bleeding spleen. Tricky things, those spleens, especially in young children. But the child had recovered completely, praise God.

"What child?" Bart Kowalski, the respirator technician, slid into the seat beside Mercy, spread out a napkin on the table, and set down a chocolate-covered donut as though it were a piece of jewelry he wanted to have appraised.

"That kid with the spleen. Jerry, this is Bart. Bart, Jerry."

"Hobo."

"Hobo?"

"The kid with the spleen — Hobo."

"You remember?"

"Sure I remember. Almost died because of our stupidity. One of many. You hear about that guy doing an amputation down in Florida, cut off the wrong foot? Praise God, that's what I say."

"Bart, eat your donut."

At the same time Bart was taking the first bite from his donut, over on Sycamore Street Bo was watching TV puppets counting backward from ten to one. At Hadleyville High School, Ann Templin was closing her locker with a bang. Marge was at home painting her fingernails, and Eddie was turning on the lights inside Worthco Appliances.

In the hospital cafeteria, Jerry Cassada asked Bart, "What happened? Can you tell me what went wrong, exactly?"

As though anything could be recounted *exactly*. Bartholomew Kowalski, Mr. O_2 Man, smiled to show his crooked front teeth between the scruff of his new beard, and told Jerry Cassada what he could remember, knowing all the while that by doing so he'd be pointing the fan toward the shit, as Gordon Metzger, emergency department resident, would say; *spilling the beans,* as Bart himself liked to say when he was handing out jelly beans to patients on the pediatric ward. Testifying as to the incompetence of said trauma team. With pleasure. Truth be told, he disliked Gordon Metzger, knew him to be a lousy doctor. Could Bart help it if someone wanted to follow the trail of incompetence from point C to point B to Gordon?

Jerry Cassada jotted notes on yellow Post-its. He called Joe Simmons later that day, and Joe called Eddie Gantz. Eddie didn't have much to say in response, only approving "yeps" as Joe ran through the information. After he hung up the phone Eddie wandered into the kitchen and asked Marge what she was baking.

Gingersnaps for the neighbors. The smell of spice and melted butter filled the kitchen. The timer on the counter ticked off the remaining two minutes while the cookies browned in the oven and Marge rinsed off the dishes and arranged them in the dishwasher. They'd better hurry, Eddie reminded Marge, or they'd be late for bowling. *Ding!* Marge lifted out the cookie sheets, waited for the thin cookies to cool slightly, then lifted them with a spatula, one by one, onto the racks.

Up in the city, while Erma spread peanut butter on pancakes, Miraja poured her milk into a saucer and showed Bo how to drink like a cat. Sam was watching the news on television. During the commercials he'd limp over to the front window and look around the edge of the curtain as though expecting to find someone standing at the bottom of the porch steps, watching his house.

"Stop that!" Erma said loudly in the kitchen. She was talking to her granddaughter. "Clean up that mess now."

Over in the hospital, Dr. Platt replaced a critically ill baby's shunt that had become spontaneously infected. The anesthesiologist reminded him that an hour and thirty minutes had passed. Down in the emergency department, Bart, who had nothing better to do, made a fresh pot of coffee for the staff and then spit in Gordon's cup for the hell of it. Dr. Amy Ratigan filled out paperwork on an appendicitis case and wondered if she could really spend the rest of her working life in this department. Mercy's voice could be heard in the background: "A quiet night, praise God."

On Douglas Street, Judge Wright, who would preside over the case of *Gantz v. Gilbert* in March, was reading a paperback novel, a thriller about a couple in Illinois named Chris and Peggy Hollister. In the opening chapters the Hollisters seem to be good, middle-class Baptists. They take in foster children, and at the beginning of the second chapter they report one of the children missing. The police focus on a neighbor, a former felon who served twenty-three years for murder and who has recently moved into a trailer down the road. The felon is fifty years old but looks eighty, with a long, lamb's wool beard, sunken cheeks, and strange glassy skin smooth to the touch but visibly scored by tiny lines. His eyes are always squinting, and he rarely speaks above a whisper. He is the obvious suspect when the foster child, an eight-year-old boy, disappears.

Too obvious, Judge Wright felt, easing himself back against the cushions of his sofa. The first suspect in a novel is sure to be innocent. As he read on, he began to focus on Peggy Hollister, the foster mother — though the writer didn't admit it directly, there was something furtive about her, an insincere note in her expression of concern. And those dogs she raises — a kennel full of Dobermans. Seven foster children and a kennel full of Dobermans. What kind of life was that?

Back at the hospital, Bart sat cross-legged on a bed inside an oxygen tent with a one-year-old pneumonic child, singing, "Three green speckled frogs . . ." while the mother wandered off to find a phone and call her husband. The child, a girl, gazed at Bart with her chin thrust forward, her head tilted, a bemused smile on her face.

Gordon Metzger, sipping the coffee Bart had made, read a story in the paper about the Pope. Mercy restocked a cabinet with airways and thought about Jerry Cassada and the way his brown eyebrows merged on the bridge of his nose.

Over on Sycamore Street, Erma watched the children eat their pancake supper. She heard Sam get up from his chair in the living room. "You expecting someone?" she called. He came into the kitchen, rested an elbow on the counter, picked up a fork, and thrust it at a piece of Miraja's pancake.

"Oh no you don't, Gramps," Miraja said, curling her arm around her plate to guard it from the predator.

At the bowling alley in Athens, five miles south of Hadleyville, Eddie lifted Marge's coat from her shoulders and went to hang it in on a hook. When he returned his wife was already standing at the end of the practice lane, extending her arm to mimic the motion of the release while Dorrie Jelilian called from the bench, "Stan's way ahead already!"

Alone in his house on Douglas Street, Judge Wright read greedily, eager to confirm his suspicion that the foster mother, Peggy Hollister of Granville, Illinois, had a hand in the child's fate. But how and why? His mind wandered, even as he absorbed the unfolding story of the novel, to his own family. His wife had died ten years earlier. His son lived out in California. Shortly after his wife's death he'd learned that she'd carried on a twenty-year affair with a man in Syracuse. Judge Wright would never know for certain if he was his son's natural father. He preferred to go to his grave without knowing for sure one way or the other. The trick was to convince himself that it didn't make much difference.

In the book that Judge Wright was reading, Peggy Hollister takes to drinking. One evening her husband smells whiskey on her breath but the argument that ensues leads nowhere. With forty pages left in the book, the felon dies in a fire set by friends of Peggy and Chris Hollister. Judge Wright couldn't stop reading. He had to be at the courthouse at seven-thirty the following morning, but he read past midnight, helplessly engrossed in the book and enraged at it when the author disclosed the secret: that neither Peggy Hollister nor the felon was to blame for the child's disappearance. In the last chapter the child is discovered living with his mother, a drug addict, in a filthy apartment in Mexico City.

Judge Wright threw the book down in disgust.

On Sycamore Street, Erma Gilbert, unable to sleep, wrapped herself around her husband's sleeping body, closed her eyes, and tried to see into the future. Down the hall, Bo dreamed that he was walking a fox on a leash. Josie, asleep at the end of Bo's bed, twitched, woke up, and settled back down inside the curl of her tail.

In Hadleyville, Marge and Eddie slept without dreaming. Outside, an opossum, ghostly pale against the driveway gravel, slunk toward the garbage bins.

At that hour of night most of the houses on most of the streets were dark — except for the house on Douglas Street, Judge Wright's house, a ramshackle stucco Tudor covered with vines. Some of the vines were a foot in diameter, others as thin as wire and without their green leaves looked like an elaborate web spun over the walls and roof. The light in a front window on the second floor shone through the web — Judge Wright was in his bedroom, thinking of nothing particular, or at least nothing he could have put into words. But at that moment, as he stepped into the legs of his pajamas, the decision he would reach six weeks later in favor of Marjory Gantz, the decision everyone involved expected him to reach, took root in his mind. The evaluator hadn't finished her report, and Judge Wright knew no particulars about the case at that point, especially not what would be revealed toward the end of the trial: that the counsel for Marjory Gantz *has learned, Your Honor, of a drug-related arrest made on the premises of the Gilberts' house in May of 1992* — a young man named Taft, a relative of the family, busted for possession of cocaine. However important this disclosure should have been, to Judge Wright it would be no more than validation for his opinion. The novel irritated him, and his irritation made possible an irritating acceptance of the significance of matrilineage. No wonder most judges still awarded custody to the mother, and so they should. "There is but a twilight zone between a mother's love and the atmosphere of Heaven," the judge in the case of *Tuter v. Tuter* wrote way back in 1938. Of course Judge Wright wouldn't have put it that way, wouldn't even have alluded to the subject if there'd been someone else in the room with him. It was merely a belief he had about the father's uncertain presence in the life of his child, a belief that would determine his response to the arguments presented by both sides in the case of *Gantz v. Gilbert* and would keep him from considering how in a just world, albeit an unreal world, Bo's father would have a chance to speak in his own defense.

PART FOUR

Kamon Gilbert woke up on the morning of the last day of his life at 6:19, and in the minute before his alarm went off thought something to this effect: to exist in space, to have a body that can be aroused, senses that give proof of joy, to be in love, to be in love and alive, to love Jenny Templin and to know Jenny loved him, to know the feeling of love, to know they'd have a child soon — why, it was all a fortunate accident, luck, a gift of chance, one sperm out of millions, one egg with the odds against it, the world already crowded, stasis always easier than growth, nothing always dominating something, so life could never be more than a minute fraction of its own potential —

"... 'cause Sunshine Boy got the weather for you right after ..."

Kamon slammed his hand down on the clock radio's snooze button. Jenny stirred beside him but remained asleep. She'd thrown off the sheets and blankets during the night, and Kamon had only to lift her T-shirt a few inches to reveal the mountain of her belly. He lay beside her, resting on an elbow, and with his free hand felt the taut skin hiding the form that would be their child in two months. And he went right on thinking:

An image like stepping-stones, patches of light on custard skin drawing his mind not from foreground to background as it would have if he'd composed the shot (knowing as he did a little, far too little, about monocular perspective) but from foreground to that dimension behind any image — the past. All images had stories to tell, causes to explain. In the case of Jenny's swollen belly the cause was, as Kamon had put it to his friends, "bumping without a body bag." He was proud of what they'd done, their exquisite faith in each other, and, yeah, he'd been dismayed when she refused to have it undone, yet by then he was hopelessly in love with her, loving their dark-and-pale symmetry, loving what he hoped to make her, bringing her along up through life as he went up instead of kicking her to the curb, which is what his cousin Taft told him to do. Oh, Taft liked to give her the red-eye now that they were living in his apartment, never mind what he said. He enjoyed Jenny Templin's good looks even if he liked to say that Kamon's life was damn well over, an opinion that became to Kamon an energizing challenge. He was just beginning — he knew this for a fact, knew that while other guys would have walked away from the situation he was going to stick it out with Jenny, make himself a family to take care of, and go on loving what he already loved: the girl made of velvet opening her legs to him, going up with him when he went up.

Don't mind that she's white.

Loving her not because of the color of her skin, though not in spite of it either. He'd admit there were times he minded. He'd even found himself wishing, once things started to get heavy, that she'd spent longer in the oven and been roasted to a darker shade. But he loved what they became together, their contrasts, the balance of light and shadow. Stepping-stones of light. He knew how to look at them together, his hand on her belly, the picture enhanced by contrast. Yet what he really wanted was to move the image through the lens of a camera and save it once and for all on paper.

He just had to keep himself from going too fast. Had to learn all he could about the behavior of light during an interval of time. Had to take advantage of time and get himself properly educated. He could look all he wanted, but he had to get educated if he meant to turn looking into a trade and move on up from the bottom. He never doubted his potential. He was busting with talent, everyone thought so. Kamon Gilbert, seventeen years old, acting day in and day out like a celebrity, pretending that he couldn't help being as handsome as his daddy, smart to boot and quick and good at everything he tried out, his special destiny written all over him, bringing girls over to his table at a bar to ask, *Who are you? You must be someone famous.* . . .

Not yet, baby girl, but soon, as long as he didn't lose his way. Sticking to a white girl who was having his child might have added to his journey an extra loop, but he hadn't stopped heading up. If anything, Jenny made him more bent on doing the best he could. Maybe she wasn't busting with talent like Kamon, but she had a kind of courage he could learn from — the courage to try anything, to pick up and start over. She was no average recruit. Why, look at her. Keep looking. The soft point of her chin. The curve downward at the corner of her almond eyes. All the shades of yellow and brown in her hair. Her lips slightly parted. Her tongue moving inside her mouth as she dreamed of love.

Dreaming, wasn't she, of what they'd done? Kamon lying flat as a carpet runner while Jenny licked the salt off him. Jenny straddling Kamon, Kamon straddling Jenny, two bodies rubbing together, building up wet friction, feeling the thrill, again and again, of making love as though for the first time, brown nipple filling his mouth, bodies lying side by side, front to back, upside down, the furnace inside her, cold toes curling against his calves, lips latched onto the ridge of his collarbone, thoughts all jumbled by pleasure, his pleasure shored up by his faith in eternity and hers by fear, Kamon assuming they'd love each other forever, Jenny assuming that something this good couldn't last.

Kamon watched her sleep, thinking about how they'd climb back into this same bed at the end of the day and make love as best they could, lifting themselves up and over the custard mountain of their baby, and when they were done they'd wonder how that mountain would ever come out of her, the baby growing bigger every day, the doctors at the clinic keen on *natural* childbirth, natural hell. "Wake me up when it's over," Jenny would say, tucking her knees up, closing her eyes, preparing to sink into a good night's sleep.

No denying their lives would have been easier if Jenny had agreed to give up that clump of cells inside her before it got itself a soul. But she wanted a baby, so Kamon made himself want what she wanted, accepting fatherhood as another challenge and thinking ahead, trying to imagine the face of his child but unable to sort through all the possible images to find the one that would greet him in two months, reminding himself as he lay there, his hand still resting on Jenny's belly, that he sure had plenty to learn about photographic composition before his child was born, especially if he wanted to make a record of the baby's opening act. And this kind of thinking made him consider how proud he was to be fathering a child who'd be as lucky as this child, what with Kamon and Jenny and all of Kamon's family loving him as they would, Kamon and Jenny heading up in the world, up and up and up.

Yeah! exclaimed the baby, shifting abruptly, pressing an eager foot into the wall of its sac, a motion that felt to Kamon like a mouse bouncing against his palm, transforming his pleasant, lazy contemplation into awe. A body inside a body, one asleep, the other awake — fucking weird, man! He'd like to catch that on film somehow, some way: motion inside stillness. Except he'd used up his allotment of contact paper at school and couldn't afford to buy more and had sworn off begging extras from his art teacher, Mr. Manelli, a white hot-sauce boss who made it all too clear that Kamon was his favorite.

Which reminded him, oh shit, that he was supposed to have finished *Hamlet* for his English class. *See you later, peanut!* He pulled the sheet over Jenny's bare belly, kissed her lightly on the cheek, and turned off the pending alarm on the clock radio. He dressed quickly in jeans and a ratty T-shirt under his flannel shirt and walked in bare feet along the cold hallway of his cousin Taft's apartment to the kitchen. He made coffee in the old Hamilton Beach pot he'd picked up a few weeks earlier at the Salvation Army and while the coffee was dripping he ate two big bowls of cereal and paged through the final scenes of *Hamlet,* got as far as the sparrow's providential fall, and chose to spend the last minutes before he left the apartment not finishing the play but instead grooming himself in the bathroom, for wasn't it more than likely that his English teacher would assign him the role of Hamlet during class? He'd already read the parts of Romeo and Julius Caesar. And now this: *If it be now, 'tis not to come; if it be not to come, it will be now.*

At 3:05 P.M., two old women in the East Avenue McDonald's waited at the counter for their order. One said, "I got mice. Mice!"

"The live ones?" the other asked.

"In my apartment. They wake me up at night."

Kamon stood behind them but moved forward when a girl appeared at another register to take his order. He bought a milk shake and fries and walked to a far booth so he could be alone and spend a few minutes calming himself down, untying the knot of anger, loops as tight as the muscles in his neck after a day spent at the snake pit that was his school, every student there bent on bringing Kamon down, hating him, if they were white, because he was a nigger, hating him, if they were black, because he was exceptional when measured by the teachers and their standardized tests against the rest of them. Kamon Gilbert this and Kamon Gilbert that. *Kamon, you're jack shit, busting your balls over white pussy.* So he kept to himself between classes and had stopped eating lunch altogether so he wouldn't have to face the cafeteria mob. And at the end of the school day he always ended up here, at the McDonald's across from the garage where he worked, so hungry that he ate two fistfuls of fries as he walked to a table.

A few minutes later he took the lid off his milk shake and shook the last bit into his mouth. He stood up again, noticing with some pleasure that the white lady with mice in her apartment reached for her purse and placed it securely on her lap as he passed behind her chair. She kept her back to him, but her friend followed

Kamon with her eyes, that ancient terror making her hands tremble just enough that a few drops of coffee splashed out of her wobbly cup and she had to set it down.

Don't you lay a hand on me, black boy!

Ah, lovely ladies!

Kamon couldn't leave without saying hello. He stopped in front of the door, swung around, and as he pulled on gloves, filthy black woolen gloves snipped to leave his fingers bare, he said, "Afternoon, ladies!" They didn't reply. "I was wondering if you knew the time?" They were silent for a period that threatened to stretch into tomorrow, until the lady with the mice finally turned to look straight at Kamon and without glancing at her wristwatch said, "Three-eighteen," grinning warmly as though to signal her forgiveness.

"That's all right then," Kamon said, returning the smile, thinking to himself that if he smiled in just the right way he might give false courtesy a palpable heat and make the ladies feel the flames dancing at their feet. But his smile was ineffectual, or else the lady proved more resilient then he'd expected. She kept grinning, leaving him nothing else to do but nod his farewell.

At the garage he found the owner, Paul, at his computer tapping numbers into the Customer Alpha Service program. "Fucking gas thief," Paul muttered, banging his index finger against the enter key in an attempt to pound information out of the computer. He snatched a set of keys from a drawer and threw them at Kamon, who had yet to speak.

"Tan Honda Civic, '87 or '88." Paul scribbled the license number on a piece of scrap paper. "Get the bastard," he growled, pressing the paper into Kamon's hand.

So someone had driven away without paying for their gasoline. Another fucking runner, another gas thief, petty stuff — the police had better things to do than respond to such a complaint. If Paul wanted the money for his gasoline he had to track down the thieves on his own. He'd copy the plate number from the video and try to find the owner's name in the computer's bank — with a name and address, he could send a nasty letter. Without the information, his only chance of reimbursement was to catch the crooks on the road. And since Paul himself had better things to do than go chasing cars like a dog, he usually sent one of his mechanics, whoever happened to be close by.

Kamon took Paul's Corvette and headed in the direction Paul had pointed him, knowing that he didn't have much of a chance catching up to the Civic but thinking that if he did, he'd force the guy off the road, flashing that friendly smile of his, waving through the window, mouthing happily, *I'm gonna kill you!* Problem was, Kamon couldn't read Paul's handwriting, so when he did spot a tan Honda Civic a few miles down the road, he couldn't be sure whether the driver, a middle-aged Asian woman, was really his fugitive. He decided against a confrontation, just drove on in a leisurely way for a while, thinking that he didn't mind working for Paul, not just because the pay was good or because he got to take Paul's Corvette for a spin once in a while, but because the other mechanics didn't despise him. In the garage, unlike at school, Kamon was considered *good enough,* not worse because he was better than the rest of them in any obvious way.

Good enough to grab a quarter-inch ratchet from the toolbox for Paul's cousin Jeff, who when Kamon returned to the garage was in the process of prying off a brake shoe, but not so good he could upload the idle speed into an engine computer or scan information about a malfunctioning ABS brake system or change the setting on a lock. Good enough to raise a car on the lift, but not so good he could disassemble the wiring. Good enough to work the alignment machine and balance the wheels on an '89 Ford Escort, good enough to plug in the AVR machine to analyze the charging system on the '82 Toyota, good enough to check the setting on the main air compressor in the pump room and, of course, to straighten up the drawer of mid-sized screwdrivers, but not good enough to explain to an owner of a '92 Saab that because the value scanned from the engine computer of his car was incorrect he would have to pay one hundred and thirty-eight dollars just so Paul could take apart the fuel-injection system to find out what was wrong.

"Kamon, buddy, grease the rod ends of this dinky, will ya?"

So Kamon pulled the grease gun away from the bulk oil dispenser and started filling up an outer rod end, stopping a second too late — thick black grease bubbled out of the ball joint and splattered his shirt. Paul was still on the phone with a customer, Darryl had stepped behind the alignment rack to help Jeff with the brake shoe, so no one noticed Kamon's mistake. He wiped the grease with a gloved hand and moved beneath the car to get at the inner joint, listening as he worked to a song on the radio:

"My snake-hipped, red-lipped, wild revolutionary man . . ."

"You know why surgeons get paid so much?" Paul had hung up the phone and come over to inspect Kamon's work. Kamon pressed the trigger carefully, filling up the ball joint until the grease seeped to the edges, and stopped.

"Why's that?" he asked.

"Because they got to listen to back talk." Paul pushed on the front fender of the car on the lift. "Maybe we work harder than your typical surgeon. But the fact of the matter is, we don't have to listen to back talk."

Paul was honest and fair, though permanently angry at the world, with his spongy features bunched up in a scowl and his voice crackling with resentment. By his own account he never recovered from the change in the industry, twenty years ago, to the metric system. He had two large cabinets for tools — just to see them made him mad, since back in the old days a mechanic needed a single drawer of tools, sizing was simple, and an experienced mechanic could measure a socket with his eye. With the metric system, the fucking metric system, nothing was simple. Yet Paul continued to blame himself for the confusion and slammed his hand against something hard whenever he grabbed the wrong ratchet. *What's experience worth when everything's changing so fast?* He'd tried out that question on Kamon more than once, and Kamon had tried out an answer:

You learn from experience how to learn from experience.

Kamon, what the fuck are you talking about?

What was he talking about? Smart-ass Kamon, he should have learned from experience to keep his mouth shut, since what he couldn't do was explain himself accurately. He was quick at calculations, could write an elegant sentence, could take a fine photograph, but he couldn't explain how to do any of it and so couldn't make himself understood. No wonder the other students hated him — strutting around like royalty, working from the unspoken assumption that he had special rights.

"Except sometimes on the phone," Paul went on. "The things customers are willing to say on the phone, you wouldn't believe it. Face to face, they're as polite as can be. But on the phone."

"You got to put —" Kamon said.

"Paul!" interrupted Jeff.

"What's that?"

"I need you to check the settings on these brakes."

So Paul went to work on the computer to upload the data stream on the brakes, and Kamon finished greasing the front rod ends, then moved to the rear of the car, listening as he worked to a song by Blind Willie Johnson on the radio — *"Jesus, make up my dying bed . . ."* And while he squirted grease Kamon started thinking something like this: how much easier it would be to give up all his ambitions, drop out of school, and work for Paul full-time. If he kept working in the garage the rest of his life he'd be a good enough mechanic, nothing special. He'd earn good enough money, enough to support his family, and if Jenny went back to work they'd have more than enough, and maybe they'd have a few more babies and eventually they'd buy a house of their own, his folks would watch the babies so Jenny and Kamon could go out, catch a movie, go dancing, they'd have friends who wouldn't hate them, they'd have fun, and the only pictures Kamon ever took would be the ones for Jenny to put in their albums to serve as a visible measure of time.

"I went to the crossroads, fell down on my knees, I went to the crossroads, fell down on my knees . . ."

"We're low on grease," Kamon called.

"Use some of Jeff's snot," Darryl shouted back across the noise of the air compressor. "There's plenty of it."

6:25 Kamon and Jenny ate sausage and pepper pizza and watched a reporter on the local news make a pitch for an animal shelter, asking viewers to consider adopting one or more of the dozens of cats taken from a filthy house on the south side, the owner a feeble, eighty-seven-year-old woman. Then at

6:37 Jenny went to pee and Kamon began his homework, reading the assigned chapter about ionic bonds, the donation of electrons, the positive ion of sodium, the negative ion of chloride, the miracle of sodium chloride, the process of molecular dissociation. While he was reading Jenny tiptoed behind him and started to massage his shoulders, and Kamon would have given himself over to her if Taft hadn't walked in right at

7:00, ducking into the kitchen, snatching a piece of cold pizza from the table in front of Kamon's textbook, muttering his end-of-the-day greeting, something like *heya,* or *hey there,* before sinking his teeth into the pizza and disappearing into his bedroom, leaving Jenny and Kamon alone again, though now Jenny had turned back to the television and with the remote changed the channel to a game show, which she and Kamon watched until

7:15, when a commercial for Worthco Appliances came on and Jenny said about her stepdad, "I wish that asshole would drop

"Here's a tip, Darryl," said Paul, still tapping at the keyboard. "Jeff's a champion wrestler."

"Phone!" Kamon called.

"I got it," Paul called back, stepping to the corner of the shop to pick up the phone.

"Jeff, you're making me hungry."

"Darryl, you're so sick," Kamon scoffed.

"Anyone know what time it is?" Jeff asked.

"Somewhere around five maybe," Darryl answered.

Memphis Minnie sang, *"I'm a bad luck woman."* Kamon checked with Darryl, who said he could go ahead and lower the lift, then Darryl stepped outside to smoke a cigarette. Jeff lowered the alignment rack, and Paul sat at the desk out front, checking the computer in the office for information about the gas pumps. Kamon lifted the edge of his gloves and pulled them inside out and off his hands, then held his dirty hands close to his face to breathe deeply that intoxicating smell of oil and gasoline and grease.

Yeah, this would be a good enough life, he thought again. As good a life as any he could imagine.

dead," and Kamon said, "Make peace with him — maybe he'll give us a washing machine," and Jenny said, "Yeah, right," both of them watching in silence until

7:30, and then Kamon continued with his homework and Jenny lay on the sofa and read a magazine. The basketball game started at

9:00, so she and Kamon sat on the sofa together and Taft sat in his Taft-throne, a plump, ragged, pin-striped armchair he'd found on the street. They shouted at the television, cursed the referees, cheered on the players, and threw pillows across the room when someone missed a free throw, until

11:15, when Taft offered to pay Kamon twenty dollars just to go out and get him some cigarettes, so Kamon put on Taft's jacket and his own orange ski hat, kissed Jenny good-bye, and headed to the deli, thinking as he went that his cousin Taft was dumber than dumb and bullish enough so that Kamon didn't feel badly about taking advantage of him, charging twenty dollars for an errand that would cost Kamon no more than fifteen minutes. Not a bad deal. But shit, he hadn't expected it to be so cold, and as he walked away from the apartment house he pinched the collar of his coat closed and ducked his head against the wind, continuing at a pace just short of a jog, so at

11:24:07 he had reached the corner of Buffalo Avenue and Raymond Street, and at

11:24:12 the door to the deli on the next block opened and at

11:24:15 Kamon saw the two figures hurtling down the sidewalk toward him. His first confused thought, having spent the last two hours watching basketball, was that he was witnessing a calculated play in some kind of game, with the boys instructed by a coach to run just as they were and at some point to pivot as they continued to run and look back at the deli, gesturing with their handguns at the door that was still in the process of easing shut on its springs. What they hadn't planned on was this: by the time they had turned their heads in the direction they were sprinting, Kamon had already arrived on the scene and by his mere presence interrupted the smooth play, forcing the boy in front to sidestep to avoid him and causing the one behind to cross his right leg in front of his left and stumble, catch himself, then hit a patch of watery ice, so his left foot slid out from under him and he fell down hard on his ass in front of Kamon, who, still confused, reached out a hand for the boy in order to help him to his feet, and at

11:24:23 recognized, or thought he recognized, between the scarf wound around the boy's mouth and nose and the ski hat pulled low on his head, the eyes of someone he knew at school—what was his name? — someone who belonged to the mob of students who hated Kamon Gilbert, someone Kamon hadn't bothered to distinguish as an individual, so now he couldn't come up with a name, despite his sense of recognition. *Who are you?* Kamon wondered as he bent slightly at the waist, preparing to lift the boy by an elbow, since the boy hadn't accepted his hand. *Who are you?* Feeling at once a sharp sensation of pity because the boy was obviously scared of Kamon, though Kamon meant no harm and wanted to reassure him, started to consider what he might say, perhaps introduce himself, though if Kamon recognized the boy, then the boy surely recognized Kamon, everyone at school knew Kamon, *Kamon Gilbert this and Kamon Gilbert that*, and in fact he looked at Kamon now with a glittery squint as if to beg Kamon not to recognize him, a look so amusing that Kamon drew in a shallow inhalation, the kind that usually precedes a chuckle, and he would have started to laugh if at

*   *   *

11:24:45 he hadn't become suddenly aware of a pain in the side of his back, only afterward hearing the sound of the first shot, as though time were moving in reverse and whatever had just happened was already starting to undo itself, the pain returning to the sound of the shot, the sound preceding the catch of breath, the inhalation preceding the pity Kamon felt for the boy who'd slipped on the ice, the boy slipping in front of him but going up instead of down, rising toward the bare branches of the maple tree in front of the Presbyterian church while Kamon fell between two parked cars. He heard a brief clatter that reminded him of himself as a boy shaking a fistful of polished stones his daddy had given him, felt a spasm of pain at the same time along with a new confusion, for the backward sequence had reversed itself again, but instead of moving forward, everything was happening at the same time, and the simultaneity seemed natural, as if life had always been this way — instants of multiple sensations, hearing and feeling and seeing the progression of an event within one moment, and within that same moment remembering with dreamy haziness, as Kamon did, that the two players running from the deli had been holding guns, realizing as he fell that he'd forgotten about the guns when he'd been moving to help the second player to his feet, but the gun must have been there somewhere, on the ground, inside the boy's sleeve, somewhere, anywhere, yet the boy had been paralyzed with fear, so he couldn't have had the nerve to pull a trigger. Which immediately brought to mind the capability of the forward player. Yeah, it was possible that the shots still being fired as he fell were coming from the forward player's gun, a clatter of stones, pain within and without, the branches receding, the street rising up between two cars to smack him in the face at

11:24:52 as the boy he'd been trying to help scrambled to his feet and ran away after his teammate, the two players resuming the game that Kamon had interrupted, maybe just practice for the real thing, the important game scheduled for Saturday. You couldn't blame them, really, Kamon had gotten in their way, though you couldn't blame Kamon, he hadn't done anything wrong, he couldn't think of a single thing he'd ever done wrong in his whole life, so at

11:25:03 he asked himself, *how did I come to be here?* The last thing he remembered was the impulse to laugh, but already he'd forgotten what was so funny and felt a residual smile disappear from his face, like a fly taking off after picking up a crumb, leaving behind the itch, which Kamon would have scratched if he could have figured out how to get his hand to his mouth. He'd had a hand once, yeah, and he'd extended the hand to a boy who'd fallen on the sidewalk. But how could that be? Had he extended the hand to himself, left his body in order to lift his body to his feet? Where was he now? Outside with the pain or inside with the night? It was so dark inside, close to midnight, he figured, and he'd done just as his ma expected: *What do you do when you leave the room, Kamon?*

11:25:08 *Turn off the light,* so the room was the color of the grease overflowing from a ball joint, and somewhere in the lightless corner Darryl was laughing at his own bad joke, maybe the joke that had almost spurred Kamon to laughter himself, whatever it was, something that had to do with Jenny. Kamon couldn't feel her but he could feel how he wanted her to hold him, to warm him with her electric warmth, for wouldn't you know that when pain leaves the body it transforms into cold, drawing snow from the sky, brittle flakes moistening his cheeks, he would have brushed them away but he had misplaced his hands somewhere between his home and the deli, yeah, he'd been going to the deli, he remembered that much, to the deli for a carton of cigarettes, he'd made a deal with his cousin Taft and would earn twenty dollars for this errand. Go ahead, push Kamon around all you wanted, you owed him twenty dollars, twenty fucking dollars, now if someone would please find his hands

*　　*　　*

11:25:17 he'd get up and finish what he'd started, a life beginning with the clatter of stones, a fistful of polished stones and the bark of a magnolia scraping his arm as he climbed, the dribble of a basket-ball, the echo of voices in windowless hallways, the endless waiting, a beer and a red hot smothered with onions, sodium chloride, con-tact paper, the shock of a mouse bouncing against his palm, the pop of a lightbulb, a darkroom, the pissing, the shitting, busting his balls over white pussy, a squirrel caught under the wheels of a moving car, food stamps in an old woman's purse, lemonade, cigarettes, music, magic tricks, and always the waiting, Jenny waiting for him to come home while Kamon waited in line for the Jack Rabbit and looked for-ward to the next ride, though the last time he'd coasted straight into a wall and ended up flat as a fruit roll. He'd have to pinch his skin and pull himself into a solid shape, Jenny would expect as much, but he discovered only then that he had lost his stuffing, there was noth-ing to hold his body in place, he couldn't even stand up, he would never stand up, he would never find his hands again,

11:25:18 he would never be himself. He felt now what might be called *panic* but was a feeling too peculiarly Kamon's to be attached to a word and have sensible meaning. The recognition that he would no longer be who he'd been, even as he was still close enough to himself to understand this, produced a change in the pattern of his thinking, a change that felt palpably real, developing as it did from the experience of loss, understanding as it happened that ex-actly when 11:25:18 became

11:25:19 the wafer of glass upon which his mind rested shattered, and thought burst from its reservoir like floodwater, traveling through the hollow package of his body in pursuit of the pain,

11:25:20 draining out of him onto the curb, so if he had been able to open his eyes he would have seen the last shreds of his comprehension lying in a wet pool of blood, insoluble thoughts, thoughts that only Kamon Gilbert could have thought, past thoughts and all the potential thoughts that would have come to him over a lifetime, leaving behind a brain as hollow as the body, knowing nothing about what had happened to him or how it had happened, unable to postulate what would become of the boys who had done this to him, boys who would live into their old age, each of them spending time in jail for other crimes but not for this, and who, by murdering Kamon Gilbert, had deprived him of the one wish he would have wished for, if he'd had a chance:

11:25:21

PART FIVE

Imagine yourself looking up from the bottom of Hadley Lake at the frozen surface. It is raining, and the rain on ice makes the sound of cards being shuffled. From below, the surface is milky white, but gradually the ice grows transparent as the rain washes away the peaks of frozen snow. You can see a layer of murky water accumulating above the ice, and above that, coils of mist dance in the wind. Eventually it stops raining, and for a couple of days cold sunlight turns the thin layer of ice an iron color streaked with rust, the ice thickens, and a storm covers the ice with snow. Below the ice the water is gelatinous, lightless, silent.

Then the rain returns and works upon the ice like wind upon stone, grinding, eroding, breaking the solid mass into separate islands that shrink over the course of a few days. And then at the end of a warm afternoon the lake is fully liquid once again, dimpled with foam, sloshing and spilling around you.

Now imagine you are a four-year-old boy, and through him see the sun rising over the lake. Listen to the silence of water and then the sharp creak of wood and clank of metal against metal. Listen to Eddie Gantz curse when he jams his thumb against the oarlock. Imagine you can see vanilla mist rising from the lake, the sun an orange bulb behind the screen of leafless willows, Eddie pushing off from the dock with an oar, Eddie rowing. Listen to the slap of wood against water, Eddie coughing, the peeping call of a blue-winged teal flying overhead, the sharp intake of breath as Eddie rows. Notice the tips of unfurled lilies poking just above the surface and the clump of bulrushes. Keep listening to the slap of wood against water, wood against water, *metal grinding against wood, Eddie's grunts, the rattle of rod and line, the sound of waiting, the silence of water. Imagine you can feel the liquid glove of cold with Bo when he dips his hand into the dark water. Hear the sudden fish splash and Eddie's muttering pleasure as he reels in the line. See the glimmering scales of the fish, the hook lodged in the wall of the fish's mouth. Listen to the slight ripping sound as Eddie pulls out the hook. Watch as Eddie throws the fish back into the water.*

Fish splash.

Rattle of rod and line.

The silence of water.

Now imagine that it is night and you can hear the muffled snap of floorboards, as though the house, along with its occupants, were settling into sleep. Imagine you can see the moonshine on the windowsill in Bo's room, the faint outline of the bureau, the various shapes of the frames holding photos of his mother, the shadowy heap of blankets gathered into a bundle in his arms.

Imagine you are dreaming his dreams.

Marge named herself *Grandma* but she gave that up after a few days. Eddie only called himself Eddie. They called Bo *Michael,* his middle name, if they called him anything at all.

Eddie said, "Marge, we're out of syrup. The boy needs syrup, don't you, Michael? Do you like pancakes? Do you ever answer when someone asks you a question?"

So Marge replied, "Here's more syrup, Eddie. Here's plenty of syrup. Shall I cut up your pancake, Michael? Go on and eat, we believe in eating a hearty breakfast in this house, don't we, Ann?"

"I gotta go to school. See you, Bo."

"Michael, call him Michael."

"He's used to being called Bo, aren't you, Bo? Ho-bo-bo. Mind if I kiss you on the cheek?"

"No."

"See you in a while, crocodile Bo."

Bye-bye.

"Bye-bye, Bodeebodeebo."

"It's not so bad here, is it, Michael? This is the home where your mama grew up, and you're going to grow up here, too. You can be happy here. We want you to tell us whenever you're not happy. Now why don't you take a bite of the great big pancake Eddie made for you?"

"No."

"That's all you can say? No? I made it special for you. A perfect pancake. How about cereal then? Scrambled eggs. How about some ice cream? Yeah, you'd like some ice cream for breakfast, I can tell. All right, you can have it, you can have anything you want in this house."

"Eddie, don't go overboard . . ."

"What? He deserves some special treats for a while, all he's been through."

"I suppose . . . but kids —"

"Must have been pretty scary for you at the hospital, the things they did to you. We're going to make sure they apologize. We got some lawyers working on it as we speak."

"He doesn't need to hear about lawyers, Eddie."

"You're right, Marge, you're always right. That's the thing you'll learn about your grandmother — she never makes a mistake."

"Come off it, Eddie."

"And wait till you taste her apple crisp!"

"I know it's a change for you, Michael, but you'll get used to us, I promise. Don't you like the lake? Don't you like going fishing with Eddie? Isn't it lots of fun?"

"He has fun, I guarantee it. Here you go, little man, here's what I call a Special Eddie. How about that? I bet those other folks didn't give you ice cream for breakfast, did they? When you're in my house, all you got to do is ask."

"Can you say thank you, Michael? Say thank you, come on, Eddie would appreciate a thank you."

"That's all right. He's got to get used to us. I mean, can you blame the kid? All he's been through, and the way the doctors cut him up for the hell of it."

"Eddie!"

"There I go again. It's just sympathy making me talk. Now I better go get ready for work. And if you want more ice cream, you just ask. But remember the one rule we have in this house. You know our rule, don't you? You know we don't allow smiling in this house. That's our number one rule. No smiling. That's the way it is around here. You're not allowed to smile even when someone tells a joke. No smiling whatsoever, do you hear? 'Cause you know what happens if we catch you smiling? Then we give you Special Eddies for lunch and dinner, and maybe some popcorn, too, and maybe if you keep on smiling Marge will have to make her chocolate chip cookies."

"He'll come around, Eddie."

"Poor little guy. All he's been through. How's that ice cream, eh?"

"I'm taking him in for a checkup today, meet the doctor, maybe he'll give us some advice on how to —"

"Ask the doc if he knows anyone up at the city hospital."

"Eddie, the lawyers —"

"I'm just curious, that's all. We'll be seeing you, then."

"Can you say good-bye to Eddie, Michael? Can you say bye-bye?"

"Oh, don't bother the kid, he's eating."

"He'll get used to us."

"He sure will."

And Eddie went to work just as he did every morning except for Saturdays, when he went fishing, and Sundays, when Marge and Eddie took Bo to church. After three weeks living in his new home, Bo knew the routine like he knew his ABC's. Marge, he thought, looked like the man in the moon. Eddie always looked like he wanted to be doing something different from whatever he was doing.

When it wasn't raining Marge took Bo for a walk along the lake and showed him where beavers were building a dam in the pickerelweed. When the geese flew in honking V's overhead, she said the geese were singing their spring song. And once a white cloud of swans flew across the sun.

Then March turned into April, and Puss and Kitten moths started to flutter around in the yard. On the trunk of a willow tree up in the high meadow Bo found a giant caterpillar the size of a grown man's thumb and the color of raw hamburger. He pried the caterpillar off the bark along with some red galls and showed it to Marge, who shrieked and told him to put it down, for God's sake.

As she said it, Bo suddenly saw his own mama in her face, and all at once he felt himself to be the victim of some terrible lie, having long ago been told a story about the whereabouts of his real mama and for all this time believing it to be the complete, undeniable truth.

Which caused him to suppose that the truth must have been the opposite of what he'd been told, and his mama would be coming back to pick him up and bring him home. He wanted to believe this version rather than the other, and in that same moment easily persuaded himself that the course of events leading to her return was as inevitable as the movement of the hour hand on the clock. You wouldn't think the hour hand moved at all, but it did, with mysterious slowness. Bo, after six weeks in his new home with Marge and Eddie and Alligator Ann, began to wait.

The sun shone, and Bo waited. At nighttime, in his dreams, he waited. He waited inside when it rained and outside when Marge worked in the garden and up in the meadow when she searched with binoculars for migrating birds. He waited while Eddie made him ice cream sundaes and while Ann talked on the telephone. Sometimes he stared at Ann's back and imagined that she was his mama and would turn around and find him standing there, after all this time.

He wondered if Eddie was the reason his mama wouldn't come back. The more Bo listened to Eddie, the more he noticed in his soft voice the ticktock of Eddie's thoughts, from *Come over here* to *Stay out of my way.* Eddie read a storybook to Bo each night and patted him on the cheek and wished him sweet dreams, and four times already they'd gone fishing on Hadley Lake, Bo sitting bundled in an adult-sized life preserver in the front end of the canoe, the dark water inviting and dangerous, like Eddie's voice.

He was always glad when Aunt Ann came home in the afternoons because she called him Bo and tickled him under the arms and let him watch television with her, or at least he played with his Legos on the carpet while the grown-ups smooched and shrieked and moaned on the TV screen and Ann did stretching exercises on the couch and waited for the phone to ring.

Josie took to scampering out the kitchen door between Marge's feet and disappearing into the wet meadow for hours at a time, so one day Bo decided to do the same. He climbed beyond the mowed yard up through the prickly grass until he got snagged in a thornbush and Marge came to get him. The next day he snuck along the narrow path made by the deer who came to nibble the new buds off the azaleas — Marge caught up to him just when he was about to enter the woods. Later that same week Ann led him through the woods, along a wide, muddy trail, and down the side of the ravine to a creek, where Bo collected rocks and tried to catch fish in his bare hands while Ann sat on the trunk of a fallen tree and smoked cigarettes.

Then April turned into May, and Bo went on waiting and waiting, eventually grew so used to waiting that he just lived in time without thinking about the future.

On May twenty-first, Eddie's birthday, Bo learned that if you sneak down to the basement when you're supposed to be watching television and look beneath the Ping-Pong table you hadn't even known existed, you will find a dusty Ping-Pong ball. And if you carry the Ping-Pong ball up to the kitchen and drop it into a narrow glass vase and collect some cardboard, string, a magnet, and a bottle of apple juice, you will discover, after maybe ten minutes spent trying out various methods, that a Ping-Pong ball doesn't stick to a magnet, the string won't make a proper loop, and the cardboard is useless, but if you pour the apple juice from the jar into the vase, the Ping-Pong ball will bob up and up and up and finally tumble with the gushing juice onto the table.

Then, of course, Eddie will come into the kitchen and shout, *What the hell!* and grab your wrist, making the plastic bottle of juice drop from your hands and bounce across the floor. Which, in turn, will make Eddie even madder — *What the hell!* — so he'll jerk your arm in an attempt to pull it loose from its socket, and you'll do what you have to do. You'll spit in his face, spit a good thick gob that lands right on the corner where his lips disappear into a fold of rough skin, and Eddie will stop bellowing *What the hell!* and he'll look at you with eyes that express precisely a sentiment that Eddie didn't even know he felt — *I hate this child* — so you'll say it back, a vocal echo, "I hate you!" Words so thrilling you'll say them again, "I hate you," and again, "I hate you," perfect words because they prove that you have found, at last, something to hate with all your strength.

Bo's aunt Ann once said, *At your age, kiddo, life is never boring,* and she was right.

Bo didn't understand why his gran and pop had given him away to Eddie and Marge, yet he sensed that this, too, was right. They did it because they were supposed to do it. And now, after ten weeks and two days in his new home, he had finally arrived at a point as close to certainty as he could hope to come.

Even though Eddie yelled at him, Bo assumed he still had the advantage. Maybe he didn't know in any precise way the meaning of *advantage,* but he had a sense of his power and the pliancy of his subjects. *I am King Bo. Kneel before me!* Just like Aunt Ann said, life was never boring. He could look out his bedroom window and see a mama deer and her two fawns stealing silently along the edge of the meadow. He could watch videos while Marge baked chocolate chip cookies. He could collect rocks in a bucket. He could eat the maraschino cherries straight from the jar. He could drop a bottle of apple juice and watch it bounce across the floor. He could spit in Eddie's face.

Just remember, Mr. Macaroni, the story of the explorer who lost his way trying to find the South Pole.

Bo couldn't remember — *Tell me again, Pop.*

Or the story of the artist Jack Frost, who painted with ice and gave his paintings away for free.

Bo would have liked to hear about the emperor who disguised himself as a beggar.

We couldn't help spoiling you, Bo, giving you whatever, fooling you into thinking that all you had to do was wish upon a star.

The reason Gran and Pop never came to see him was because they were afraid of the law. The law carried a gun and shot whatever it caught by surprise. So the trick was never to let yourself be surprised, to keep looking in front and around whenever you are out walking, and don't confide in people you don't trust, for they could call in the law at any time.

Then he poured apple juice into the flower vase and learned that Eddie hated him and he hated Eddie.

So he went up to the attic to play by himself, and he found a dusty rag quilt that must have been more than one hundred years old. He opened the window, dangled the quilt over the sill, and beat it against the side of the house to shake off the dust. "Please stop!" the quilt cried. "If you stop beating me, I'll take you for a ride." So the boy spread the quilt on the attic floor, sat cross-legged upon it, and sure enough, he felt the quilt rise beneath him, and they flew out the window and soared over the trees.

Oh, there you go, teasing him with magic!

No one had to explain to Bo that as soon as you stopped believing the quilt was magic, it would lose its power and plummet to the ground, taking you down with it. Bo knew the difference between magic and reality. He knew, for instance, that by storming from the room Eddie had found a way to avoid hurting Bo. But in came Marge, who scolded, "Never, never do that again, Michael Templin —"

Who?

"If you ever spit at Eddie again, or anyone, if you ever spit, we'll . . . we'll . . . you get up to your room, get on."

Testing the limits of his power in the real world, Bo refused to budge, so Marge picked him up and carried him upstairs herself while he punched the doughy flesh of her back.

"You bad boy. You sit here until you're ready to apologize!"

So Bo sat. Sat on his goddamn ass on the bed where his mama used to sleep, thinking about how he hated Eddie and he hated Marge and he hated his mama for ever having had a bed that Bo had to sit on. He threw his pillow across the room at his mama's picture, but the pillow just bounced off the bureau drawer and fell to the floor. This, more than anything else Bo had done since he'd been living in his new home, felt like a catastrophic failure, and he began to cry.

When you cry out loud, someone always comes to comfort you, but when twenty minutes passed and no one came to him, Bo gave up. He sat on the radiator cover, pulled his knees to his chin, and gazed out the window at the meadow. He sucked on the side of his thumb and thought about fish. He imagined that he was a circle of bright orange light growing smaller and smaller — now he was the size of a dime, now the head of a pin, now, poof, he had disappeared.

King Bo, are you there? Your majesty?

There was no reason he could understand why he would be allowed to fade away to nothing. The other times he'd felt alone didn't compare to this, for in the past he'd been left alone by accident and now he was being punished with loneliness. That he'd lost everything and his mama had kept him waiting for longer than eternity — this was his fault because he no longer believed in most magical powers, including the ability to fly or to breathe underwater. How could he believe in things so implausible? He needed proof. If he had proof, he'd believe anything.

Proof could be as arbitrary as finding the drawings he'd made on the floor of his old bedroom — if he rolled up the carpet from the corner and found his drawings on this floor, he'd know what to believe. But the wall-to-wall carpet was secured with tacks, and no matter how hard Bo tugged he couldn't loosen it. He returned to the radiator and stared out the window and as he thought about his loneliness he discovered, all at once, the bitter pleasure of pity.

Poor Hobo, all alone in the real world, unloved, unwanted. He cried just thinking about himself crying, a sorry sight that would evoke, in memory, enough self-pity to sustain him for a lifetime. Oh, he was a miserable child. Think of all he'd been through, all the waiting, his daddy no more than letters carved in stone, his mama gone off somewhere, his grandparents scared away by the law. Weep for him, if you're susceptible to pity. But don't let your eyes grow so foggy that you miss the subtle transformation taking place, the transformation of pity into something far more powerful than even Bo could have anticipated, a kind of anger that distinguished itself from the magisterial anger he had felt just minutes earlier, this anger born out of the loneliness Bo couldn't bear to feel anymore, an anger that would have prompted immediate violence if Bo had been ten years older. But because of his youth, its effect was directed inward, resulting in no more than a barely apprehensible tightening — his jaw tightened, the muscles in his torso and neck tightened, and his fingers tightened, the skin lightening to a lemon color around his knuckles.

One moment a pitiful, scarred, unhappy child. The next moment a wolf, with thick paws for his hands and feet, his body covered with gray fur.

"Michael, are you ready to apologize?"

He growled, bared his dagger teeth.

"Say you're sorry, come on, look at me, say, *I'm sorry.*"

He prepared to pounce, to sink his teeth into her throat.

"Okay then, I'll say it for you. *I'm sorry, I'll never spit in Eddie's face again.* That's a good boy, Michael. Now you come down and have some cake and ice cream, and we'll all be friends again."

Marge led the way downstairs. Bo entered the kitchen snarling, glared at Eddie, and saw with pleasure Eddie's comprehension. Yes, Eddie was properly afraid of Bo because only Eddie knew how hatred had made the tame king wild. They spoke the same language, Eddie and King Bo, though they'd learned it separately, in private.

I will kill you.

Get out of my house.

I will tear your head from your neck.

Stay away from me!

Light fled from the room, as Eddie would have if he'd even had that much courage. But he was too scared to reveal his fear. Through the dusk, Marge appeared with a cake carpeted with fire. "Happy birthday to you," she sang, a lone voice, while Eddie sat silently, his face lit up by candlelight, and Bo stood at the opposite end of the table.

Marge and Eddie blew out the candles together, the overhead light flashed on, and Ann appeared in the doorway.

"Did we miss anything?"

"Ann!"

"This is Mervin." She made room for a scrawny teenage boy with pink skin, wispy blond hair, and a tuft of a beard. He bowed slightly, looking directly at Bo with a half smile. Bo liked him instantly. He cocked his head to study him from an angle, and after a couple of seconds felt his first impression confirmed.

"Well then, come along, have some cake, Mervin. This is Eddie, Ann's step-dad. I'm sure you've heard —"

"Thanks much," Mervin interrupted, stepping up to the chair Marge had pulled out for him. Eddie leaned back and pulled open the utensil drawer, found the cake knife, and waved it in the air above the cake, a gesture understood by Bo to mean, *Maybe I will kill you first.* In the fat triangle of the blade Bo saw his reflection for an instant — wild King Bo stretched across a surface of metal — and then saw himself plunge into the froth of whipped chocolate butter cream, recognized at once the humor of the image, for even if he was a wolf capable of ripping to shreds anyone who displeased him he was no less a silly little kid who loved to eat cake. When his piece of cake finally arrived on a plastic plate he took the fork Marge handed to him, discreetly dropped it on the floor, and plunged into the cake for a second time, face first, filling his mouth with frosting, coating his eyelids and cheeks and the tip of his nose with frosting while Ann and the boy named Mervin hooted in support and Marge ordered him to "stop it, stop it right now, Michael Templin!"

Who?

He raised his head only when he needed a gulp of air. He

didn't need to look at the blade of Eddie's knife or into Eddie's scowling eyes to know exactly what he looked like — a mad, wolfish king covered with sweet mud — even if he didn't know all the words to describe it.

This is the way to eat a piece of cake: He plunged again, this time shaped the piece into a boat with the mold of his face, tore through the butter cream with his teeth and filled his mouth, rose again for another breath, and saw through the curtain of his sticky lashes Marge holding the wrist of Eddie's hand that held the knife, restraining him, while Eddie struggled to his feet. Bo couldn't believe what he was seeing, so he wiped his eyes with the back of his sleeve, looked again and saw only this: Marge moving to grab Bo's plate away, Eddie rising from the table, Mervin picking at his cake with a fork and grinning, and Ann sucking frosting from the bottom tip of a candle. There was nothing else for Bo to do but laugh and laugh and laugh.

Born in 1930, the year, he liked to remind others, when the planet Pluto was discovered, Edward Gantz had experienced only indirectly the hardships of that hard decade. An uncle of Eddie's lost his land to foreclosure and brought his family to live on Eddie's father's farm. A neighboring dairy farmer campaigned for a socialist candidate. And when prohibition was repealed, Eddie's father proposed an ordinance, unanimously passed, to keep the county dry. But throughout the Depression the Gantz family held on to their land, and Eddie learned from the example of his father the importance of vigilant work.

Eddie's mother, in contrast to his father, treated life as one long frolic and became more susceptible to fad and rumor with every year that passed. She danced when King Edward abdicated, wept when she heard the news of the Hindenburg disaster, and in 1938 dragged her family up to the Canadian town of Callander to see the exhibition of the Dionne quintuplets. In 1940 she had the kitchen in their farmhouse redesigned to include three work centers — a sink and dishwasher center, a range and serving center, and a refrigeration and preparation center. She wore nylon stockings and contact lenses and once a year went with her three sisters on an extravagant weekend trip to New York City.

Eddie, everyone agreed, had his father's sober temperament, and as he grew older and more self-aware, his disapproval of his mother's behavior grew more pronounced. She wanted whatever advertisers told her to want; she laughed too raucously, dressed too flamboyantly. Still, Eddie always showed her proper respect and mourned with proper sorrow when she died of heart disease in 1961. His father died two years later, and Eddie and his two brothers inherited the farm. By then Eddie had his job with Worthco and had moved to Hadleyville, a town dry in practice if not in law. He sold his portion to his brothers, and they turned around and sold the farm a year later. Eddie came to believe that his brothers had swindled him in the deal — since 1970 he hadn't spoken to them, though the wives had continued to send Christmas cards.

In general Eddie expected little from life, and he accepted the losses and betrayals as his burden, having learned that God always gives the afflicted their right and those who hearken and serve Him will complete their days in prosperity.

The most powerful love he'd ever felt, besides his love of God, was his love for his first wife, Isabelle, a small-hipped woman with chestnut hair and a spray of freckles across her nose, a woman who matched him in sobriety and honesty. He'd loved her according to the covenant of marriage, but he'd found himself loving her even more after she passed away, finding that love could be nurtured by absence and believing as he did that her spirit had knowledge of his most secret thoughts.

But even such ethereal love couldn't be sustained. Twenty years passed between her death and his second marriage, and by the end of that time Isabelle Gantz was a hazy presence in Eddie's life. Eddie turned to Marge for distraction — she took Isabelle's place and gave him a new sense of purpose, especially in those first few years when Eddie still enjoyed sinking into the warm cushion of her body. And when he lost interest in the physical aspect of their marriage he found in Marge a perfect companion — reliable, dutiful, attentive.

And then the child arrived to disrupt Eddie's perfect world, to test the limit of his previously unlimited patience. Eddie would suffer because of his efforts to help this boy, and out of suffering would come redemption. The strain of depravity in the child must have a purpose, Eddie believed. All suffering had a purpose. If nothing else, Eddie would learn from the experience of raising a wicked boy that there was a limit to his influence. And if at the end his efforts to help the boy failed, he would have to accept the failure. He was no more than God's humble servant, a worthy man only by the grace of God.

If your right eye causes you to sin, pluck it out. Answer *yes* or *no* when you are challenged — anything more than this comes from evil. Only the godless in heart cherish anger. Eddie was not angry. Spit in his face, go ahead, you won't rouse him to uncontrollable anger. God despises no one.

But listen to the boy laugh — that's the devil! A perfect portrait of evil. Filthy, hysterical child — spit in Eddie's face again, go ahead. There is no darkness where sinners can hide!

When Bo was still a novelty in the Gantz household he represented to Eddie the potential fulfillment of his dream — at last, a child of his own to raise. A son! Marge's children had been beyond raising by the time Eddie came along. But this child, Michael Templin, this little lamb of Christ, poor orphan boy, Oliver Twist, why, he was clay in Eddie's hands. He would be what Eddie wanted him to be. They went fishing together, Eddie made him pancakes and ice cream sundaes, and he read to him the books that had been his own childhood favorites. So what if the child had been conceived in sin? So what if his skin was the color of a rotten peach? Eddie wanted to be his friend and held nothing against him. When the child arrived in the house, he was, in Eddie's view, completely innocent.

And strange, yes, there was, he had to admit, something strange about the child. Even in those first few days, Eddie found himself wondering whether there were something irrevocably wrong with Michael Templin. The way he let his mouth hang open while he stared stupidly at Eddie, with malice dancing deep in his eyes. *Like an animal,* Eddie thought. Fish, horses, deer, squirrels, bears — they will stare at you without interest, look right through you, and still look at you as though centering you in a rifle's sight.

Well, maybe he didn't completely take to the boy straightaway, nor the boy to him. "Give it time," Marge recommended. But the more time he gave it, the less they liked each other. Still, Eddie didn't lose his temper. For three months he ignored the boy's transgressions and worked hard to spoil him. And what do you think?

"The kid took the bit in his mouth and ran!"

At a town meeting early in May, Joe Simmons warned Eddie that this would happen. But by then it might have been too late to correct the situation — the child considered himself invulnerable.

"It's never too late," Joe said, reasoning that the boy would learn eventually that he had to please those who took care of him.

Eddie privately disagreed. If the salt has lost its taste, how shall its saltiness be restored? But still he went home prepared to make a little soldier out of the boy. Guess what happened?

"The little demon spit in my face!"

He said this to one of the salesmen at his appliance store. He didn't tell how the boy had dropped his head in a piece of chocolate cake and laughed as only the devil could laugh. And a few days later, wouldn't you know, his lawyer told him that he didn't think the hospital would settle anytime soon. In the first deposition the surgeon insisted that the boy's treatment had been entirely proper, that the attending physician had admitted him for observation, as they'd do in any similar pediatric case, and that at every stage the nurses and doctors had responded briskly and appropriately to his condition. More than eleven thousand dollars later, they'd declared the boy healed. Now there's a way to make a profit! The whole medical business disgusted Eddie, and now the boy disgusted him as well, with his butter cream face and his devil's laugh.

So the case would go to court, where a jury would decide upon the hospital's liability. Thousands of dollars were at stake, Paul Krull had reminded Eddie — they should not be surprised when the initial negotiations broke down. The matter would take time, months, maybe years, to resolve.

Eddie himself had a scientific mind and when he considered the matter privately, lying in his bed in the dark a few hours after he'd received the call from his lawyer, he understood why the hospital would risk a trial. *The powers of man are limited, and it is necessary to limit what is to be observed to a portion of the universe.* Had Eddie read that somewhere? He couldn't remember. But in order to make sense of an external event a man must accept his bias, Eddie knew full well. Doctors call their bias a hypothesis, which, when confirmed, becomes a diagnosis. Truth was no more than a proposition in the world of science; therefore a doctor could propose as fact the lie that the treatment of young Michael Templin had been entirely reasonable.

It would have helped if the boy's injuries had attracted publicity. Too late for that, just as it was too late to give up. You don't give up when justice is at stake. *Believe you me I'm not in it for the money!* Eddie would have said to anyone listening. But Marge was still downstairs doing whatever she did after everyone else had gone to bed. Women have an appetite for loneliness. His first wife had been the same way — grateful for every minute of solitude. Eddie would have preferred working through the knot of these circumstances with his wife at his side. *Believe you me,* he wanted to use the money to repair the horrendous damage that had been done to the child. But now he knew that neither instruction nor reparation could save him. Too immature to throw off the force of evil, young Michael would have to wait years before he could make the decision to behave. Until then, he'd exist in a perpetual state of war with the world, spitting, kicking, punching, intent on hurting those who were only trying to help him.

However frustrated Eddie felt, he didn't lack sympathy, for he recognized something of himself in the boy, saw in the child's unruly manner the person Eddie Gantz might have been without the grace of God. Sympathy, though, was hard to sustain when the devil laughed in your face. But no matter what, Eddie would retain self-control and therefore would remain superior to the child, who assumed that by losing control he could bring Eddie Gantz to his knees. No, Eddie Gantz would never kneel before the devil. Eddie Gantz had God on his side.

* * *

Four days after his birthday, Eddie sold five sets of washer-driers, two dishwashers, three ranges, and a microwave oven — not quite a record sale but close to it. He stayed late at the store making phone calls to follow up on earlier sales and was pleased to find that all of his customers were one hundred percent satisfied with Worthco's products. What a day! He went to celebrate with Joe Simmons and his other pals at Angelina's Grill down in Athens, drank his usual 7-Up, played darts, watched two innings of a baseball game, and arrived home in a cheery mood at about eleven o'clock to find Marge sitting alone in the kitchen with the lights off.

Nothing unusual about that. Eddie announced his success, watched her shadowy figure for a nod of approval, which didn't come, so he kissed her briskly good night and headed toward the stairs.

"May I ask you something, Eddie?" Now *that* was unusual — her voice sounded tense, faintly accusing.

"What is it?" He reached for the wall switch and turned on one set of track lights.

"Where have you been?"

The simple question stunned him. Where had he been? He'd made a hefty commission that day, and she wanted to know where he'd been? The question implied more than suspicion. By asking him to explain himself, she indicated that she thought him capable of behavior deserving concealment. Not only would he lie about where he'd been, he'd been doing something so terrible he couldn't even speak of it!

"What do you mean, where have I been?"

"Exactly that. Where have you been, Eddie?"

She said his name as she would have uttered a foul word. He returned across the kitchen, stood over her, and felt in that moment indignation that gave him such immediate pleasure his cheeks burned. He wanted to hit her, a desire he'd acted upon in their few previous arguments only by threatening her with his fist. He would never actually hit her — he'd seen his own father hit his mother and perceived how such an act earned a man no more than humiliation. But he enjoyed the desire enough to let it flare. He'd extinguish it in good time. All in good time.

"Where do you think I've been?"

"Why won't you tell me?"

"Why? Why?" Although he wouldn't have admitted it even to himself, he enjoyed, along with his anger, the escalation of an argument, especially when he knew he would win it. "I'll tell you why!" Ahead of the situation in his mind, he knew exactly what he would say and distributed his words carefully, each to a full second. "Because I don't want to tell you."

"Bastard!" She turned her face away and whispered, but Eddie still heard her.

Bastard. Eddie Gantz, a bastard? He didn't say the obvious — that the true bastard of the family was upstairs in Jenny's old bed. Instead, he met his wife's insanity with an equanimity designed to torment her. He sighed audibly, shook his head, and said, at last, "What has come over you, Marge?" expecting with this question to prod her into tears. But she just matched his calm with a fierce smile of her own, and Eddie was struck by the uncanny resemblance — how similar she looked to her bastard grandson.

Now he had to scramble to keep up with the associations set in motion: that Marge had gone mad because of the boy, that the boy had driven her mad, that Eddie should never have gotten involved with the boy, that it was too late to back down now. This last recognition had enough weight to put a crack in Eddie's sturdy surface; with a roar he swept his hand backward, away from Marge, and sent a glass mug half full of warm coffee soaring across the room, to bounce against the wall and onto the floor and roll to a stop, still intact, missing only its handle.

"Dorrie Jelilian saw you there, Eddie." Marge bent over, gathering in her hands the mug and handle.

"What are you talking about?"

"She had to go to Gifferton to pick up her son from a basket-ball game. She saw you and Joe going into Romeo's in the company of two ladies." She reached for a paper towel to clean up the spilled coffee.

So jealousy, soap-opera jealousy, was propelling Marge. Eddie would have laughed — laughed and laughed and laughed — if he were a different sort. Instead, he caught Marge by the wrist, whirled her around, and said fiercely, "You know me better than that!" certain that this simple statement would remind her of the weight of her obligation to him as his lawful wife.

"I don't know you at all," she muttered.

He released her wrist as he would have cast away a stick after finding it crawling with insects. He left her alone in the kitchen and went outside, letting the screen door swing shut with a loud crack behind him. The night was dark, the sky tinged with brownish red from the cloud cover. Two cats sat on the back rail — one was the boy's, the other a stray. Eddie grabbed the stray with one hand and heaved it into the yard. The cat landed on its feet and raced into the field while the boy's cat slunk beneath the deck.

Eddie walked into the yard, uncertain of his next move. Was it possible? Had his life changed this much, this abruptly?

He walked around the house and down the driveway, kicking through the gravel, finding in the area made visible by the living room lamp an image that gave sense to his confusion. He existed within a murky patch surrounded by darkness. The boy was hidden in the darkness. Yes yes yes, the boy was out there finding ways to hurt Eddie, to ruin him. Everything happening was happening be-cause of the boy. Marge had turned against Eddie because of the boy. Eddie was walking in the dark instead of lying in his own bed because of the boy. Dorrie Jelilian had told a deliberate lie about Eddie because of the boy. It should be otherwise, what with the pincherry blossoms scenting the night air, the earth garbed in spring finery, joy available to all who would let themselves feel it, gratitude as natural as heat emanating from fire. Whatever had gone wrong had gone wrong because of the boy. And the boy — *admit it, Eddie, fess up, come on* — was living in their midst because of Eddie Gantz's monstrous greed. He, yes, virtuous Eddie Gantz, yes yes yes, was responsible for the turn of events because he, Eddie Gantz, had brought the boy into his home to prove himself righteous.

He tried with the force of his vision to blow the darkness open to dawn. By the grace of God ye who walk in the valley shall confess your evil thoughts! In a corner of his mind he'd known his intentions were wrong and still he'd persisted, brought the child, little lamb of Christ, into his home so he could pursue the case against the hospital and punish the offenders.

Wait a second! The trouble with this version of events was that the child truly deserved compensation for his pain and suffering — Eddie believed this absolutely — and only Eddie had had the foresight to pursue a malpractice suit. Without his involvement, no suit would be brought, and the hospital would go on doing to other children what it had done to little Michael Templin. Eddie Gantz was the key to justice — for this he should be praised. And yet for this he should be damned. He recognized clearly how he'd allowed pride to determine his actions. It had never been the indemnity he wanted — filthy money, he hadn't earned it and it wouldn't add up to much anyway. No, Eddie Gantz had wanted nothing less than to play God. And now, having recognized his pride, he renounced it with a click, click, click of his tongue. *Shame, shame, shame.*

An animal — a squirrel or a bird — shook the branches of a locust tree, startling Eddie back into time. It must have been close to midnight by then; he didn't intend to walk forever. No, he belonged in his own bed. He hadn't even reached the end of Hanks Lane when he made himself turn around and head back to the wife who didn't know him and the child who despised him. He walked straight back toward the thick of it, right toward the mess he'd made, feeling better now that he'd come to understand his motivations. He who through faith is righteous shall live, and he who is without sin should cast the first stone, and God shall lead every willing man to repentance. Salvation surpasses innocence, and virtue must prove itself not once or twice but over and over and over. Eddie savored the blessing of repentance and thought about what he might say to Marge, how he would gently lead her through the darkness of her suspicion back to faith and understanding.

He entered the house through the front door, which they never locked. She must have heard him, but she didn't emerge and Eddie had to go looking for her. The kitchen was empty, though the light had been left on. The other rooms were dark, so Eddie headed upstairs, figuring she'd gone to sulk in the comfort of her bed. He looked for her in the bedroom, in the walk-in closet, in the master bath. He returned to search the downstairs again, turned on the outside light to illuminate the backyard, checked the garage to make sure both cars were there. Had she fled to Dorrie Jelilian next door? But the Jelilians' house was dark, as still as a boulder, so Eddie went back inside and upstairs, realizing just as he reached the second floor that he knew exactly where to find her, wondering at the same time why he hadn't thought of it before.

He opened the door to Jenny's room and in the sheet of light that spread across the room in front of him he saw Marge's stocking feet at the end of the bed, toes pointing toward the ceiling. It took another moment for Eddie to find form within the dark corner, to see, with effort, his wife lying beside her grandson, her head propped on a pillow, her arm bent to cradle the sleeping child. Eddie could tell from the stiffness of her body that she was awake and still resentful, that she considered Eddie an intrusion and wished him to get out. So he got out, retreated to their bedroom, where, after a brief hesitation, he dove face first onto the mattress in an attempt to smother the memory of what he'd just witnessed. A woman, his wife, lying with her sleeping grandchild, a harmless scene that in different circumstances would have provoked in Eddie a sweeter sentiment but now seemed to him unbearably perverse, not because of any physical intimacy but because of the implication of exchange: Marjory Gantz, seduced by the devil, unable to distinguish between wrong and right, between truth and falsehood, between guilt and innocence, had traded her husband for the child.

The king is dead! Long live the king!

The weather turned hot — hot and dry and still — the lake glassy, algae slopping at its edges, trees buzzing with cicadas and Marge buzzing with hot resentment, though not because Dorrie Jelilian claimed to have spied Eddie entering a bar in Gifferton. Marge had seen at once the obvious innocence in Eddie's face and had persisted with the accusation only because it gave her unexpected pleasure to drive Eddie toward fury. She'd wanted to make him rage, fume, sputter, stomp, while she sat calmly by, watching him spin loose, out of control.

Eddie was right about one thing: little Kamon Michael Templin had changed Marge. But change depends upon changelessness, and Marge considered the possibility that she had resented Eddie ever since he'd sent Jenny away. Maybe she'd resented Eddie from the moment she'd agreed to marry him and had accepted resentment as an inevitable aspect of their marriage, perhaps had even nurtured it so she'd have something to give color to her solitude. She'd been strong enough to drive her first husband from the house and to raise her family alone; with Eddie, she'd been strong enough to deceive him into thinking she was weak.

Not strong enough to defy him, as it turned out. She'd let him send Jenny away, convincing herself that in the long run Jenny would learn a necessary lesson about responsibility. And that's exactly what happened: Jenny learned that if she wanted to be a responsible mother and hold down a job, then she had to drive from the mall to the city to pick up her son and drive home to Arcade on a wet night in April when the roads were slick. But if Marge had been strong enough back when Jenny was pregnant, then Jenny would have learned about responsibility from the refuge of the home where she'd been raised. If, then. Follow the logic to its source and you'll find Marge letting Eddie push her around.

Not anymore, thanks to Kamon Michael — Bo, as she'd come to call him. He had indeed changed Marge, strengthened her with his own resentment. He didn't like her — he had no reason to like her, given her record of disinterest. Yet he couldn't help but prefer her to Eddie. Dangerous Eddie. As sure as the weather would turn cold again, he would turn against the child. Marge found herself savoring the premonition along with the corresponding intensification of meaning. In such a dangerous world anything could happen, and risk made ordinary activities seem freshly poignant.

And then in a different sort of mood Marge stopped relishing the possibility of danger and simply accepted the situation. The tension, as she explained it to herself, was entirely natural. Eddie couldn't be blamed for his inexperience with children; Bo couldn't be blamed for his inexperience with adults. They were at odds and would remain so, like two houses on opposite shores of the lake. Nothing would happen, and accusations would wither away for lack of proof. Consider Dorrie's gossip: how wrong she'd been to include Eddie in Joe Simmons's escapades. Joe could make a fool of himself, but not Eddie. Eddie Gantz was not the philandering sort, never had been, never would be. Neither would he let himself hurt the child, and Marge was wrong to consider him dangerous.

Hot, still, dry summer days. Marge drifted idly, sometimes imagining the worst that could happen, other times anticipating nothing out of the ordinary. She let Ann baby-sit for Bo while she had lunch with her friends. She worked in the kitchen and the garden, took daily walks, sat in a deck chair and drank iced tea while Bo played with his cat in the backyard. She wondered how she could doubt Eddie, wondered how she could trust him, wondered what she could do to make everything turn out all right, wondered what she meant by *all right,* decided that the case against the hospital should be dropped; no, that the boy deserved whatever the lawyers could win for him; she contemplated the dust, a dry summer after a wet spring and now all this dust, dust on her eyelashes and in the creases of her palm, dust on the counters, dust giving the boy's black cat a brownish sheen. She imagined the lake evaporating, shrinking away from its shores, transforming into a muddy swamp. Sometimes she feared the devastation of a terrible drought; other times she enjoyed the slow, hot days and wanted summer to last forever. She felt content, suspicious, pleased, anxious, proud, aghast, strong, weak. She wondered how she was changing and what part of herself would never change; she wondered what to do, what not to do, what to expect and what to discount out of all the things she heard over the course of any one day.

And then one hot August morning Ann announced that she would be moving in with Mervin. Bo was watching television, and Marge had just started to make lemonade when Ann came down to the kitchen in her oversized T-shirt and declared her plan. She would be turning eighteen in two weeks and had a right to make her own decisions. She'd live with Mervin, study in a food services program at a nearby business college, Mervin would learn to cook, and someday they'd open a restaurant together.

"Don't pull this on me, Ann."

"I'm not pulling anything. I'm just telling you the facts."

"I need you here."

"Yeah, and I'm like, like the perfect baby-sitter, cheap and available."

"That's not what I mean."

But it didn't matter what Marge meant — Ann had made up her mind, made it up without giving a thought to her family, and nothing Marge said would dissuade her. So without another word Marge continued twisting a half lemon in the juicer, sensed the cold stare of Ann's eyes on her back and a few minutes later felt herself released, though she hadn't heard Ann leave the room.

Marge waited a long forty-five minutes before she went upstairs to find her daughter. Instead of Ann she found Ann's boyfriend, Mervin, lounging on Ann's bed.

"How long have you been here, Mervin?"

"Hi there, Marge. I didn't hear you —",

"Where's Ann!"

"She's in the bathroom."

"Then I'll talk to you, Mervin. I think Ann should stay at home. She's better off at home, and if you care about her, if you really want —"

"Aw, Marge —" Ann had come in from the shower wearing shorts and a bright red tank top, a towel draped over her wet hair. "We've made up our minds. But anytime you want us to watch Bo, you just bring him over."

"I'll let him play my drums," Mervin added, tapping a rhythm in the air — *tah tah tatata tah ta ta.*

"He's a good kid. You were right, Marge. He's better off here. Settling finally, I'd say."

Marge watched her daughter rub her hair dry, watched Mervin watching Ann, felt herself weakening as she watched them, tears glazing her eyes, so she turned toward the open window. Once she could control her voice again she said, "You're leaving because of Eddie." The silence that followed confirmed what she feared, even though after a long minute Ann said, "I wouldn't do anything because of Eddie."

Oh, but you would, Ann. What Eddie wants — Eddie being the sort — you being the sort — Mervin offering — and all the dust, the dust, the goddamn dust!

She left them in the bedroom that would soon stand empty. Instead of going directly downstairs she stood in the hall, not intending to stay and listen but unable to stop straining to hear what they were saying, their low voices buzzing, wordless, the sound conveying no more than the fact that they didn't want anyone to overhear what they were saying.

Marge sidestepped to peek into the room and saw within the frame of the doorway Mervin sitting on the end of the bed, his thin arm stretched out toward Ann, who had her back toward him, his hand dipping into her shorts while she tugged a comb through her hair.

"By the way," Marge burst out, abruptly entering the room. Mervin drew back his hand, pressed it under his thigh as though to subdue it, and Ann whirled around. "I was thinking you'll be wanting, you'll need —"

"Could you knock, please, Marge?" Ann muttered.

"Linens, towels, that sort of thing, yes? Let me see what I have to spare, some towels, maybe a couple of blankets, yes? Pillows, you'll need pillows and washcloths, whatever else, feel free to ask . . ."

"Fine, that's great, thanks, Mom."

Who?

She'd never gotten used to that name and felt flattered, as though she'd been mistaken for a movie star. She returned to the hallway, chewing lightly to contain the grin on her face, and started sorting through sheets in the linen closet, pulling out supplies for Ann. With a dry washcloth she wiped her forehead. Still an hour until noon and here she was dripping with sweat.

Later, Marge liked to think a premonition brought her back downstairs to check on Bo, but more likely it was just a sense of time — she'd been upstairs long enough and so went downstairs, crossed the living room to pull the drapes closed against the hot sun, heard the crash-bang of the television show, and went to offer Bo a glass of lemonade.

He wasn't on the couch where she'd left him. He wasn't on the floor behind the couch, where he sometimes hid. In the first few minutes Marge felt annoyed at him for hiding and ignoring her calls, making her search high and low — in the kitchen, in the basement, upstairs in his room, downstairs beneath the dining room table, behind chairs, on the back deck, in the backyard.

"Bo! Bo, come here! Bo! Ann, where is Bo?"

How he loved to play hide-and-seek, to sneak away when he thought Marge wasn't looking. "Bo!" A cunning child, pretending to vanish into thin air. But he never wandered far, never —

"Ann, where is Bo? Ann!"

"What?"

"Where is your nephew?"

"I don't know."

Smack of cold fear. The child was gone, really gone this time! He'd wandered beyond calling distance, out of sight, out into the world. Maybe he'd gone down to the creek, yes, that's where children went when they ran away from home, to the creek to wade in the silver water! If not to the creek, then down to the lake. A small child alone by the lake. The lake ate children, swallowed them whole, devoured one or two each year and spit them back in pieces — a sneaker, a headband, a ring, a limp, naked body. A small child alone by the lake. Or the creek. The world was too dangerous for children, who couldn't comprehend the risk of life.

"Bo! Bo!"

Marge sent Ann to search the creek, Mervin to follow the path into the woods, and she ran down to the lake, drops of sweat stinging her eyes, her breath coming in huffs, her breasts flopping, a scene that in hindsight would make her laugh — thick, foolish woman jiggling in a panic down the lawn, across the road, down the steps to the pebble beach, waving her arms and calling to Frank Jelilian, who was steering his boat toward the south end of the lake. He couldn't hear her above the noise of the motor and just kept on going, unaware that a child might be drowning, Jenny's child, Marge's grandson, the only one in the world who still needed her.

Think, Marge, think. There was no sign of him on the shore, no overturned bucket or spade, whatever he might have brought along with him, if he'd brought anything, if he'd even come here to the lake. Probably he hadn't come down to the lake, for wouldn't Frank Jelilian have seen him and headed straight over to find out what Bo was doing, a young child alone at the water's edge?

If not the lake, then the creek. Marge climbed back up to the road, walked up the driveway because she didn't have stamina left to run, and headed across the backyard into the field. "Bo!" she called. "Ann!" Her heart had sprung loose from her chest and lodged in her throat. "Bo!" She cut through the meadow, pushed aside the brambles that had grown over the path connecting the field to the old logging trail, headed down the trail, and met up with Ann around the first bend.

"He's not," Ann said, gasping for breath. "He's not."

The sun shone like melted gold behind the glaze of white clouds; the cicadas buzzed; a blue jay screamed; gnats swirled across the trail. It was so dusty and hot, and the dust clung to Marge's skin like a thin wet cloth.

Children disappear and sometimes they magically reappear and sometimes they don't. Sometimes they run off to the creek without telling their mother where they're going. Sometimes they disappear forever down a dark, empty road. Now Bo had disappeared, and Marge would be to blame for it. She'd let him slip away, let him wander off into the dangerous world.

"Oh!" she said, her voice barely rising above a whisper. "Oh." She tottered back along the path to the meadow, dragged herself through the crackling grass with Ann close behind, and stopped to rest against the maple tree at the side of the backyard. This tree, rough bark against her hand, leaves hanging limply in the dusty air — its solidity appalled her. That it should stand so brazenly alone while a little boy might be running for his life, yes, this was the only way Marge could imagine him, a little boy running along a path, across a lawn, down a sidewalk, running anywhere, stumbling, scraping his knees as he fell and picking himself up to run some more, running away from death, a monstrous thing near enough to cast a shadow across the boy but still outside the frame of the scene as Marge imagined it. Bo running, running, running. Marge ran, too, ran back inside the house and picked up the phone and started dialing one of the numbers posted beside the phone, the number of the sheriff's office.

She got that lousy Myrna Joyce on the line, the secretary who was trying to steal Joe Simmons away from his wife. Marge tried to explain but couldn't put the words together to make sense, so Ann took the phone from her and gave Myrna the information — the boy missing for a good hour by then, a boy dressed in navy shorts and a striped cotton shirt, a four-year-old child who was small for his age, a brown-skinned boy, black hair needing a trim, the son of Jenny Templin and —

Kamon Gilbert. The Gilberts! Of course, why hadn't Marge considered it? Those Gilbert folks, damn it! She tried to take the phone from Ann but Ann resisted, listened to whatever Myrna was telling her, and then slammed the phone in its cradle.

"Those damn Gilberts!" Marge shrieked.

"We're suppose to wait here," Ann said, peering over the sink to see through the open window into the backyard.

"Oh!" puffed Marge, picking up the phone and hitting redial, shouting as soon as Myrna answered, "Go find those Gilberts, the ones, you know, you know, they've stolen my grandson." Myrna told her to sit tight, Joe would be right over, and Marge said, "Go to hell," and hung up the phone.

"Oh!" Marge had to sit down; she had to stand up. Didn't anyone care what happened to her grandson? Why weren't sirens wailing, people shouting, police gathering in her front yard? She'd lost the child of the child she'd lost a year ago, and no one cared, not even Ann, who had gone back outside to smoke a cigarette. All of a sudden she desperately wanted Eddie with her, wanted to hear his quiet, decisive voice making plans, devising strategies, promising her that he wouldn't sleep until he found the boy. He'd be angry with her for letting the child out of her sight, but his forgiveness would be quick and total. He'd forgiven her for accusing him of lying, hadn't he? He'd forgiven her for taunting him and ignoring him. He deserved a better wife. Why he put up with her she couldn't say.

She snatched a cigarette from the pack Ann had left lying on the counter, pinched it tightly to keep it from trembling between her lips, and lit the end with a kitchen match. She stared at the phone, prepared to make the call she wanted to make to Eddie, but her right hand hovered in midair and Marge just kept on staring at the dull black plastic and puffing on the cigarette, her first in three long years. She wanted to call Eddie and would call him soon, but first she'd finish her cigarette. She rehearsed what she would say: *Eddie, I need your help. Bo . . . Michael . . . little Michael has —*

The ring of the phone startled her, causing her to drop her cigarette, and the ember left a small brown welt in the linoleum. The phone rang four times before Marge finally picked it up.

"Hello?"

"You're there." Eddie's voice. Eddie always speaking nothing but the truth.

"Yes."

"Joe called me. Now I know you're worried, Marge, but just keep yourself steady and he'll turn up. I'm coming home."

"I'm thinking that those Gilberts . . . they've stolen him."

"You're thinking that?"

"Yes I am."

"Those Gilberts are Christian folks, whatever else you want to say about them."

"They could have snuck inside the house somehow . . ."

"You tell Joe what you're thinking when he gets there. He'll look into it. I'm coming home now. I'll be there in, what, about twenty minutes."

"Eddie —" He'd hung up. Into the silence of the dead connection Marge said, "I'm sorry."

Joe arrived and Marge followed him on his search through the house, listening to him tell about the time a mother had called to report a missing child, an eighteen-month-old baby that had fallen asleep between the plush cushions of the couch. No one saw him there for a good hour until a deputy sat down on the couch to begin filling out a report, and the child began to cry. And then there was the time that the Jelilian boy ran away from home and hitched a ride with a trucker to Cleveland. And Marge's own daughter Jenny, remember how she'd gone off with Tony to the creek and Marge called to say she'd been kidnapped?

No, Marge hadn't forgotten. Goddamn Tony. She'd felt so foolish then and would be happy to feel just as foolish again, if someone would only return her grandson.

"Anyone home?"

Marge rushed into the kitchen just as Mervin stepped in, broad moons of sweat darkening his T-shirt, Bo clinging to his back.

"Oh!" Marge exclaimed, lunging for Bo, peeling him away from Mervin. Bo pushed out of her arms and ducked behind the island.

"That's right, tramp," Mervin said. "Are you in for it now!" He raised himself onto the island, flattened his belly against the counter, kicked back his legs, and teetered with his head extended over the opposite edge so he could look down on Bo, who was cowering in the corner. "Hey you, tramp. Shall we tell them?"

"Mervin came out of the woods by the quarry" — Ann was standing just outside the open door on the deck, smoking another cigarette — "and found him walking up along Webber Road. That's over a mile from here. He sure knows how to get around!" She laughed with an irritating squeal, but behind the counter Marge heard Bo's echoing laughter and felt all that she'd been feeling until then — the fear, the guilt, the irritation — softening into foolish relief.

"Another happy ending!" Joe said.

By the time Eddie arrived home Bo was watching television, Mervin and Ann had gone to visit a friend, and Joe Simmons was finishing his glass of lemonade, blinking his gray-blue eyes, pulling at his mustache and laughing at a joke he'd just told Marge. Joe Simmons the philanderer. He only made her feel more ridiculous in front of her husband, but she hardly minded. Embarrassment was a mild punishment for all she'd done wrong, and if Eddie didn't return her smile it was because he had done nothing wrong and had no reason to waste even a fraction of his dignity on this ridiculous event.

A happy ending to the hot, dry summer, as well as a beginning: the first rain in two months drenched the region the next day, refreshing the land and marking the turn toward colder weather, while Bo, having discovered the pleasure of flight, decided to repeat his journey not just once but over and over. Marge could lock the doors and windows, but still Bo managed to sneak away, running from the yard when she was gardening, through the garage when she was bringing in groceries, right out the front door when she was talking on the phone. Residents of Hadleyville soon became familiar with the sight of Bo trotting along the side of a road and made a game out of finding him. They competed to be the one who caught him and brought him home, and boasted of their rescues at every opportunity.

And everyone laughed at Marge — a thick, hysterical lady who couldn't keep track of a four-year-old child. Why, every time Bo was returned to her, Marge just felt sillier, and the more that people poked fun at her, the more convinced she became that she needn't be so worried.

H*i.*

Hi.
Where you heading?
Don't know.
You lost?
Nope.
Just walking?
Yep.
Scuff scuff scuff scuff.
Nice day.
Yep.
Scuff scuff scuff scuff.
You like to walk?
Yep.
Just for the hell of it, eh? Most kids will walk only if they're walk-
ing somewhere. But you . . .
Scuff scuff scuff scuff.
Aren't you scared? No one else around . . .
Scuff scuff scuff scuff.
I can bite your face off.
Really?
You better run for it, quick, quick, up here behind these bushes!
Wait!
Hurry, come on!
What's wrong? What are you running from?
A car. Cars are to run from.

Why?

It's gone now. Let's go.

Scuff scuff scuff scuff.

Once I laughed from nothing.

Really?

Once I wished and a star fell out from crying. Ask me what I want.

What do you want?

I want to be back when I was. Poke your eyes out, yah! Deedle deedle pee pee pee. I used to believe in ghosts but now I believe you just stop crying. And every time a car comes I'm a wolf and hide in the bushes. There's saying please, that's good. Please play with me. You can be whatever you want.

Scuff scuff scuff scuff.

You hungry?

Nope.

Thirsty?

Nope.

Scuff scuff scuff scuff splash!

That was a big fat puddle!

Yes.

I like puddles.

Squish squish squish.

You're sure you're not lost?

Nope.

So you're just going to keep on walking?

Squish squish squish squish squiff squiff scuff scuff scuff.

How long is forever?

How long do you think it is?

Not so long.

Scuff scuff.

You don't want to fall and get all messed with blood. That happened to my knee once when Gran was making pancakes. I have a gran and a pop and a Josie. I tried to make Josie follow me but she just ran up a tree, stupid cat. My mama gave me Josie at the grocery store.

Josie was a kitten in a box outside the grocery store and Mama picked her up and gave her to me. I remember that time when Josie was. Also other things.

Like what?

Scuff scuff scuff scuff.

A penny, a penny! It's mine, I saw it first, I want it, it's mine!

There's a truck coming.

Move out of there, I want my penny!

A truck —

Losers weepers penny, I got it, I got it!

Officer Casella found him walking along North Lake after dark one day. Brian and Mary McCloud found him. Rosa Pascalli of Rosa's Restaurant found him. Hilda Sagamore, Realtor for Gifferton County, found him. The Peach children found him. Archer Dodge, a technician for Safari Heating and Cooling, nearly hit him with his van. Lou Cisco found him. And a man who called himself Vincent found him and invited him into his car, but Bo ran the other way.

There you are again.

Scuff scuff scuff scuff.

It's almost nightfall. You don't want to be out walking after dark, do you?

Scuff scuff scuff scuff.

Whatcha thinking about? Hmm?

Nothing.

That's impossible. Thinking is always thinking about something.

So what?

Scuff scuff scuff.

Da-da-da-da-da la. La. La.

Scuff — *La* — scuff — *La* — scuff scuff scuff — *La la la.*

Don't you go, she yelled, she was so mad.

Scuff scuff.

Don't you never go off with a stranger, she said, and he fell down and this monster came along crying and shot him in the head, pow, pow, pow!

Scuff scuff.

Don't you never go off, she said, she was always saying it so he ran away and found a million dollars, a zillion million dollars, he just looked and found it in a pile on the ground and he picked it up and kept running and she yelled, Bo, Bo, get back here, Bo, you Bo, goddamn you, she was always yelling, yelling and brushing my hair and always saying don't you go with a stranger no matter what, you hear?

Dorrie Jelilian found him at the end of her driveway. Les Goodman spotted him walking along North Lake Road in the rain on a Friday morning. Three middle-school students chased him up Bacon Drive and lost him again along Amberton Road. Rebecca Horton, who lived alone with her two parakeets in a cottage by the lake, met up with Bo along North Lake Road when she was out for her evening walk. She found him again when she had climbed to Hightop Meadow to clip wildflowers. She found him a third time at the fork of North Lake and County Road #35.

When Hugo Miranda, a driver for USA Mattress, saw him squatting on his haunches on the side of Route 62, he thought at first Bo was a big old woodchuck that had come up to the road to have a look around. Hugo would have driven right past, but Bo stood up as Hugo's truck approached and then Hugo saw him clear as day. It looked to him as though the kid meant to dash out in front of the wheels, turn himself into roadkill and Hugo Miranda would be the one to blame. So Hugo veered toward the center line, made a wide screeching arc around Bo, and pulled up a hundred yards past him. Bo ran into the woods. Hugo jumped from the cab and ran after him. He would have lost him there in the thick undergrowth if Bo hadn't given a fine little sneeze, *achew!* Hugo caught him by his collar and dragged him fighting and cursing all the way to his truck and took him straight to Joe Simmons, who called Eddie, who when he got to the station acted like he was claiming something he didn't even want.

The reason is I don't know, maybe why not. I'm going to be a comedian when I grow up. Knock knock, who's there, wolf, I mean cow, cows say moo not who. Pow pow, rat tat tat tat tat. I spy a white stripe. A little tree. A big tree. Pow pow pow! Did you know the most safetest place is the top of a big tree? Can wolves climb trees? Big fat stupid tree. I can skip — watch me, look at me, look! And stand on one foot. And hop on one foot counting one two three four five six seven. The highest I got once was twenty-two. Do you know me? Ya ya ya! Play with me, please, you can be whatever you want. I'll be a wolf. You bad, get away! Once I was afraid of night but not now, I'm not afraid of nothing now, not even strangers.

Star Dayton, a nursery school teacher, found Bo at the edge of the grocery store parking lot. Carol Clack was waiting for her car-pool ride at the intersection of North Lake and Main, pouring out the remnants of her diet Coke, when Bo walked by. Joe Simmons found Bo when he was responding to a fire alarm. Marilyn Cady-Shearing and her teenage son Andrew caught Bo around suppertime on a Friday when he was trotting across their backyard toward a rusty old set of monkey bars.

Rebecca Horton found Bo a fourth time one day at the end of September when she'd walked up her driveway in her slippers and bathrobe to check her mailbox. She was a woman who liked to characterize herself as *broad awake,* despite her frail health. And even though she hadn't had her eyesight checked in seven long years, she didn't fail to notice Bo whenever he happened to be near.

Bo was staring at the ground as he shuffled through the grassy ditch. Rebecca Horton called a sharp "Hey there!" He turned and would have run away but fortunately she dropped a magazine and he climbed out of the ditch to pick it up for her. They talked for a few minutes. Rebecca invited him into her house to meet her parakeets and have some cookies. Bo willingly gave her his hand and would have accompanied her but just then Eddie pulled up in his car. He thanked Rebecca kindly for her help, though as she would tell her sister on the phone later that night there was no kindness in his voice nor in his arms when he restrained the boy and carried him to his car.

"So you see how it is in this lake country?" Rebecca Horton said to her sister. "There are those of us who have come here to die, and those of us who would risk everything to escape it."

You have to do what I do. Push the blanket down and put your foot on the floor and then the other foot. Step but the door doesn't move so turn the lock because there is always a lock on the inside and I already figured out how. Step until you come to the stair and then step down one at a time no jumping or you'll get it. Follow me. Put on your boots because you don't have to know how to tie them, they aren't tied boots. Go to the front door because there is two locks on the inside and you need a chair and can reach the high one and then the other. Open the door after me. Come on. Pretend you are made of nothing. Now run, run, come on, follow me. When Eddie finds you will he be mad, you can bite his face off and stay running, that way you won't get cold.

Now you know how. Then when someone says you got to go back you can do it all over.

So it became what he did, what he was known for, the expertise that made him famous in the community. "Ain't for nothing Jenny called you Hobo," Ann joked. "Tony would be proud." Bo didn't know Tony but Ann said that once in a while, every few years or so, he wandered down to Hadleyville to borrow money from Marge. Next time

Tony visited, Ann would introduce him to Bo. "You'll hit it off," she promised. "Two peas in a pod."

Ann had gone to live with Mervin, who was teaching Bo to play the drums. Bo stayed with them on days when Marge went out to lunch with her friends. It never occurred to him to run away from Ann and Mervin. Only from Marge and Eddie. Bo kept running away from Marge and Eddie because he understood it to be a wonderful game that he would win no matter what. Even when he was caught and brought back. Even when Eddie dug in his fingers and tried to rip the skin from his shoulders. The harder Eddie dug, the more points Bo gained against him.

And then the crisp splendor of late autumn disappeared into the bottomless hole of wintery cold, and Bo felt less inclined to jump into that hole. Instead he watched TV and pretended to be a wolf pretending to be a boy, and Marge brought him a cup of hot chocolate. In Bo's make-believe, Marge didn't exist. Only Eddie existed, and Bo with a subtle effort tried to provoke the great battle between them that would lead to Eddie's absence. Sooner or later Eddie would have to go away. Bo had given him plenty of opportunity to learn how to escape with his own example. But the difference would be in the way people responded when they saw Eddie running along the street. No one would stop him and bring him home like they did with Bo, and Eddie would just keep running.

On Thanksgiving Day Bo knocked over the gravy boat, but Eddie hadn't come into the room yet and as Marge mopped up the mess she insisted to Bo that the accident remain "our little secret." So instead Bo begged a piece of bubble gum from Mervin and blew a bubble — his biggest ever! — while Eddie was saying grace. *Bang!* Eddie ignored him. Bo stirred his milk with the tip of the drumstick, which earned nothing but humiliating laughter, so he propped a wad of stuffing on the end of his fork and catapulted it over to Mervin's side of the table. That was enough for Marge, but instead of taking Bo upstairs herself as she'd done before, she asked Eddie to do this service instead, a request met by a potent silence. Eddie just stared at his meal, and the rest of the family stared at Eddie. Finally Ann said, "I'll —" but Eddie immediately slid out of his chair while Bo slid further into his, came around the side of the table, and lifted Bo up by his wrists.

Was this it? Bo wondered. The battle of battles? He squirmed, twisted to free himself from Eddie's grip, heard Ann yelling something, and watched the blur of his aunt as she jumped from her chair and ran at Eddie, though what she did to him Bo couldn't see; he just felt Eddie jerk forward and himself slip out of Eddie's grasp back into his seat.

By then Marge had joined in shouting, and there was too much noise even for Bo; he slid further down, out of his chair and beneath the table, a space where he felt immediately safe, a den sealed off from the fray by walls of white linen. The only set of legs remaining at the table belonged to Mervin, who sat quietly, his knees wide apart and his feet propped on the gray rubber heels of his sneakers.

Crack and crash of voices, squeals, storm of adults raging with words that sounded oddly pleasant to Bo when he covered his ears with his hands. He tried flapping his hands open and closed, enjoyed the broken sound for a minute, then pulled his hands away altogether, for by then the roar of argument, still loud, had lost all meaning, and Bo listened to it as he might have listened to a gusting wind, thrilled by the power of nature and pleased to have found shelter.

He lightly touched the tip of Mervin's sneaker and when nothing happened Bo lifted the end of one lace and gently pulled. He kept pulling until one side of the bow was loose, then pulled out the other lace and with the wedge of his finger he separated the laces. When he'd finished with the right sneaker he moved to the left, pulled one lace from its knot and was about to start on the other lace when Mervin suddenly shifted his legs. The roar of argument continued, Mervin's feet settled flat on the rug, and Bo tried to pull loose the one remaining bow. But every time he reached for the lace Mervin tapped that one foot nervously, and Bo had to wait until he settled again. Finally he caught the plastic-coated tip of the lace between his thumb and forefinger and managed to pull it just as Mervin pivoted his legs around to the side of the chair and stood up. Bo barely managed to contain his laughter as he watched that pair of sneakers march, laces dragging, across the floor behind Aunt Ann's stomping boots, into the living room and straight out the front door, which closed magically, on its own, with the sound of a snap unsnapping.

He noticed the argument had stopped only when he heard the clinking of dishes and silverware, noises that were soothing and distinct, like notes tapped out on a piano. No one was talking, and Bo couldn't be sure who was left in the room. He waited for someone to look under the table, kept waiting until the only sounds he heard came from far off in the kitchen. He felt himself growing sleepy so he lay on his side, curled his legs beneath his chin, and waited for someone to come find him, doubting more with every minute that anyone would ever find him in such a secret place.

When he reached his arm out to pull Josie's warm body next to him she was amazingly there, and this increased his pleasure until he felt happy enough to sleep. Sliding into sleep inside a secret cave was nearly as enjoyable as kicking along the side of a road. Scuff scuff scuff. He didn't have to leave the house to disappear. He could come here and drift on a linen raft across the wooden water.

Twenty-two, twenty-nine, twenty billion belly buttons bump bump bump, loodle lee, loodle lie. Shut your mouth! It's scary over there so shut up. Go when they aren't looking. You know just because how it is and when you taked things they will get you so go before they can. Go go go go go. Go go go go go.

He would have slept for hours, would have preferred to sleep in his quiet den rather than eat Marge's pumpkin pie, would have chosen to sleep forever if he were offered the choice, but just as he was about to slip into a dream Josie gave a shriek and darted away, and Eddie's strong hands pulled him by his shirt out into the open.

"Who do you think you are!" Eddie yelled. "Huh? Huh? Who do you think you are!"

Too confused to resist, drugged by his fatigue, Bo let Eddie lift him by his waist higher and higher until he could almost touch the ceiling. He wasn't scared. He knew himself to be as invulnerable as a stuffed animal, felt magically safe inside his padding and tight seams as he swished and swayed in Eddie's hands and then went soaring across the room, nothing but a white wall blocking him from the sky.

When the phone rang in the house on Sycamore Street, Erma Gilbert wasn't dealing blackjack as she liked to do on Thanksgiving Day in that lull when the potatoes had been set to boil, the turkey rested beneath foil, and the gravy simmered on the stove. She wasn't out in the living room enjoying the company of her family right then. Nor was she fishing around in the foamy pot with a fork or mincing turkey gizzards or arranging the silverware or scolding Miraja for leaving peanut shells everywhere or tapping her two-hundred-and-eighty-pound nephew Taft on the side of the head because he'd used unfit language in front of the children.

When the phone rang Erma Gilbert was just finishing her business in the bathroom, and she didn't hear the phone's jingle over the noise of the flushing toilet and so didn't go find Sam to ask him who had called. Instead she dallied in front of the mirror, examined the mole on the side of her chin, compared her reflection to her memory of herself as a young woman and thought it strange that the changes in her life had left no obvious traces.

Here she was in a house full of family and friends, the world a hop-skip from the next millennium and folks everywhere working themselves into a panic over the calendar's grid. Here was one woman's life reflected back at her, a life worth as much as anyone's, no more, no less, and thanks to God and to the circumstances of history, it was a life fairly blessed with health and love. And yet she might as well have lived in the midst of war, for though she'd survived, she'd lost so much — her youngest son killed, her grandson stolen. That was more than enough for one woman to handle.

She blinked back her tears and set her mouth straight from its ugly grimace. Why waste her sorrow on herself? When she took it all into account she recognized the bounty of her life as well as the need to resist the forces that had conspired to break her, though sometimes she liked to imagine Kamon's voice to help her along.

Come on, Ma!

So out she went to join the crowd in the living room. Alcinder and Taft were watching football on the TV. Taft's younger brothers, Johnny and P.J., were playing poker with Merry and Sam. Erma's sister Leonore hadn't been able to take time off from her nursing job in Buffalo to come along, so she'd sent her boys on their own. Add the three grandkids and Merry's husband, Danny, and there would be eleven sitting down to dinner, including Erma and Sam. Twelve, if Kamon had been there. Thirteen with Bo.

Erma stood over the card table, watched her daughter deal a hand, and looked across to Sam, who had returned from the kitchen with a bowl of peanuts and was just settling back down in his chair. And right away, because she knew Sam as she did, knew the few wrinkles that decorated his relaxed face, knew how he should be breathing and blinking and shifting back to stretch his arms, she saw that something was wrong.

At that point, however, Sam didn't think anything was wrong. Nothing wrong with the hand Merry had just dealt him, a queen up, an ace down, thank you! Nothing wrong with having company on Thanksgiving Day. Nothing wrong with peanuts and bottled beer. And nothing necessarily wrong with someone calling on the telephone and hanging up after a long, long pause without saying anything. Probably a wrong number and the caller knew it from Sam's voice: *Hey-low . . . hello . . . hello there!*

"Higher than high on the hog . . ." he sang, scraping the pile of coins over to his side of the table.

So why did his wife stand there looking at him so strangely? Not saying anything like *time to carve that fat bird.* Just staring at him. Not sashaying over, wrapping her arms around his neck, and announcing that she'd hit the jackpot when she married Sam. Just staring.

"Hey, lady."

"What do you want, Sam?"

"What do *you* want is what I'm thinking!"

"Nothing."

"That turkey ready for the knife?"

"Not quite. You go on stealing money from your family."

"I call it winning fair and square. Isn't that right, Merry?"

"Sure, Dad."

Erma headed into the kitchen then, and Merry collected the cards for another round, but this time Sam begged out of the game and went after Erma.

"Anything I can do?" he asked.

"You could give the gravy a stir," she said. So he stood over the stove, the steam from the potatoes rising and spreading across his face, glossing his skin, and with a spoon he broke the skin just starting to form on the surface of the gravy. He drew in the good smells of the feast they were about to eat, thought to himself, *nothing wrong with this food,* and yet started to feel sure that there was something wrong, he just couldn't put his finger on it. Something to do with that phone call.

Erma reached around him and turned off the knob for the right burner. She drained the pot of potatoes and went to work breaking and fluffing them with a masher. The physical effort comforted her at first until her mind found its way back to the thoughts that had absorbed her earlier: all that she'd lost. She wished her nephew Taft had stayed away today. She didn't like to have to look at him and remember the trouble he'd brought into her home.

She glanced at Sam and felt the old urge to pack up and escape with him, though they had nothing in particular to escape from, nothing but history, and *you can't run from that,* Erma told herself. Better to keep on doing what they were doing, living their lives and financing the appeal that might, just might, bring Bo back into their home.

"Why don't you go ahead and cut her up," Erma said. "Sam?"

"Yes ma'am?"

"Did you hear me?"

"What?"

"You can start carving."

"Sure, sure."

Something to do with a hang-up call on Thanksgiving Day, Sam decided as he slid the knife back and forth over the sharpener. Thanksgiving Day. He liked holidays, liked to have a crowd in the house, liked to win at blackjack, and didn't mind washing dishes and picking up peanut shells when it was all over. Today was Thanksgiving Day, and he felt his usual gratitude. He missed his boys, sure, but he didn't dwell on missing them and kept his hopes focused on the lawyer — as long as she stayed on her toes, everything would work out, and Bo would be back home before his next birthday.

Sam eased a drumstick around in its socket, searched with the knife tip for the joint, and began cutting. While he worked he felt Erma's eyes on him again. Standing there and staring. Just staring.

"What's wrong?" he asked.

"That's just what I'm wondering," she said.

Sam tugged at the turkey thigh and cut through the last fold of crisp skin. He laid the leg on the platter and started in on the meat of the breast.

"It's something," he confessed after a minute.

"Something to do with . . . ?" Erma prodded.

"This being Thanksgiving Day," he said.

"Makes the missing harder, I guess."

"I don't know." Sam shrugged and caught a slice of meat on his palm.

Erma shifted her weight, put her elbows on the counter, and formed an envelope with her hands in front of her mouth. This being a holiday with their family, but not their whole family. Thanksgiving Day.

"Need help?" Merry pushed through the swinging door from the dining room holding a full ashtray of cigarette butts.

"You could finish setting the table," Erma said.

"Hey, Dad, who called earlier?" Merry asked as she collected a handful of spoons from the drawer.

"Just a hang-up call. Merry, do me a favor and scratch this itch on my face, will you?" She lightly scratched his cheek with a long red fingernail, and Sam thought, *now that feels good,* but didn't say it because he sensed his daughter would come back with some sly rebuttal.

"A hang-up?" Erma asked.

"Yeah. They heard my voice and decided they had better things to do than talk to me. Oh, Merry, don't stop."

"I got better things to do, sweet Daddy of my dreams."

Erma held the door open for Merry, who carried an armful of napkins and silverware to the dining room. She let the door ease shut, releasing it at the last moment so it swung toward her before settling back in place. With her mind groping to make sense of the uneasy feeling plaguing her, the swinging door supplied the image for the hang-up call that Sam had just told her about. Silence on the line, a door swinging shut, a conversation never taking place. Nothing new about that. A phone ringing, no one taking responsibility for calling, the silence of hesitation, the click of an ending.

Nothing new about any of it, Sam thought to himself. Someone calling the wrong number and hanging up. There was a difference, though, between someone hanging up right when Sam answered and someone waiting on the line long enough for Sam to say, "Hey-low," and again, "Hello," and a third time, "Hello there," the caller listening to him break up the silence with his greetings but not willing to try out his or her own voice. Maybe there was something unusual about the length of the wait before the person hung up, Sam decided. A little bit unusual but not so unusual that he needed to waste his time thinking about it, especially now that the rush of the meal had begun, with the dishes still steaming, the table set, everyone eager to dig in, wine to be poured, milk for the children, and had anyone seen the ladle for the gravy boat because dinner was ready!

The accomplishment, Erma believed, was not in the taste of

the food but in its warmth, everything served piping hot to dissolve the cold of this November day, unrelenting cold for two long weeks, making it the coldest November in fifty years, according to yesterday's paper. She announced this to the others at the table, and Alcinder said the county had budgeted for a warm winter and had reduced its supply of salt for the roads.

"Speaking of salt," Sam said, "Joe, can you send it over?" Joe, Merry's son, was fourteen, already an expert jazz pianist, rambunctious on the keyboard but a quiet kid on his own. Joe passed the salt to Miraja, who passed it on to Sam. Miraja was the chatterbox, took after her grandfather in this way, and as soon as she'd filled her plate she announced that she had a joke to tell, a knock-knock joke. It was Sam's job to say, "Banana who?" seven times before Miraja brought the joke to an end with *orange*.

Sam chewed on his turkey leg and thought about that period of time after the accident when Bo wouldn't respond to his stories. Sam had sat with him and kept right on talking in hopes that he'd say something ridiculous enough to prompt a question from the child. Sam couldn't remember the stories he'd told, he'd told so many there at the hospital and then back at home, talked at his grandson without knowing whether the boy understood what Sam was saying, unsure in those early weeks whether Bo had been damaged in some permanent way by the accident, fearing that language had been ripped out of him.

"Knock-knock," Miraja said, and this time answered herself, "Who's there?"

Erma asked, "How's the turkey?" Everyone erupted in compliments, except Miraja, who after the praise died down said, "How's the turkey who?" Amid the laughter that followed, Sam kept thinking about Bo's silence. He felt Erma watching him again. She stared at the new wrinkles that had formed on Sam's forehead and wondered why he wasn't laughing. But how could he laugh when he was thinking about that time when his youngest grandson wouldn't utter a single word? Erma wished only that Sam would tell her what was wrong, Sam thought that what was wrong had to do with Bo being unable to talk. Erma wanted to take Sam aside so she could ask him, Sam figured that speech had returned to Bo only when he'd stopped being afraid, and Erma gestured toward the kitchen, nodding toward Sam — they could talk out there; he'd tell her in private what was wrong.

Sam rose and excused himself from the table; Erma followed. In the kitchen he picked up the phone, started to tap out a number, and hesitated.

"What's that code for call return?" he asked.

"Code . . . ?"

"When you want to find out —"

"Trace a call?"

"Trace it, yeah . . . yeah . . ."

Erma reached over her husband and pressed the numbers herself. Sam motioned with an empty hand and Erma found him a pencil and scrap of paper and watched while he listened to the computerized voice and wrote out a phone number. She felt a strange suspicion grow as she watched the pencil nib making its marks, felt with each new numeral her suspicion slowly turning into recognition. Yes, she knew that phone number. It was a number she'd memorized when Bo was taken away, a number she'd never dialed.

"Jenny's folks," she said, still staring at the paper. Sam stared hard at her, waiting for her to look up and see what he was trying to tell her with his eyes.

He could be, couldn't he, some-one in someone else's story? And maybe in that story he died and became an angel. So what if angels aren't really true? It was only a story, one version out of many, a catastrophe loaded with meaning by the author of the tale. If he hadn't been able to pull himself up off the floor and run away after Eddie threw him against the wall, then the meaning of the story would be born out of accusation, Eddie to be the one accused, the end. But Bo didn't like that story. He wanted to live on as an angel, for he knew it would be much better to be an angel than a boy — then when he soared across the room he would keep flying right through the wall and up into the sky, and that's the kind of surprise a good story needs! Just when you think the hero is doomed. . . .

Also his tears turned into diamonds and dropped on the ground as he ran. The next day another little child, a poor, barefoot, hungry child, would find the diamonds, and he'd go live with that nice old woman and her parakeets in the cottage by the lake, and they'd have enough to eat forever and ever.

While Marge and Eddie fought with each other Bo had run from their house. This time he headed toward the lake. When he'd run away before he'd gone everywhere else except to the lake, per-haps because he preferred to stick to the road so he'd have some-thing to follow, a paved path leading away from the beginning. When you got to the lake you couldn't go anywhere but around it, Bo knew — around and around. Now, however, he was an angel so he could fly across it if he wished. Besides, the lake was different from any of the roads he'd walked along, and he wanted something different, a new story, a happy ending. So to the lake he headed, hop hop, bunny hop.

Funny, happy story. It could be that he was a dead child crumpled on the dining room floor, and Eddie Gantz was guilty, the end. A dead, not-knowing child, and Marge was still bending over him, begging him to come back to life, but he refused, the end. It could be that he was a story in the newspaper, nothing more. But who wants to hear that kind of story? You're expecting something amazing to happen and what do you get? A not-knowing child. Forget it. Don't tell that story, please. Bo had turned into an angel — that's the story he wanted to be in, so that's the story to tell, and it was only just beginning.

He ran. No, he didn't. He danced lightly over the earth, with each step sprang three feet off the ground, for angels are virtually weightless, or even if they have weight gravity applies only to the living, and an angel is something else. Hop hop, bunny hop. He ran so fast, so effortlessly, that the birds stopped flying and settled on branches to watch him. But he didn't run fast enough to leave behind the voices. Voices you remember are faster than angels, and Bo still remembered what he'd heard no matter how fast he ran, and remembering made him aware of the throbbing pain in his head.

Poor not-knowing child. Stop! That's the wrong story!

Bo ran down the hill and across North Lake Road. See how simple it is? A child ran like an angel. An angel ran like a child. When you're a child you don't mind contradictions. Like an angel, like a child, Bo ran, leaping high in the air with each step, defying the pounding in his head. He snatched at a chickadee perched on the bare branch of a dogwood but missed, descended to earth, leaped high again. Hop hop, bunny hop. Josie ran after him but soon fell far behind. Cats aren't as fast as voices. Still Bo remembered the voice crying *Stop!* as he'd been sailing toward the white wall. How did that story begin? Bo couldn't remember the particulars, but he knew Josie had been in it. A cat, however, isn't as fast as an angel, and Bo ran on, discovering to his relief that even when you think you know what's going to happen, you're bound to be wrong. Look! There was ice on the lake! He hadn't expected that. Strips of ice laid side by side over the water. Ice like packing tape, like empty highways, like blank pages, like empty maps. He didn't need to fly after all. He could just walk one step in front of the other. Slide. Skate. Kick that hockey puck right into the goal, and everyone would cheer!

Yet how quiet they were. He stopped, listened to his audience listening, stood on the page of the book and looked up, tried to see them but saw only gray tree limbs looming overhead. Tree limbs like arms about to snatch him and crumple him and throw him out.

To save himself he danced. Tapped and spun on the ice in an effort to entertain his silent audience, imagining as he performed how he would look from above: a tiny figure spinning in a music box. Then he remembered that no harm could come to an angel, so he stopped. That's when he noticed he'd lost the voices and could hear only the sounds of the world — branches creaking, wind hissing — and his own panting breath. And then it occurred to him that he must be invisible. Of course! Invisibility was one of the many advantages angels had over children. That's why he was alone, at least until Josie caught up with him. His audience had gone away, having concluded — incorrectly — that the story had ended because they couldn't see Bo anymore when in fact here he was, standing on the ice of Hadley Lake, a regular comedian who had just performed a major disappearing stunt!

Sooner or later he'd like to come back and be seen again, but for now he'd enjoy himself and explore the emptiness. Maybe his head didn't hurt so badly anymore. He knelt on the ice, touched his tongue to it, relished the metallic taste of cold, and tried to see all the way to the one place forbidden to angels. There it was, goddamn hell, as dark as the space underneath his new bed.

Run! Run away from there! So he ran and slipped and fell, dragged himself up off the cold sheet of ice and ran again toward the center of the lake, trying and failing to work up the speed that would enable him to jump high and far enough to reach the other side in a single superman bound. Ice is like a bad joke, like a bully, like a headache, like a story that won't end. You keep running and slipping and getting nowhere, even if you're an angel.

So what you do is step carefully one foot in front of the other like you are sneaking out of your bedroom when everyone else is still asleep. You run away by walking.

He made slow progress, but when he finally looked back to shore he was surprised by how far he'd actually come. Josie was still heading toward him, stepping delicately across the frozen lake. Somewhere near here Eddie had pulled fishes out of the water, wrenched the hooks from their mouths, and thrown them back. The birds had chortled and beavers slid below the surface with a soft splash. Not now. Everyone and everything had gone away, and Bo was a lonely, wingless angel stranded between Heaven and hell. That was as it should be, for the story had reached the point when anyone listening would start to worry. But Bo, despite his real fear, wasn't worried, for he knew that any story worth telling has a happy ending, and already enough had happened for him to be convinced that in this story everything would turn out all right in the end. Just the fact that he'd escaped the other story, the one that left him crumpled and not-knowing on the dining room floor, was enough. Having come this far he couldn't go backward or begin again. So on he went —

— and saw the glint of fresh water rippling ahead of him, black water sprinkled with diamonds, a lovely sight that drew him forward, luring him with light, sparkling light that reminded him of the light he'd seen between his fingers when he lay crumpled on the dining room floor and Marge had covered him with her body, weeping over him, calling, *Bo, you Bo!* as if he were already far away. Then with a roar Eddie had pulled her up, they'd staggered away, locked in each other's arms, and that gave Bo a chance to escape.

All life is going somewhere, even when you are sitting in one place, even when you are hanging upside down, even when you are sleeping, so it was funny to Bo how sometimes you go in circles and end up seeing the same light sparkling ahead of you. This comforted him — the simple, unexpected repetition of things — just as the light had comforted him back in the beginning, representing all that was beautiful in the world and drawing him out from underneath the weight of Marge's body, spurring him to run. He'd run through the lights and out the door and now here were the lights again.

There is magic and there is what happened. Sometimes the two come together in a glittering sheet stretched out ahead of you, and you run through it, or over it, and are transformed into something else.

Yet this time Bo didn't feel the urgency to fly away; there was no Eddie around, no wall, no ceiling he could almost touch. There was just the gray ice, the blue sky and cotton clouds, a far-off voice, a cat stepping toward him across the ice, and the glittering black strip of water ahead. He watched the way the setting sun danced off the edge of the ripples, felt with each sparkle that he was witnessing a magic trick, the black water shedding tears of diamonds that flattened into stepping-stones of light for him to skip across.

He could do anything, go anywhere, hang upside down in the bubble of a car, pass through walls and dance across the water, and no one could stop him, not even Marge, fat old Marge.

"Bo!"

Why, that's her! Look: she wasn't just a remembered voice anymore. While Bo had been watching the diamond lights, she'd made her way to the edge of the frozen lake and now stood there bellowing for Bo to come back. But he knew that back there was a dead-end crumpled story lying at the foot of a white wall, while here he was near enough to stepping-stones of light and with one giant superman leap could . . .

"Don't!"

Or fly . . .

"Stop! Bo, you Bo!"

How could she see him when he was an angel, the color of air, and she was Marjory Gantz, whose bulk made the ice crackle like rice in a hot dry pan as she stepped toward him? She was what she was and Bo was no longer what he'd been, yet still Marge managed to point her big fat self in the right direction and approach him. Did it feel to her like walking toward a mirror that should have held her reflection but instead reflected only the background? Walking toward emptiness. *Stop, Marge!* She drew closer, decorating the ice with silver cracks every time she shifted her weight onto her forward foot. She extended her hand toward Bo as she would have for a timid colt, tempting him to come closer to see what she might be holding. Bo wasn't fooled. Neither was his cat, who with one last awkward, hindquarter push hurtled herself against Bo's leg and turned her head to the side so she could rub the slope of her forehead against his pants. Giddy with the pleasure of contact, she tried to curl herself into a knot around his ankle, kept spiraling round and round Bo's leg, her tail a rope that tightened and then slipped loose. Bo reached down to touch Josie on the nose while the voice of Marge begged him to please come back to the beginning, to a time even before the white wall, a time before Eddie.

She was only about twenty sliding steps away by then. Bo tried to move in the opposite direction but discovered that somehow Josie had managed to wrap his legs in thread so fine he couldn't even see it and so strong he couldn't wiggle free. A web spun by a cat? It was magic, and magic could happen in a story about angels. *You, Josie!* Evil, clever cat, fooling him with affection while she trapped him.

"Come on, Bo, come with me. I'll keep you safe. Please believe me."

What should he believe? What should anyone believe?

To someone standing on shore watching this, the picture might seem a painter's embellishment: puffy clouds against a deepening blue, late-afternoon sunlight angling from between the far hills across the ice, a young boy standing on the frozen lake, a small black creature — a dog? — dancing around the child's feet, and a woman scooting slowly toward the pair. But even from a distance of two hundred yards the tense, high pitch of Marge's voice could be heard, and the onlooker would have to wonder, What is going on? *So he'd stop and watch more carefully to make better sense of the scene, and the first thing he'd think strange would be the fact that the boy had left his house without a hat and coat, which would arouse in the man an acute, sympathetic discomfort. He'd immediately blame the woman, for wasn't it her job to dress the child appropriately? And then he'd conclude from her lumbering manner that she understood her mistake and had come to correct it and call the child inside again. But the child was a defiant sort, apparently, and would not come when called. So the woman had no choice but to go out and carry him off the lake herself, and oh would that kid be in for it back home, that rascal, whoever he was. If the man happened to be from around these parts he'd probably recognize the boy, though if he hadn't lived in Hadleyville for a while he wouldn't know Bo but most likely would recognize Marge. Marge was an old-timer, she'd lived in the village for more than thirty years and had hardly changed at all, had only grown wider as she'd grown more satisfied with life, though maybe the man would remember her as a lovely young woman, movie-star quality, that's what people used to say, and once in a while, he might recall, Marge would really get going. If the right music were playing and her mood matched the opportunity she'd dance on tables, she'd spin, yeehaw! and kick her feet up,* causing Bo to wonder what she had in mind, kicking her one foot high in the air and then pulling the other one up, too, so for an instant that in Bo's impression seemed to defy the usual rush of time, she hovered, weightless as an angel, in the air. And then with an "oof," she landed splat on her big fat ass, her body folding at her hips, one leg crossing over the other as the ice gave way beneath her, and she plummeted into the black water in a single smooth motion, as though someone had pulled a panel out from beneath her, *so from the shore she seemed to have fallen into a space designed by a magician to give the illusion of disappearance, a secret drawer with an exit to the space beneath the stage,* voila! She was gone. The man held his breath and waited for her to reappear. The child waited as well, staring at the place where any moment the woman would be standing, intact and dry, as thick and satisfied as ever. Only the dog moved — no, a cat, a cat scampering away from the boy, slipping, dragging itself away from the broken ice back to shore. The man's disbelief corresponded with his *growing awareness, so he went on waiting, telling himself that what* *had happened couldn't have happened, not while he was watching.* *Then it became suddenly, brilliantly clear to him that he must do* *something, so without considering the peril he stepped out from the* *shore and swept with agonizing slowness across the ice,* the magical ice that was and wasn't and now was again, though broken, like Bo, who watched the shards of gray ice bob to the surface and understood what had happened. Marge had gone into the water and would never come out again unless he helped her. So he tried to step forward, but the silk spun by Josie the cat would not yield, and he fell forward, catching himself with his hands. He felt the hard surface shifting beneath his weight, and he heard the water slurp and splash in the hole where Marge had disappeared. He moved toward the water until he could stretch out a hand and curl a finger over the ragged edge. The cold! He wouldn't have believed cold could be so cold! To go into such cold would be much worse than flying headfirst into a wall, no one deserved to endure that cold, and Bo must pull out Marge not the way Eddie pulled out a fish but with his own bare hands.

He gripped the rim of the ice and pulled himself closer. Cold, slurping hell. Slosh of water. Creak of ice. A gull called above him, called, *there, there she is!* The glow of her flesh appeared and then receded like a distant torch into the darkness. *Stop!* Would he have to go after her just like she'd come after him? Would he have to decide not to go into the cold and so prove himself a coward? Still he stretched out farther, stirred the water into a froth with his hand, and then, with the suddenness of a cough, the ice crumbled beneath his chest and he felt himself falling, falling forward into the cold, then falling backward across the ice, sliding, as though the whole surface of the lake had suddenly tilted. Was this what was supposed to happen? It was a true story. Or a fake story. He had slid into the water long ago, in a dream, and so what was happening now was meant to happen. Or he was in the midst of a story told to him, a story he'd made up, or a fairy tale, a riddle, a joke.

Life had been promised to him — that was the only thing he knew for certain as he felt himself being pulled by one ankle away from Marge, away from the cold and from the hero he might have been. He didn't struggle as he slid up off the ice and into the embrace of a stranger, a man, a bearded man who clambered up from his knees and with wobbly strides started across the ice, clutching Bo, whispering into his ear, "You goddamn kid, you goddamn stupid kid." A stranger who was not a stranger. And even though he cursed Bo, he would not hurt him. Bo hung in his arms, let himself go wherever the man cared to take him. This man wearing a faded red baseball cap, this man who smelled of smoke and lemons, this man, a stranger, not Eddie, not anyone Bo knew. This man cursing him. This man carrying him across to the shore. This man did not frighten him because in the only story Bo really believed right then, the story that was happening, this man belonged.

PART SIX

Do you hear the rain striking the ice? Do you hear the ice melting and the sputter of whitecaps? Do you hear anything at all? Do you see the gray mist rising from the lake? Can you describe your underwater world, the sleepy fish gliding past in slow motion, the muddy bottom, the liquid cold? Didn't you know the ice wasn't thick enough to support your weight? Why weren't you more careful? Why are you gone, Marge?

Did you know that your ex-husband was watching you from the shore? Tony Templin, drunk as usual, but not so drunk that he couldn't stagger across the ice and rescue Bo. Did you see Tony standing there? And what about Eddie? Where was Eddie Gantz while you were drowning?

Why, he was dialing the phone number of Sam and Erma Gilbert to tell them to come get their grandson — *devil child* — and take him away. Eddie didn't want anything more to do with him.

Where's Eddie now? Why didn't he say anything when Sam Gilbert answered the phone yesterday afternoon? Why did he just hang up? What had he done that he didn't want to admit?

Tony said that Bo slipped and hit the side of his head on the ice, thus the bruise and swollen eye. But what does Tony know? He's never sure of anything.

What do you know, Marge? Do you know why Eddie converted his certificates of deposit to cash this morning? And why is the dining room window cracked? There's a story that should be told, isn't there, Marge? What does Ann need to know?

Tony won't be much help. He remembers yesterday as a hazy

dream—you swooping into the air and falling back through the ice, the blur of sound, a clapping noise like applause at a concert heard from outside the gates, and the kid, your grandson, Tony's grandson, too, though Tony had to wait until Joe Simmons arrived on the scene to learn about the family connection. Wasn't it just like Tony to disappear for years at a time and then reappear to watch you drown?

Listen, Marge: your daughter Ann wants to know why you are gone. She wants to know what you would have done differently in life if you'd had a second chance. What will you miss most? What was your highest bowling score? Why did you marry Eddie Gantz?

And what about Tony? How did that all start?

Tony was useless when it came to the facts — he couldn't say whether or not Marge had recognized him standing on shore, and it turned out he couldn't for the life of him remember the first time they'd met.

But you remember, Marge, and Ann wishes she'd paid more attention on those occasions when she was alone with you and you started reminiscing, your cheeks puffing with a mixture of pride and love and scorn as you thought about your misguided sense of the future back then, mid-1960s and you were already an old maid, twenty-seven years old and single because no man was good enough to be your mate, not until Tony came along, snappy Tony Templin who happened to be sitting next to you on a Hudson-line train that stalled en route to Albany. *As luck would have it* — that's what you used to say about meeting Tony Templin. *As luck would have it,* he was sitting in the seat across the aisle from you, and the train broke down and didn't budge for two hours.

You married him because you loved his promises; that's what you told Ann. You told her other things, too. She wishes she'd been paying more attention. She would listen now, Marge, if you'd just set the record straight and begin at the beginning, the stalled train, Tony sitting across the aisle, the two of you talking — and then what?

Something about Tony reading your address on your suitcase tag and calling you the next day.

Ann hadn't paid attention to you, Marge, because she didn't want to hear you go on about your foolishness. Clucking, shaking your head, chiding yourself for believing Tony Templin's pack of lies. All those promises about happiness, and that billboard on a hill near your rented house in Penn Yan, an advertisement showing a young couple buzzing along in a motorboat — for a while that billboard was the image of Tony's promises. And then and then and then.

Marge, tell Ann what happened. Tell it start to finish, and while you're at it let your daughter know that her suspicion is right: Eddie Gantz is to blame for everything.

Does anyone know where Eddie is?

Do you hear the slight hissing sound of melting ice? It is supposed to rain through Sunday, and then another cold front will move down from Canada. The divers must find you before the ice seals the lake for the winter.

Tony isn't sure what happened — all he knows is that he arrived at the lake in time to see Marge fall through the ice, that the child he carried to safety is his own grandson, and that the mother of the child, his eldest daughter, died in a car accident nineteen months ago.

Bo went up to the city hospital with his other grandparents to be checked over. Eddie wants nothing to do with him and last night called the law office of Krull and Krull and left a message on their machine directing them to drop the malpractice case against the hospital. Just like that. Paul Krull called this morning to talk it out, but Eddie had already left.

Ask Eddie and he'd say, *Leave judgment to Almighty God.* So where is Eddie anyway? Whatever he'd done, his sin had not been so grave that the merciful Lord saw fit to consume him in punishment. Eddie escaped unharmed. Not Marge, though. The way Eddie told it to Joe Simmons last night, Bo was a devil child who had lured Marge out onto the thin ice and laughed when she fell through.

No, Tony had corrected him — Bo hadn't been laughing. But what did Tony know for sure?

He knew about the beef Stroganoff Marge used to make back in the old days. Her roast duck. Her Sally Lunns and soda bread, her corn dodgers and mont blanc and blancmange and pineapple soufflé. The good old days.

Ask Marge's next-door neighbor Dorrie Jelilian, and she'll tell you about how at the end of a meal Marge would fill finger bowls with water scented with geranium leaves. Marge could entertain like you wouldn't believe!

Tony remembers this: that Marge used to call him her *funny lover. Funny lover, stand up straight and dance with me!*

Ann remembers Marge's song about the rain.

Does it always rain the day after someone drowns?

Try this: was there ever a time, Marge, when you were lying in bed watching the television screen fade to black and Tony came in from the bathroom wearing his boxers, smelling fresh from the shower, and he climbed up from the end of the bed, ducked his head under your nightgown, ran his tongue along the inside of your thigh and crotch, kissed you, sucked you, played in you with his fingers, and then pushed in his dick as you lifted your hips? Tony remembers something like that — the wild, mucky fun of it all. Dancing the Watusi in the living room. And of course the money you would give him when he came by for a visit after the divorce — a wad of twenty-dollar bills secured with a rubber band.

But that was nothing compared to the money you sent to Jenny twice a year. And did Jenny ever pick up the phone to say thank you?

What is true, what is misremembered, what is a deliberate lie? Who can be trusted? What would you change if you could live your life over? Why didn't you ever learn to swim?

What happened, Marge? What did Eddie do to you? He did something terrible, didn't he? Where is Eddie now? And why won't Tony get up from the kitchen table and come join Ann and the others at the lake? And who does Dorrie Jelilian think she is, passing around a tray of fudge brownies to the deputies like it's coffee hour at the Presbyterian church? And that old Rebecca Horton wearing her frisette of white hair — what right does she have to weep? And there's Joe Simmons leaning against the hood of his car, squinting through the needles of mist as though he expected to see Marge climb out of the water intact. And Mervin, just back from smoking a joint — don't even think about putting your arm around Ann right now, Mervin!

Marge, are you there? Ann wants to know what flowers to plant in your garden next spring and who would you name as a friend and why is the dining room window cracked?

You should tell her what happened. You should tell her how Eddie held you back when you wanted to run after Bo.

Wherever Eddie is, he will not drive more than five miles over the speed limit, he will keep his registration updated, he will not smoke a cigarette or drink alcohol, and he will find a church service to attend every Sunday. In his own assessment he is devout, not fanatical. He doesn't have to be born again to experience the grace of God. All he has to do is go his own way — faith will keep him well.

Listen to the raindrops singing you to sleep.

There will be talk all right, plenty of talk, there's no stopping it, the gossip, the accusations and assurances, and every time someone turns around there's Dorrie Jelilian offering a fudge brownie.

Marge fell through the ice and the world turned upside down. Now people are standing on their heads, feet in the sky. Is that what it looks like from inside the lake?

Go ahead, Marge, say it. Tell Ann that yes indeed you saw Tony Templin standing on shore. You saw him, didn't you, in that moment after you slipped and were falling toward the ice? At least you could have seen him. In that brief suspension, before you plunged into the water, you could very well have seen Tony's red cap, the one he'd bought at McCurdy's years ago. Even from a distance of one hundred yards, you could have seen with the kind of clarity possible only in moments of intense fear Tony's three-day beard and the smirk of his lips, the cigarette dancing between his fingers, even the dirty stains on the knees of his jeans.

And if you'd seen that much you would have seen the trees behind him, the gull soaring overhead, the smoky ice, the bruise purpling across your little grandson's face, the confusion in Bo's eyes. Isn't it true, Marge, that as you fell you saw everything there was to see, a confluence that would have to be called miraculous if each distinct part hadn't been, on its own, so ordinary?

Tell your daughter what she deserves to know, Marge. Tell her that Eddie Gantz is the reason you are gone.

First there was the uproar, beginning with Bo throwing food and ending with Ann and Mervin walking out. The startle of unrepentant hatred, the complete sundering, an entire dinner left to grow cold. And all Bo had done was flick a forkful of dressing across the table. Such a streak of wildness in that child, no denying, though after enduring Jenny's wildness and Ann's stubbornness Marge didn't put much stock in discipline. She was always frank about her resignation. Children will do whatever they please. Still, she wasn't about to tolerate bad behavior on Thanksgiving Day, all the trouble she'd gone to, and if Bo couldn't mind his manners he'd sit out the meal in his room.

So maybe Eddie lifted Bo a little too roughly. Maybe he looked like he was trying to pull the boy out of his skin. Still, Marge would have continued to insist that there had been no need for Ann to pounce the way she did, coming up from behind Eddie and slamming her fist against his back, right between his shoulder blades, *bam!* Oh, the fight that followed, the shouting, the names Ann called her stepfather, *pile of shit, fascist, pervert,* nothing that had any relation to reality, Marge tried to point out, moving to Eddie's side to defend him. But Eddie didn't need anyone's help. In the same calm voice he used to order meat at the deli he ordered Ann to get out of the house, to get out for good. She shouted that she could do what she liked, she was eighteen years old and her own boss. So Eddie told her to sit down, and Ann yelled that she was getting out of there for good. So out she stomped with Mervin at her heels, and Marge didn't try to stop them, just as she didn't try to stop Jenny when she left home. She just folded her arms and scowled as Mervin saluted good-bye and pulled the front door shut behind him.

The whole meal spoiled, and Marge had worked so hard — that's what annoyed her in those first minutes of quiet. An eighteen-pound turkey, fresh cranberry relish, sweet potato rolls and pumpkin pie made from scratch. The only person she thought about was herself as she calculated the waste. And her bad mood expanded to include everything she'd ever done, all of it a waste.

No one cared about you, Marge, no one noticed your efforts. Your fifty-ninth Thanksgiving Day, and look at the mess of your life.

Marge and Eddie were both silent as they carried dishes into the kitchen and wrapped uneaten food in cellophane. The anger weighed heavily; Marge felt the weight of Eddie's fury growing, though his face remained as placid as ever. He grew frustrated trying to make space on the cluttered shelves in the refrigerator — he slammed the door shut, leaned against it, and punched his fist into his open hand.

Marge assured him that everything would be all right, *things take time,* whatever that meant, and Bo would *come around eventually.*

What about the kid? Blowing bubbles, throwing food. The little brown hoodlum. So where was the kid?

Hiding underneath the table — Marge had to suppress a giggle when she told this to Eddie.

Now would Eddie stack the rinsed dishes in the dishwasher as he did after every meal? This was the nightly routine, one of many, and Eddie was always reliable. This time, however, he had a more important job to attend to first, a lesson to teach a child who did not understand the range of consequences that follow any significant cause.

With the dishes piling up on the counter, he abruptly left the kitchen, and Marge turned off the faucet to hear him. A few seconds later he was shouting. What did he say? Marge couldn't make out his words, heard only the roar of his voice, an animal sound, not hateful exactly, more like the roar of a challenge: *Come on and fight!*

Marge wiped her hands on her apron and hurried into the dining room, arriving just in time to see Eddie raising Bo up over his head.

Sure she screamed — screamed like nobody's business — and she caught Eddie's arm, slowing but not stopping the motion. Eddie heaved that little body across the room, and the side of Bo's head hit the wall with a terrible thump, then the child twisted so his feet came round and snapped against the window, forcefully enough to crack but not shatter a pane, and his whole body dropped and lay motionless. Marge thought for certain Bo was dead. She stared at him, forgetting completely about Eddie, who stood rooted to the floor beside her. She tried to derive from the tumult of her thoughts an adequate response.

Then Bo began to cry, whimpering at first, then wailing, a beautiful sound, the sound of a newborn baby. Marge threw herself over him, squeezed his arms and legs, smoothed his hair, kissed his face. There was no blood, no obvious injury. Marge could feel his little muscles bunching, his fingers flattening as he tried to push her off. Big fat Grandma Marge. Here she was so full of gratitude she nearly smothered him.

Maybe Eddie was worried about the same thing, for he pulled Marge up by her wrist, and Bo sprang to his feet as soon as he was free of her weight and ran out of the room. *Bo, you Bo!* She called to him even as Eddie dug his fingers into the flesh of her arms, she tried to lean to the side to see where Bo was going, she begged him to stop. But the next moment Marge couldn't speak because Eddie had pressed his lips against hers. Eddie, who hadn't given her more than a good night peck for years, kissed her with the kind of passion seen in old movies, grinding with closed lips, bending her backward. She felt him shaking, then he straightened and shook his head, gulped a broken sob.

He was sorry, he said, he couldn't help himself. *Please, please, please. Please,* Marge echoed. *Please would Marge explain to Eddie what had happened. Please would Eddie let Marge go. Please, Marge, please, Eddie. Please.* He tried to kiss her again, but she turned her head away. He grabbed a fistful of hair and held her so she couldn't move. She tried to slip out from beneath the manacle his arms made, but he held her tight.

What did he want? He was desperate to want something, to decide for them both what would happen next. How could he have been anything else than desperate after his astonishing loss of control? He was a stranger to himself, and as a stranger he could do anything he pleased. He pulled Marge's hair, tripped her, and as she fell to the floor he fell over her. She landed on the hardwood floor between the living room and dining room, with the arch of the entranceway looming overhead.

She tried to fight him off, but this only enraged him, and in his fury he ground the top of his head against her clavicle, breaking it, Marge thought, for she heard a sickening crack, though she didn't feel much pain there, not yet. She was too busy pounding at him with her hands, tried to wedge a knee between his legs, but he must have realized what she was attempting, for with a strength Marge didn't know he could muster he flipped her over onto her belly and pinned her to the floor.

She gave up quickly, but her acceptance came too late, she'd already incensed him, he'd lost his mind, he'd lost himself. He tore and tugged at her clothes and yanked down her panty hose, actions that struck Marge as no worse than bizarre; Eddie was an old man with a weak heart, and just as she could have warned him, a minute later he collapsed in exhaustion.

He lay on top of her, mucus rattling in his throat. She felt dizzy, her collarbone ached. She tried to remember who Eddie was — someone she knew, but who? This compression of flesh against flesh was improper, she suspected, though she couldn't think clearly enough to be sure. She tried to remember what they'd been doing before they fell to the floor. With a great effort she traced the motion backward — Eddie had grabbed her hair, before that he'd kissed her, before that he'd grabbed her wrist. And that's when she remembered Bo.

Eddie rolled off her when she curved her back, and he lay on the floor like a sack of sawdust, though as she stood he roused himself from his stupor and begged her to stay, even reached out and tried to help her pull up her stockings. He asked her what had happened, what he'd done, as if it were up to her to explain. He said he was sorry, so sorry, couldn't she see how sorry he was. He began praying softly, still tugging at her sagging panty hose. *May the Lord come with all His holy myriads and convict me of my deeds of ungodliness. I will wait for the mercy of our Lord Jesus Christ unto eternal life.* But she easily slipped her leg loose, whirled around, and started to run toward the kitchen, for that's the way Bo had run, through the kitchen and out the back door, out into the dangerous world.

She felt nothing for Eddie. It was as though all memory of him had been swept from her mind, and when she turned one last time to see him cowering on the floor, his face buried in his hands as he muttered his prayers, she wondered if she'd ever see him again. She knew what she was supposed to feel. It occurred to her as she slid into her black flats that an acceptable action would be to go up to the man and give him a good strong kick in the jaw. She paused, trying to figure out if she had to do this or if she wanted to do this. She couldn't decide. And to think that all her life she'd believed she could choose what to feel. So she just left Eddie there and went on, ran out of the house after Bo, and as she'd done every other time she'd gone in search of him, she headed straight for the lake, the place she had come to fear most.

When the upper layer of a lake cools in autumn, the surface water sinks, its density begins to decrease, and the near-freezing water at the surface turns to ice. Thick ice and snow screen out light, causing winter stagnation, or *winterkill*. Plants and animals die due to lack of oxygen. The cover of ice prevents the wind from circulating the water. Beneath the surface, the liquid world is dark and still, disturbed only by the occasional form of a pike gliding across the lake in search of food. It is like the inside of an ancient temple that is visited only by centipedes and rats. The stillness seems eerily permanent. Nothing worthy can live in such a place, and the few creatures that do survive here are like phantoms themselves, shadowy, evil, immortal. Except that there is no evil here because there is no true singularity. Water, the universal solvent, dissolves singularity. Everything that exists in a lake is always on the verge of becoming something else. Algae is eaten by mayfly nymphs and beetles, the small insects are preyed upon by fish and dragonflies, birds and mammals eat the fish, and everything that dies and is not eaten turns into protoplasm that becomes food for the plants.

Marge would be happy here, drifting suspended in the water, free at last of her big, ungainly body, which the divers would retrieve before the freeze. She'd be as happy during the quiet of winterkill as she would be during the spring overturn and the abundant summer, passing continuously with other molecules between plants and animals and the water that sustains them, existing in a state of constant change, dissolving, being absorbed and dissolving again, no part of her untouched by change. Change was total in this world, inexorable, and whoever said change depends upon changelessness didn't live in water.

Marge would be happy because all she'd wanted as she drowned was to be free of herself, to leave her singular life behind.

You want to know about happiness? Happiness is a stone sinking into the water; that's what Ann would say. If you're flesh and blood, too bad.

No, Ann will never swim in Hadley Lake again. But she can't stop looking at it, searching it for evidence of what has been lost.

Marge, are you there?

There she is, rising through the wintery mist on the wings of a wood duck taking off to head south.

Ann is no fool. She doesn't believe anything for the sake of comfort. She doesn't even believe she's capable of spontaneous feeling. If she feels anything at all it is the sludgy anxiety of being awake for two days. She isn't hungry or thirsty, she doesn't love Mervin anymore, and she doesn't know what she feels about her mother.

Marge?

Ann is no fool.

All Mervin has ever wanted to do is smoke pot and hang out. Now Ann wonders if she'd be better off alone. Marge never liked Mervin anyway and she'd be pleased to know that Ann and Mervin might be on the verge of breaking up. What else would Marge like to know? That Ann isn't going to let herself fall through the ice. Also, Tony has had nothing but coffee since he's been back home. Also, Sam and Erma Gilbert arrived at the lake shortly after Joe Simmons and the rescue crew, and Erma rode with Bo in the ambulance up to the city hospital. There would be no more argument about custody — Eddie doesn't want anything to do with the kid. Fucking Eddie. Where is he? He left a crack in the dining room window. Left town, left his job, left the state, folks say.

Marge, please explain to Ann why you married Eddie Gantz.

At the west end of the lake a hawk plummets through the dusky air and disappears into the marsh. A moment later it rises, beating its narrow wings against the air, clutching only muddy grass in its talons.

If Ann could have chosen she would have been a turtle, for in aquatic food pyramids they are the top carnivores, feeding on smaller animals but rarely being eaten themselves. Unlike Marge, however, Ann doesn't think she has much of a choice about anything.

For example, Ann wouldn't have chosen to work as a cocktail waitress in Gifferton, but that's what she does. Marge should have seen her wearing a wrinkled purple tulle skirt and an ostrich feather in her hat. The owner keeps inviting Ann to his house for dinner — luckily she has Mervin as an excuse. Mervin is still useful in some ways, even if his only ambition is to buy a Jet Ski and spend the summer zipping around the lake.

A brown bittern stepping along the slippery shore stops when Ann coughs. Ann tosses a pebble onto the ice near the bird; it stands stock-still, its tiny legs half submerged in the rainwater that has collected on top of the frozen surface; the bird keeps one black eye fixed on Ann. She whistles at it, but still the bird won't move. Only when she stomps her clog through the thin lip of ice does the bird take off in a panic.

That's as close to swimming in the lake as Ann will ever come. She used to be a strong swimmer and had even competed one season on her high school swim team. Marge had never learned to swim, though she'd lived up the road from Hadley Lake for more than thirty years. Now Ann understands her mother better. All the icky, slippery life within this shallow lake. You have to share the water with fish and water snakes and rats. Yuck! And the bottom inhabited by snails and bloodworms. And the ice! The murky chill! No thank you! Ann plans to keep herself dry and to grow old in a delicate way, like that old Rebecca Horton who lives alone with her parakeets.

She watches the gray surface bulge and flatten, the ice transforming into mist and swirling away. In the center of the lake, a dozen or so white gulls have tucked in their wings and float lazily, draped by the silky mist.

Ann has never been superstitious, but she can't help remaining open to the possibility that she'll be given some direction from her mother. She needs her mother to tell her what she is supposed to feel. She stands a distance from the activity on shore and concentrates on salvaging what is left of daylight, tries to hold the images with her eyes so she will find what is hidden. The half-frozen lake, the mist, dusk pressing in, a world of shadows and uncertainty. She watches a diver's slick head bob up and disappear. The divers will keep searching for the body until nightfall, and if they don't find her today, Joe Simmons has promised Ann, they will find her tomorrow. But Ann is determined to find her mother on her own and learn what she needs to know in order to feel again.

Marge? Are you there? Ann is waiting.

Oh, Ann, I'll tell you what it's like to be a musty chlorella drifting through the water below glimmering discs of ice, no place you have to be, all of winter to get there, no noises to bother you, no one drawing you into conversation, nothing but the weak bursts of minute bubbles rising from the deep mud and dissolving, the echo of motion when a fish passes nearby. And then after the thaw you can look forward to joining the surface film and feeling the footsteps of a strider dimpling your skin. It's a fine way to wile away the time. And then to dissolve and take your place on the tip of a philonotis. Then the next thing you know your head is buried in the mud and your tail is wagging above, crooking like an index finger in invitation, then straightening and disappearing all at once into the mouth of a hungry leech. And after awhile, there you go, you're silt again, settling into the rich humus and then traveling up and up and up on the spike of an un-furled water lily, then flattening into a rubbery carpet on the surface, where you take a nice sunbath and sag a little beneath the weight of a tiny frog.

Yes, it's wonderful here in the lake, so don't be afraid for me. As for the cold, well after the first shock you just stop feeling it, you stop feeling any discomfort, instead you're treated to the very simple certainty that you should be exactly what you are, even as you're changing.

PART SEVEN

Look at me!" He clutches the bar and in a fierce wriggling motion lifts himself up until his chin touches the metal. Then with a nimble turn he curls his legs around the bar and hangs from his knees, stretching his neck so his face is horizontal with the ground. He grabs the bar with his hands again, unfolds his legs, and he's right-side up. Then upside down, swinging wildly. His gran calls, "You be careful!" He is swinging from his knees, pumping with outstretched arms, arcing up toward the clouds and then falling back toward the earth and then twisting up again in the other direction so forcefully that for a second his legs bounce off the bar and he recognizes the bright familiar feeling of helplessness and in the next moment the bar is beneath his knees again and he is swinging back and forth and back and forth, oblivious to danger.

He does not bother to remember what he used to be and understands only that his escape from *before* was lucky. Maybe he'll go on being lucky. Maybe not. Luck, smelling of smoke and lemons. Luck, the magician who turns *soon* into *now*. One minute you think you're in trouble, the next minute you're fine, thanks to luck. And best of all, yesterday can never be today, not even in your dreams. The time before just goes away, like a moving van full of furniture, and you have only now and the mystery of what will be.

Here's luck: he reaches up to grab the bar, lets go with his legs, curls within the frame of his locked arms, and drops into the mud, splattering his jeans.

"You, Bo!"

Here's luck: running and running across the soccer field, falling and climbing to his feet and running some more.

Here's luck: a yellow tennis ball hidden like an egg in the grass.

And now here's his cousin Miraja coming at him, tackling him, stealing the ball. The wonderful gush of tears, just like that. And then the tennis ball in his hand again, and Miraja running in the opposite direction.

He's lucky to have the ball in his hand. He's lucky to have the ability to throw the ball so far. He's lucky to find the perfect stick to use to stir the mud puddle beneath the swing. He stirs the black water into a thick mud soup. He drapes himself over the plastic seat of the swing and keeps stirring the soup until it is the consistency of chocolate frosting. In the distance he hears people chattering. He listens to their voices with pleasant indifference, as though he were listening to sparrows.

Bo pushes off with his feet and glides back and forth, dragging the stick through the mud, which separates in ripples and oozes flat. He kicks with his feet again and watches the ground blur beneath him. His sneaker skims the puddle's surface, scattering little dollops of mud across the grass. The mud smells of spring, but the air still has a sharp, wintery tang.

"Bo, stop that!"

Okay, he'll stop. He bounces off the swing and runs to the ladder, climbs three rungs at a time to the top, and then hurtles headfirst down the slide. By pressing his palms against the bottom lip of the slide, he manages to stop before he swoops into the mud.

"Uh-uh. That's not the way."

Like this?

He's back at the top of the slide. He slides on his belly, feet first, slips down the dented metal sheet, bumps off the slide onto the ground, his legs buckle beneath him, and the next moment he's sitting in the mud, and a boy at the top of the slide is grinning in contempt at him.

So what? He can hop on the shaky bridge and make it impossible for anyone else to pass. He can descend in a fast spiral down the pole. He can round his arm into a plump little muscle — see!

Bliss, disdain, vanity, cheek, timidity, recklessness, glory — he's lucky to know what he feels, even if he doesn't know these words. He's lucky to know so much and so little at once. To be here doing what he's doing, to be able to do whatever he wants to do. He can hold his breath for the count of ten. He can burp and fart and throw mud at Miraja and when his gran comes over to scold him he can burst into tears and then won't she be sorry she got mad. That's luck. So is this: a spiderweb spun across the links of the fence, a tiny dead bug magnified by a single bead of water, its pinhead body wrapped in its own black lace wings. And this: a fluffy orange dog with the tennis ball in its mouth.

"That's mine!"

The dog running. Bo running. The dog circling and dropping the ball, nudging the ball with its snout, panting, darting hopeful glances up at Bo and then turning to gaze with glassy eyes into the distance. Who needs words when you can say everything you need to say with your eyes? Still, Bo is grateful to know the meaning of the word *luck* and to have the powerful confidence generated by understanding how lucky he has been. And there's no reason to think he won't go on being lucky. Look! He can throw a tennis ball over a chain-link fence. He can lead a dog through the open gate and into the scruffy woods separating the field from a backyard. The weeds are ankle high on the other side of the fence, but Bo — infinitely lucky — has never broken out in a rash from poison ivy. Nor has he ever been stung by a bee. And all he has to do is look through the grass and he'll find something lost by someone else: a yellow tennis ball, here it is, or, over here, a rare treasure, a plastic sheriff's badge half buried in the dirt. The dog can have the tennis ball. Bo prefers to keep the silver star and as he walks back to the field he tries to hook the star to his shirt.

"You stay in sight, Bo, you hear! Wandering off like that . . ."

Run run run as fast as you can, you can't catch Bo, no one can catch Bo, Super Bo, hero of the day. Miraja, look what Bo found.

"What's that?"

"A star."

"A badge. Cool. I'll trade you. Here, you can have this ring."

"That old plastic stupid ring."

"Look, it's a diamond, a real diamond."

"That's not a real diamond."

"Sure is."

"Sure's not."

Miraja is lucky in this way: she's so much bigger than Bo that she can pry open his fingers and steal the star and run. But Bo is lucky to have a voice loud enough to scare the crows from the tree-tops.

"Give it back!"

And Bo is lucky to have a gran capable of scoping out a situation and figuring out who's to blame.

"Mir, you come back! Come over here! You're in for it, girl!"

You see, Bo is always right and always innocent. That's *his* star. Give it back! He wants his star back. "Mir, you better . . . !" Fine then, Miraja will give it back! She throws it at Bo. The badge flies over his shoulder and disappears into the grass. Disappears forever. His star, gone. A lucky star, a magic star. He's been lucky until now, but his luck just ran out on him. He'd bite and kick and pull his cousin's hair but she's already on a swing, pumping furiously. Bo shakes with sobs. He might as well die. Forget about going to kindergarten and learning to read and growing tall enough to dunk a basketball. Forget about all the tomorrows. He wants none of it. He lost his confidence when he lost his lucky star. Super Bo. Miserable Bo. There is only now, luckless empty now. Nothing really good has ever happened to him, and nothing good will happen soon. If only he hadn't been born.

"All this fuss . . ." Gran says, her voice trailing to silence as she parts the grass with the toe of her rubber boot.

She doesn't understand. No one understands. What are they supposed to understand? Even if Bo could explain, he wouldn't change anything. He collapses in a heap.

"We'll go to the store and I'll buy you another one of the same, whatever it is you lost. You stop crying, child. There's no reason to get so worked up over . . . over this itsy-bitsy trifle. Huh!" She straightens with some effort, pushing off her bent knee. "Is this here what you're wanting?" She holds the star by an edge as though it were a dead mouse she meant to toss away. Bo opens his hand to accept it. A star with ornate embossed letters and a cowboy hat in the center. A lucky star dropped long ago by a hero who must have had no more need of luck. Five points, the plastic curling around the tips like the skin of a starfish. If you stare at it long enough the star will begin to glow with a cold silver light.

With his free hand Bo wipes his wet face, smearing mud over the bridge of his nose. Super Bo, once more poised for the rest of his life.

"Look at me!" He holds the star with both hands and spins around the axle of his arms, turns around, turns faster, faster, his heart a churning motor, the funnel of air as smooth and dense as the inside surface of a balloon. If he spins fast enough maybe he will rise from the ground like a helicopter. He spins and spins, as convinced as ever of his good fortune. He has been lucky and he's still lucky. He's lucky to be spinning. Spinning. That's all. He's a kid spinning across the grass. Just spinning. He can turn in perfect circles, lifting one foot before the other even touches the ground, his head pounding with the colorful blur of the here and now.

He has not forgotten the past, exactly. Nor does he have to work at stopping the unpleasant surge of memory. It's just that the *was* of his life is confusing and he has no interest in sorting through the clutter in search of explanations. Maybe someday he will begin to wonder about those years and try to understand what happened. Or maybe not. Maybe it will be enough to know that he was lucky, luckier than everyone else. For now, he cares only about staying upright for as long as he can and will keep spinning across the open field, spinning and spinning until either he gives up or gravity relinquishes its hold.

Now the ground is spinning. Now he is on his feet again, spinning. Now he is revolving in synch with the earth. Now he is spinning and the ground is stationary. Now he is floating on a raft in the middle of the sea. No, he is soaring in a red balloon toward the sun. He is right-side up. He is upside down. He is spinning, and the world is out of kilter. Up is down, down is up, the world revolves, keeps turning and at the same time turns in reverse, the ground swells into a crest, and Bo falls. He clutches tufts of grass to keep himself from sliding off the tilting plateau of the earth, feels himself slipping feet first and flattens himself against the ground in a thrilling effort to stay put. He holds on long enough for the earth to level, then he scrambles to his feet and starts twirling again, bouncing against the air and spinning across the field and around the corner of the building.

"Bo, get over here!"

She's mad now, really mad, she's had it up to here, Bo, the way you keep running off, disappearing into thin air, one moment you're where you should be and in a split second you're gone, leaving only the space that should have contained you.

And then, of course, here he is again, *you Bo, Ho-bo-bo, you stupid kid, you good-luck charm,* spinning around and around, demanding, "Look at me!" simply because he's doing what he can do so well.

Make Believe
by Joanna Scott

A READING GROUP GUIDE

On writing *Make Believe*

Joanna Scott talks with
Leonard Lopate of "New York & Company,"
WNYC, New York

LL: At first glance this book seems something of a detour from your usual themes. Not only is it set in the present, but it deals with some very au courant issues — race, adults battling for custody of children — not the sort of thing that we've seen from you in the past.

JS: Yeah, I would like to say that I shift with each book. I don't know if it's a good thing or a bad thing, but I tend to turn my back on my last book. So, book by book, I think I'm not necessarily following any patterns. This seems in a way my next step, not necessarily a turning away from all my past work.

And it deals with one of the great themes of America and American literature, race.

Which I've dealt with before. I've written about slave ships and illegal slaving in the mid-nineteenth century. I've also worked race in in other ways. Because it's our country's concern, it's my concern as a writer.

You once said that you weren't too good at writing about yourself, and that once you got started getting into history and other people's lives you were freed as a writer. But here you have moved a little closer to home. Make Believe is not about your experience, but it's about your time.

I was a little nervous about that. . . . I'd look at this wild world and I'd ask myself: How can I write about it? I don't know the words for things. I don't know the name of that person. I don't know his story. So it required more invention, and that's what I wanted to do. I wanted to push myself away from what had, in a sense, become a crutch for me, the crutch of history, the crutch of fact. I wanted to see if I could throw the crutch away for a book.

And this very definitely relates to things that we've seen in newspaper stories recently, even though obviously you wrote the book before Elian Gon-

zalez's case came up. Make Believe *is about a black boy and a white girl who fall in love and he's shot and killed while she's pregnant with their child. His parents help her care for him. Her parents deny her, which is an atypical situation today. But soon she too is killed and the grandparents fight over custody of the child. Even though he's never met his white grandparents, the boy ends up with them — and that's a whole other matter here. You're not interested in the legal aspects of this. You don't even write about the court case except maybe the judge's literary tastes.*

I don't. I thought of that as a hinge. There are other hinges in the book too that are not visible, but they're crucial, they're essential. I try to explain why the judge makes that decision, a rational decision, but I didn't want to spend time writing a scene, a court scene, that I wasn't interested in. I was too interested in my characters to spend time in the courtroom.

Do you think that this is likely to have happened — that a judge would have awarded a child to the parents who have rejected him rather than the ones who have been raising him?

Well, I slipped in a little fact about how the white grandparents had been supporting the daughter financially. I also checked with some lawyer friends in my neck of the woods and they gave me the nod. They felt it was okay given the idiosyncrasies of law.

You have the white step-grandfather — it's not the boy's real grandfather — really being motivated by self-righteousness and a religious conviction. That's what compels him to take this child away from the grandparents who've been bringing him up and who obviously adore him. So do you think that those are things — that religious conviction is something that would get somebody to do something so outrageous?

Well, I want to say that anything I write about is a possibility. It's not necessarily a formula for the drift of religious thought. I think in this case that what you consider self-righteousness, it begins with confusion. The boy's step-grandfather wants to be a good man, and that becomes a fierce desire for him. And as it becomes fierce internally it needs some sort of external reaction response.

The way you structure the story is we meet these people and then we go back and we learn about them, much the same way as we experience people in real life. You meet somebody, you don't know much about them, and then in time you learn more and more details. You've obviously chosen that approach for a reason, but it's one that we don't find in most novels.

Tell me more about that. I'm not sure what is different here.

It seems to me that what happens is that after you introduce the character you then go back and we learn about that character — in the same way that if I meet you. First I meet you in a very particular way and then I will eventually learn all these other things about you. So it allows you as a writer to go back and forth in time.

Yes, structurally I'm kind of all over the place, aren't I? But it felt like fitting pieces of a puzzle together for me. It felt quite natural once I had a sense of how the structure would come together. The parts when I do go back in time, when I do elaborate on the lives of the people who are at that point of the narrative gone now, it enabled me, yes, to tell their stories, to fill out the characters.

But it also forces us to reassess our own sense of stereotypes and expectations.

I see what you're saying. And then this hopefully is what happens every day with us as we sit here and talk.

Things get more and more complicated.

And a reappraisal goes on continuously.

Is that something that happens while you're writing the book?

Absolutely.

You keep on throwing in complications?

And it's part of the discovery of fiction that's so marvelous, that's so exciting. You have to work with the logic of a character. You break out of that logic and either you have to create another compelling logic that makes sense or you drift into a madness for the character. But usually you stay within that logic, that way of thinking. Within that way of thinking, you can do anything.

And how much of the plot actually is known to you before you start?

You want the truth here?

Of course.

Probably not a whole lot. I tend to . . .

Because this is a novel with a big plot.

It is.

Usually plotted novels are thought out and then other things happen in the process.

Yeah. I end up throwing out whatever I planned. I do plan, I really do. I plan all the way to the end and then I drop my plans. I change my plans. I alter them.

The book forces you to consider what it's becoming.

Yeah. So I'm constantly rewriting my outline as I'm writing along in my books.

You also throw in another — well, I won't say confusing — but another thing that confounds us for a while. The characters have fantasies and nightmares and you present them as though they're the real thing. And then we figure out later that they're not necessarily. Bo even had a cat that isn't there. Other characters have things that we assume to be true and then discover are not true. That's part of the writing process?

Yeah, since I'm so interested in consciousness — where does that take me? — that involves the edges of consciousness. And so those dreams, the conversations that don't take place but are imagined — they seem part of consciousness, part of the mind's work.

And they lead to the title as well, Make Believe.

Absolutely.

You have often been linked with writers like Lydia Davis, as experimental authors. Do you think of yourself in that way?

Well, in this regard, that it is a journey into the unknown. Each book I write is something I'm trying out, it's a kind of proposition — will it work or not? I suppose you could call it an experiment. I would hope that, like Lydia Davis, like many other writers . . .

Robert Coover, your teacher . . .

He was my teacher. John Hawkes . . . Those writers, writers like Hawkes or Coover, Barthelme, are very different from one another. So the phrase tends to be used to lump together a wide variety of writers. And that's when I get a little nervous about the term.

In this book, even though it's all written in the third person, you really adjust the third person so that we're in the minds of a lot of different people. We start off in the mind of a three-year-old. Obviously you can't write in the thoughts of a three-year-old — so the third-person strategy was the way to get around that?

To a certain extent. I'd actually sat with my own young children and taken some notes and listened to the way their thoughts translated into language, if that makes sense. They would be thinking hard and the words coming out would be so wonderfully nonsensical, I guess — so free — and I couldn't quite use that language. Here and there I do. I try to evoke the wild language that a child has access to. But by using that narrator I can move in and out, and perhaps I describe a sensation that the child himself can't describe.

Another powerful emotion is the protection of your two kids. You're the mother of two kids. Did the fact that you were raising these children affect your decision to pursue this kind of material?

Yeah. The joy I feel with them, that is part of the impulse here that got me going. Their fascinating ways of looking at the world — I found myself imagining the world through their eyes, and so that helped me start to design a character, a child who is different from them. I had to make something new, something other. But certainly the fact is that they are my life and this is what I know best these days. Or this is what I want to know best, I should say — let me qualify that.

Jayne Anne Phillips once said that she wrote a book, Shelter, *out of fear for her boys because she felt so protective of them.*

That fear is great for any parent.

"What would happen if I were dead and these kids were left to the power of the courts, other people?" Sometimes strange things happen. People we thought we knew well will act very oddly.

Yeah, it's frightening. But I've learned how resilient children are and so tried to describe that.

～

Leonard Lopate's interview with Joanna Scott was originally aired on "New York & Company" on WNYC. This partial transcript is reprinted with permission.

Reading Group Questions
and Topics for Discussion

1. "Erma's first thought when she heard the news was not *thank God* or *poor Jenny* but *Now that white girl is gone Bo is mine to raise properly*" (page 38). Do you think it was reasonable for Erma to assume that she would have custody of Bo?

2. People often say that a sense of humor is what they value most in a life partner. Marge notes that "Eddie rarely laughed" (page 41). And yet she seems to consider him an ideal mate. Why?

3. Why is Jenny, at the tender age of sixteen, so ready and eager to have a baby? Do you think she's emotionally prepared for motherhood?

4. Bo thinks, "Surely Gran and Pop had always been as old as they were now, no older, no younger" (page 79). To what extent do you consider this a childish perception? Aren't there times when all of us, caught up in our present lives, lose sight of the constancy of change?

5. Ann urges Marge to think of Bo "like a cutting from one of your rosebushes, you know, transplanted, and if he doesn't take, if we're not right for him, then we bring him back, okay?" (page 103). Do you think Marge is ever actually willing to let Bo leave?

6. Do you agree with Judge Wright's decision in *Gantz v. Gilbert*? What is the significance of the thriller that Judge Wright reads several months before he issues his decision? Describe how reading that novel influenced him.

7. Judge Wright seems to believe that the maternal bond is always stronger than a child's bond with his father. Do you agree?

8. How important is the issue of race in *Make Believe*? Do you consider it central to the novel's plot or only marginal? Discuss scenes in which characters in the novel deal with the issue of race head-on, such as when Kamon encounters the white women at McDonald's (page 146).

9. Kamon Gilbert dies harboring a single wish (page 158). What do you think his wish might have been?

10. Discuss the role of fantasy in the lives of the novel's principal characters. Why do you think Joanna Scott chose to call this novel *Make Believe*?

Talking to the Dead
by Helen Dunmore

"Brilliant and terrifying, an unbeatable combination. . . . We aren't released from the author's spell until the very last line."
— Carolyn Banks, *Washington Post*

White Oleander
by Janet Fitch

"A ferocious, risk-loving novel about a teenage girl's tour of duty through a series of Los Angeles foster homes. . . . An intimate and epic novel." — Mark Rozzo, *Los Angeles Times Book Review*

The Dangerous Husband
by Jane Shapiro

"It will speak to anyone who has ever dwelled, briefly or at length, on how useful the death of a spouse might be. . . . What makes *The Dangerous Husband* so memorable are Shapiro's insights into the universal nature of marriage and love."
— Deirdre Donahue, *USA Today*

The Fig Eater
by Jody Shields

"What makes *The Fig Eater* so compelling is its eerily atmospheric depiction of Freud's Vienna and its account of the cunning machinations its female detectives must enact to pursue their covert investigation." — Leslie Haynsworth, *Denver Post*

Fortune's Rocks
by Anita Shreve

"*Fortune's Rocks* kept me reading long into the night. . . . Shreve renders an adolescent girl's plunge into disastrous passion with excruciating precision and acuteness." — Katherine A. Powers, *Boston Globe*

Evening News
by Marly Swick

"An affecting novel . . . utterly palpable and real. . . . It possesses both the psychological suspense of Sue Miller's bestselling *The Good Mother* and the emotional acuity of Alice Munro's short stories." — Michiko Kakutani, *New York Times*

Available wherever books are sold